The Lies We Bury

The Cage Foster Series

By

Stacy Green

The Lies We Bury

Print Edition

Visit the author website:
stacygreenauthor.com

Sign up for Stacy's mailing list to hear about new releases, contests and more!

say instead of "Move." Manners count.

"Where you going, pretty lady?"

He's definitely wearing beer goggles.

"Away from here." I sidestep him. His fingers brush against my bare arm.

"Why don't you hang out with us? You're local, right? Tell us all about your city." He runs his fingers down my arm, and my stomach coils. "Your skin is so pretty."

I slap his hand away. "Back off."

He laughs and holds up his hands. "Whatever. There's plenty more just like you around here."

He and his friends lumber toward the next bar, and I finally make it to the sidewalk. I'm sweating through my shirt, and the mass of people seems to double the humidity. I wipe my face with my shirt and get my bearings.

Laveau's House of Voodoo is on the right. Nothing but hoodoo kitsch to satisfy the tourists. She never lived at this building, as far as I know. Her house was farther down, closer to Congo Park. Gran swore she saw Marie Laveau's spirit walking the streets every time she visited St. Ann Street.

I've never encountered the Queen. Now would be a great time. Maybe she could fix me.

My fingers clutch the ring tucked beneath my shirt. Sweat has stuck both the ring and the chain to my skin. Gran chose the ring herself—a family heirloom she swore would protect me.

The worst of the zombies are finally behind me, but the bass and cheers are replaced by a sharp staccato. Bang, bang, bang.

Drummers. Boys camped out in front of one of the bars off Bourbon and St. Ann, beating worn drumsticks on plastic buckets. Fast and loud and digging into my brain with every rap of the plastic.

Too many people. Why didn't I just wait?

I walk around the drummers' audience, keeping my eyes down. My glasses are steamed over, making my vision more blurry than usual.

"Watch it." A female voice snaps. "Don't those thick-ass glasses work?"

I yank off the frames and rub them on my shirt. Put them back on.

A college-aged girl stares at me. I'm immediately jealous of her porcelain skin, perfect makeup that somehow hasn't sweat off, and a string of beads around her neck.

"Mardi Gras is over." I try to walk around her. The musicians slam their drums even louder. My head seems to pulse.

Bead Girl is blocking my way. "What's wrong with you?"

If she only knew how loaded that question was. "Nothing." I brace for the usual insults.

"You look like your face is melting."

That's the best she's got? "You look like you're ready to blow the whole second line for more beads. Move out of my way."

I only manage two steps before she sticks out her heel, and I hit the filthy pavement hands first. My palms burn, my jeans tear. My knee feels wet.

I stagger to my feet. The girl and her friends glare at me. "How's the pavement taste?"

I want to choke her, but I don't have the time.

"What's this?" Bead Girl is staring at something on the ground.

I don't realize the chain's broken until I see my Gran's ring in her manicured hand. My heart stops. I'm exposed. "Give it back."

She squints at it. "It looks like an antique."

"It was my Gran's. Please give it back."

She's still touching it, running her poisoned fingers over the glass. "What's inside here?"

"Doesn't matter." I step forward, a knot of nerves making their way up my throat. "Give it back or I'm calling the cops."

She ignores me and takes out her phone, aiming its bright flashlight at the glass. "It looks like dirt."

Her friend snickers.

My skin is on fire, my head throbs, my chest is caving in. I can't lose that ring.

I try to remember what the therapist said about controlling my anger, but everything's jumbled. I only see the ring in her hand, Gran's voice in my head.

"Never take it off. Carry it with you, and you will always be shrouded. Lose it, and it will be like a beacon."

I try one last time. "Please give it back."

"Or what?" Bead Girl smiles. "I bet it's worth some money."

Everything turns red. The zombies scatter, and I only see her pretty, laughing face.

I slam my fist into her mouth and smile when her lip splits. Blood drips onto the beads.

"Oh my God." She's screaming at me, her hands going to her face. I lurch forward and catch the ring before the glass shatters on the bricks.

One of Bead Girl's friends yanks me up by my hair. "You bitch."

I jab her in the throat. She lets go and tumbles into the other girls. I turn and run toward the house on St. Ann Street. I'm so close. They'll never touch me once I'm with her.

A hand closes around my arm and jerks me to stop. A sweaty cop glares down at me. "Why'd you hit that girl?"

I stare, the words stuck in my throat.

"I saw the whole thing. She was handing the ring back to

you."

Was she? I try to pick through my memory, but anger and fear blur the images.

"I have somewhere to be."

The cop raised an eyebrow. "Settle down. I don't want to have to arrest you."

He shifts, and I see the silver handcuffs gleaming. "You're just being detained right now."

Dark, black and cold. Hurting all over.

I taste blood.

I will not be handcuffed.

2

CAGE FOSTER TOOK one final look at the photograph. Two teenaged girls, smiling and happy, less than a month from graduating high school. Just hours after someone took the photo, they'd disappeared without a single scrap of evidence.

Now one of them waited on the other side of the door.

He loosened his tie and then wiped his brow. He opened the door to a small, windowless interview room. She sat in a folding chair in the far corner, arms banded across her orange jail uniform. He scanned the changes: a gold hoop in her nose, a scripted tattoo on her right forearm, a thin scar running from her chin to her left ear. Her face was off somehow: asymmetrical, her scarred left jawline off kilter. That side of her mouth pulled upward.

The thick, black-framed glasses were new.

Same shimmering brown eyes, same spattering of freckles across her nose. Her silky, black hair was longer, falling in waves around her odd face.

Her eyes narrowed as Cage grabbed the other chair and placed it just a few feet from her.

She tossed back her hair in defiance and stared at him. No spark of recognition, no cry of joy. Was it really her?

Seven years had passed—not enough time for her face to become unrecognizable. Something terrible had turned this woman into a distorted mirror image of her teenaged self.

She broke the silence. "Who are you?"

Her voice no longer had the soft quality of a teenager's. It was hardened and sharp, her accent more pronounced.

She had the same mole to the right of her top lip.

He sat down and gave her the shortened version of his new position. "My name is Agent Cage Foster from the Louisiana Bureau of Investigation. I'm here about a case in Mississippi, where I used to be a deputy."

Technically, his job at the LBI didn't start for two more weeks. But the call from the Adams County Sheriff had changed everything.

"I've never been to Mississippi. Where's my ring?" She scratched the tattoo on her arm. "I need it back."

Cage had read the arresting officer's report. A minor altercation with a couple of drunk tourists had turned into an assault on an officer when he tried to handcuff her. Her fingerprints got a hit.

"It's with the rest of your things. You'll get it back once you're released." She'd scratched the patrol officer's face. "But that might be a while. Attacking a cop is never a smart idea."

Her fingers clenched into fists. "He said I wasn't under arrest. Why did he need to put handcuffs on me?"

"It's procedure."

"Whatever. Get my ring. I need it, now."

He hadn't recognized the ring she'd made such a fuss over. She definitely hadn't been wearing it when she disappeared. "It's an antique, by the looks of it. Family heirloom, I assume?"

She leaned forward. "Is the glass cracked?"

"The ring is fine, I promise."

"Then get it for me." Her fist came down on the table, her uneven mouth stretched tight.

Cage ignored her request and changed gears. "What's your name?"

"Really? As if you don't have it in that file."

"Lyric Gaudet. You live with your grandmother in the French Quarter. She's recently deceased."

Her mouth twitched. "That's none of your business."

"I'm sorry for your loss."

She stared, suspicion in her dark eyes. "Like I said, I've never been to Mississippi. So, unless you're here to give me my ring back, you're wasting your time." She spit the words, drumming her fingers on the table. "I called Miss Alexandrine. She'll fix everything."

Cage had her case memorized, but he pretended to thumb through the thick file while his mind raced. She'd been an innocent high school kid when she disappeared. What reason would she have to lie about her identity? Was she too scared of her captors, like the girl in Utah several years ago? If Annabeth had spent seven years with the person who took her and somehow escaped—or worse, assimilated—she might still be too afraid to talk.

"I'm trying to find someone, and I think you may be able to help."

She scratched at the tattoo again. "Can you get the assault charges dropped?"

"That's an NOPD decision. But I'll try. Your cooperation with this will definitely help your case."

He let the silence hang between them.

"Whatever. But like I said, I've never been to Mississippi."

Cage placed the copy of her fingerprints on the table between them. "These are yours, taken last night after your arrest."

She shrugged.

He took out another set from his file. "These belong to a

missing young woman from Roselea, Mississippi, named Annabeth George."

"So?"

Cage put the prints side by side, never taking his eyes of her. "These two sets of fingerprints match."

Her angry mask flashed to confusion. She leaned forward, her thick glasses sliding down her nose to reveal a crooked bump where it had been broken. "I thought that was impossible. Two different people can't have the same fingerprints."

"That's right."

"What are you playing at?" Her voice trembled.

"I'm here to help you," Cage said. "But I need you to be honest."

"Your fingerprint dude screwed up."

Human error happened on prints, and since Annabeth's had been taken when she was twelve as part of a safety program in her school, there was a minuscule chance the growth in the finger might have slightly changed the expanse between the ridge lines. But the lines themselves didn't change. Cage trusted the match.

"Annabeth George and her best friend, Mickie, went to the lake seven years ago and were never seen again. Your fingerprints match Annabeth's."

She slammed her hand down on the paper and shoved the sheets at him. "My name is Lyric Gaudet. I don't have a friend named Mickie," she snapped. "Your geeks got it wrong. Where's Miss Alexandrine? She'll fix this."

He changed tactics, softening his voice. "Your tattoo, it's covering a scar. R-e-s-p-i-r-e R-a-n-n s-o-u-f. I'm guessing Creole?"

"None of your business." Her arms banded tightly across her middle, fists clenched. Even her lips had gone white.

Every person lied about something, and everyone had a tipping point. Cage leaned forward and folded his hands over the prints. "When Annabeth and Mickie disappeared, I was a sheriff's deputy in Adams County. I worked the case for months, and we never found a hint of what happened to them. And their families are still living in hell."

Guilt needled him, and for the thousandth time, he wondered if his single bad choice could have prevented the girls from disappearing.

"That sucks, but you're still wrong." She gnawed at her lower lip, tracing the tattoo with her finger, her head nodding with each new letter. "Please get my ring. I need it."

A sharp knock on the door, and then a tall, striking woman with a detective's shield hanging around her neck entered. "Agent Foster, may I speak with you for a moment?"

"Now isn't really the best time." The girl's wall was crumbling. A little more time, and he would have her trust.

"It's urgent." She looked at Annabeth, and her icy expression softened. "Please give us a few minutes."

Sonofabitch. "I'll be right back."

The detective shut the door and glared at him. "Myra Bonin, major crimes. I'm your NOPD liaison."

The New Orleans police—aside from the pencil-pushing brass—had voiced suspicion and resentment when the Louisiana Bureau of Investigation announced its newly formed Criminal Investigative Assist Unit to aid the NOPD with major crimes. Most of the NOPD resented the intrusion. Cage needed to earn their respect and trust. The last thing he wanted to do was piss off the only investigator who'd offered to be his liaison with the department, especially when the job hadn't even started.

"Nice to meet you, and I'm sorry I didn't talk to you first. I've worked this case from the beginning, and I'd like to get things figured out and bring some closure to her family."

"You're not with the sheriff's office anymore," Bonin said. "And you don't start with the LBI for another two weeks. Meaning you're on vacation."

Exactly what his angry wife had said while he rushed to get on the road. "My former captain gave me the opportunity to bring Annabeth home."

Bonin appeared unimpressed with the sentiment. "Does your boss at the LBI know about any of this?"

"I plan on calling him once I've confirmed everything." So much for that being relatively easy. He'd expected Annabeth to break her façade once she saw him and realized she was finally safe.

"That she doesn't really believe she's Lyric Gaudet?"

"Seven years is a long time to screw with someone's head. If he kept her all that time, she's probably under his control. She needs to believe she's safe before she lets us in. Did anyone notice any unusual people hanging around when she was arrested?"

"She got into a fight in front of a bar on Bourbon Street. Unusual is the norm." She handed him a file. "You'll want to look at this before you go back in."

Cage scanned the information. His head spun. "This is solid?"

"Absolutely."

He motioned for her to enter the room first, but she shook her head.

"Ganging up on her is risky. I'll watch from the video room. Then you and I can discuss what the hell you were thinking jumping on this without at least talking to your liaison first. Especially when the LBI agent in charge is a pompous media whore."

He flushed "Yes, ma'am."

"Don't call me ma'am. I'm not that much older than you," she said. "And the tattoo is Creole for 'inhale, exhale.'"

"Thanks." Despite the air conditioning, Cage's scalp was damp with flop sweat, his newly shorn hair doing a poor job of soaking up the moisture. Adrenaline pulsed through him the way it always did when a case started to break.

The girl eyed him warily as he closed the door and took his seat. "We have some new information."

"Yay." She rolled her eyes. "I'm thirsty. Can you get me a Coke? And my ring?"

"Not right now. I need you to answer some questions." He placed the picture of a smiling, suntanned Mickie and Annabeth on the table. With the photo in his peripheral vision, he now saw Annabeth beneath the strangely lopsided face and the fading scar. "Annabeth is the one on your left."

"Cool. That chick who dragged you out of here looks like a bad bitch. She's almost as tall as you."

"Detective Bonin," Cage said. "I'm working with her."

"I bet. You one of those white boys who like light-skinned women? 'Cause that one looks like she needs a good dick."

The back of his neck warmed. "I'm married."

"So? Is your wife here?"

Her stalling tactics had gone on long enough.

"If she is, maybe you could get a little three-way action." Her smirk turned into a cocky smile. "Bonin looks like she swings both ways."

He ignored the comment and opened the file Bonin had given him and laid it flush on the table. Lyric Gaudet stared back at them.

Annabeth's brash exterior disappeared. Her face paled, and she sucked in a hard, fast breath. "Who is that?"

"Lyric Gaudet," Cage said. "She disappeared in 2005 right before Katrina hit. She lived with her grandmother Charlotte Gaudet in the French Quarter. Lyric went to the store for supplies and never returned."

Cage put the photo next to the picture of the two girls. Mickie's summer tan made her skin appear darker than Annabeth's, whose biracial parents had gifted her with beautiful caramel coloring. Lyric's missing persons report listed her as Creole. Just like Annabeth and Mickie, the real Lyric Gaudet had shoulder-length, dark hair with an athletic build. They could have easily been mistaken for relatives.

Their similarities set Cage's nerves on edge.

"This is you." Cage pointed to Annabeth's picture. "How did you come up with Lyric's name?"

"Because that's my name!" She slammed her hand on the table and shoved the picture of Lyric away. "Look, I was in an accident. I'm sure you can tell by my elephant-man face."

"You don't look like the elephant-man. When was the accident?"

"Seven years, last week."

Sweat trickled down his neck. Just weeks after the teenagers had disappeared. "What happened?"

"Details don't matter. I got hurt pretty bad. Screwed up my brain. Only thing I could say was Lyric, and my gran's phone number."

An electric current rippled through him. Lyric had disappeared when Annabeth was only ten-years old. Roselea was a small community, and while Annabeth had been a popular girl and a track star, her paranoid parents also sheltered her.

He tried his best to rationalize. Was there some connection between the Georges and Gaudets? Surely, Charlotte Gaudet would have known the girl wasn't her granddaughter, and if the families were friends, had she really kept Annabeth from them all these years?

With five years between their disappearances and their physical similarities, Cage had to consider the other very likely possibility.

And it chilled him to the bone.

Annabeth's nails left red streaks across her tattoo.

"So, amnesia then?" Cage asked. Anything was possible with head injuries, especially one that had caused such facial trauma.

"Yeah, my face got busted up. And my brain got it even worse."

"I need the name of the hospital so I can confirm your story."

"Mercy Hospital in Jasper, Texas. Transferred to Tulane. Spent three months there getting surgeries and rehab. Have at it, Agent Dick." She laughed at her own joke, revealing a gap where two of her left molars should be.

Annabeth grabbed the corner of her mouth and stretched it wide open. "Knocked two teeth right out. Left my partial at home. Between that and my smush-face, I'm ready for a date." Her dark eyes gleamed, and she leaned forward across the table to slide her hand over his. "What do you say? Get me out of here, and I'll show you a good time."

Cage pushed her hand away. "I'm going to pretend you didn't say that. What were you doing in Jasper?"

She flopped back in the chair and huffed. "Wish I knew. I can't remember anything before the accident."

"Did your grandmother ever mention the name Annabeth George? Or having friends in Mississippi?"

"Gran was born and raised in the Quarter, just like me. It's in her blood, and she never traveled anywhere else."

Did she really believe what she was saying? None of it made

any sense. Lyric's grandmother must have noticed the mole above Annabeth's lip. She would have known this wasn't her flesh and blood.

"What about the rest of your family?"

"Don't have any. It was just me and her." She yawned, her eyes suddenly droopy. "Took me a long time to recover. And I'm still not right. Won't ever be, so Gran and me mostly kept to ourselves."

Cage arranged the pictures side by side again and slid them closer to her. Annabeth's frightened gaze latched onto the snapshot of Lyric, and she started digging at her tattoo again. She rocked back and forth, her lips moving silently.

He pushed Lyric's picture to the end of the table. Annabeth shot back in the chair, eyes transfixed on the photo. Tremors shook her small body.

"Listen, whatever happened that night, I'm on your side." Cage kept his voice soft, his arms lying open on the table. "But I can't help you if you don't come clean with me. I want to bring you home, Annabeth. And Mickie was your best friend. Tell me what happened to her."

"I'm not ... I don't know any Mickie." She pressed her hands over her ears, her head whipping back and forth. "No, no, no. No!"

Something feral flashed in her eyes. She snatched the pictures and flung them across the table at him. She kicked the chair against the wall as she stood and slammed her hands on the table. "My name is Lyric!"

"I'm trying to help you."

"Liar!" Spit flew from her mouth. She gulped air as if she'd just finished sprinting. "You're trying to solve your case by using me. It's not going to happen." She stomped past him and yanked on the locked door. "I want to go back to the holding cell until

I'm bailed out. And I want my ring!"

Cage pushed his arm between her and the door. He towered over her, but the rage in her eyes made her seem of equal height. "Sit down. We're not done talking."

Her arm flashed out and her fist connected with his windpipe before he had a chance to react. "Yes, we are."

3

AN OFFICER HAULED a screaming Annabeth back to the holding cell. Two patrol cops snickered as Cage rubbed his throat. The girl could pack a punch.

"So, the superstar can't handle a little girl?" One of the uniforms sneered. "Why the hell did they send you over here, anyway?"

"The LBI is trying to make your life easier." Cage sidestepped him, the stink of the burly officer's sweat-stained uniform turning his stomach.

"NOPD don't need help from the Louisiana Bureau of fucktards," the officer snapped. "Especially some white-bred Mississippi boy who's just here to look pretty for the cameras."

Cage looked him up and down. "You're whiter than me, Hoss. And thanks for the compliment."

"My grandma's half Creole, asshole." The uniform adjusted his belt. "I'm born and raised in this city. You're an outsider, and you'll stay that way."

"Knock it off, Pietry." Bonin had caught up with him. "Your shift's over."

Pietry looked her up and down, his gaze lingering on her chest. "How about you get a drink with me, sugar?"

"I'm on the job."

"Your loss." Pietry sneered at Cage. "I thought we didn't

have to deal with him for another two weeks."

"Plans changed," Bonin said. "Sorry you're too low on the totem pole to be informed."

Pietry's face turned scarlet. "Dyke bitch." He stalked around the corner.

"Welcome to New Orleans. He's just the first asshole you'll deal with. Most of the patrol cops—and plenty of detectives—feel exactly like him."

Cage exhaled, his guts slowly relaxing. "Thanks for covering me."

"I considered reporting you to the LBI myself," she said.

"Why didn't you?"

"I watched you in there," Bonin said. "You actually give a damn about that girl, and that's a rare thing. And you didn't let her comments about me get under your skin. How's your throat?"

"Sore," Cage said. "You think we can get her medical records today?"

"I sent the subpoena first thing this morning. We'll have them shortly. The grandmother had to know this wasn't Lyric."

"Grief makes people do strange things. Why didn't anyone follow through on Lyric's original missing persons case?"

"All hell broke loose during and after Katrina. This station was the only one not flooded, and they were completely overloaded. A lot of people went missing. If family members didn't keep pushing, police regulated those people to cold cases. Lyric's grandmother stopped calling." Bonin's expression was neutral, but Cage read the warning in her defensive tone.

"No judgement. I can't imagine working through Katrina and the aftermath."

"Thanks. Not everyone has that reaction," Bonin said. "The print match is solid. You think she's playing us?"

Cage's instincts rarely led him off course. And the few times he'd second-guessed himself led to disastrous consequences—Annabeth and Mickie's abduction by far the worst one. "No. I think her medical records will confirm her story." He used the file as a fan, his body damp with sweat. "Ya'll have the air on?"

"New Orleans in the summer, and this is an old building with an old system. Be thankful you won't be working here most of the time. God knows I am. You'll be working downtown at Criminal Investigations with me—once you're officially on the job. Did you get a hotel?"

"I thought we'd be on our way back to Roselea tonight."

"Call the Mason Dupey," Bonin said. "My sister's the manager. Tell her I sent you, and she'll find you a room."

"Thanks." Cage loosened his tie. "Now comes the hard part. I've got to call my wife and tell her I'm staying here."

"What about your supervisory agent at the LBI?"

Pompous media whore perfectly described Cage's new boss. He would see Annabeth as an opportunity to put the new division—and himself—in the spotlight. And that greed would outweigh his anger over Cage's unauthorized investigation. "I don't have the right to ask this—"

"Agent Rogers will preen more than the Rex King of Carnivale," Bonin said. "Annabeth's mental well-being won't be on his agenda. But he's well connected, and I like my job."

"You know she was likely taken by a serial offender," Cage said. "Lyric too. And God knows how many more."

Bonin sighed. "You have one day."

THAT'S HER.

She's been in my dreams for weeks. She stares with this demanding, urgent look and then lunges at me. My wrists burn, and then she hisses "run." Some nights the dream plays on a loop until I force myself awake.

My chest burns. The pressure in my head is building, and I want to scream and bang my fists against the wall.

I try to remember the breathing exercises my therapist taught me, but my mind refuses to focus on anything but her face.

Lyric Gaudet, according to Agent Foster. And I'm some girl named Annabeth who's been missing from his hometown for seven years.

I dig my fingers into my tattoo. I've already turned the skin raw. It's *Creole* for the only advice my therapist gave me that stuck.

Creole. If I'm not Lyric, then I'm not Creole. All of my pride in descending from a powerful Haitian Creole family, all the things Gran told me about the life I couldn't remember—was that all bullshit?

It's so hot in this damn cell. I can't get a full breath. My face feels like I've been standing over a pot of steaming gumbo for too long.

She lied. Gran lied to me. The anger's coming back. It starts in the pit of my stomach and then takes over my whole body.

And if that girl is Lyric, the other … the other is the one I never forgot.

I yank open the buttons of the stiff, orange jumpsuit. Its short sleeves aren't cutting it.

It's still too hot.

I don't know who I am. And she lied.

Did Miss Alexandrine know the truth? Does the ring mean anything? Will it really protect me?

Red creeps back into my vision. I close my eyes against it, but now I'm seeing red starbursts. I press my hands over my ears, like that will get my brain under control.

I was okay with not being normal because I had Gran and

the Quarter. Even with my freakish face and my dented brain, I had a history. I knew who I was, and I had a purpose in life.

Her face flashes in my head, but this time she's covered in red. Her eyes are narrowed and angry. "You stole my life."

I shake my head. "I didn't know."

"Yes, you did. Deep down, you knew."

"Not at first. Not until—"

The face—Lyric's face—snarls. "Exactly. Now you're going to pay for it."

I'm rocking back and forth. I don't know if this is a memory or my imagination, but it's wigging me out.

"It's too hot in here." My voice falls flat in the cell. I'm stuck in the corner of the first floor, away from the action.

"If someone doesn't bring me a fan or something, I'm going to strip!"

Once it's out of my mouth, I can't resist it. Poor impulse control. I don't give a shit right now because thinking about taking my clothes off keeps me from thinking about everything else.

But only for a second, and then the red's back.

"Will somebody bring me a goddamn fan?"

4

CAGE WAITED UNTIL the holding cell door clanged shut and the uniform walked away. Annabeth was curled on the floor in the corner, head on her knees.

"I'm not charging you with assaulting me."

She lifted her head enough to glare at him. "They made me put this shitty orange thing back on, and it's hot as hell in here." The jail suit's top buttons were open, revealing her white bra. "And they won't bring a fan."

"I'll see what I can do after we talk." Cage let the implication hang and sat down cross-legged in front of her, trying not to think of all the bodily fluids caked on the floor. "You've scratched the hell out of your arm."

"No shit, Sherlock."

"I believe you."

"My medical records must have showed up."

"Not yet," Cage said. "I'm going on instinct, and I want to help you. But I need you to tell me everything."

Annabeth edged closer, her uniform gaping open. She was either oblivious or didn't care. "You're being straight with me?"

"Absolutely."

"You can get the juicy details from the hospital."

"That's not what I'm asking. What do you remember about that night?"

"I told you, hardly anything."

"What's the first thing that comes to mind?"

She flinched as though he'd struck her. "I don't let myself think about it."

Cage softened his tone. "But sometimes you can't control that."

He let his words sink in, giving her time to think. Annabeth remembered more than she was letting on.

"Why does it matter?"

"Every detail matters. It's usually the overlooked ones that break a case open. I said I believe you. Can you trust me enough to let me help?"

She let out a defeated sigh. "Pain. My feet felt like I'd stomped on a hairbrush. Blinding lights. A screeching that made my head feel like it was splitting open."

"Do you remember giving them Lyric's name and her grandmother's number in the ambulance?"

"No. They told me about that when I woke up. I still didn't have a clue who I was. Gran was already there by then. She said I was her granddaughter and my name was Lyric Gaudet." She closed her eyes. "I was so miserable. My entire body hurt, and I had to pee in a tube. I looked like a smushed pear. But she said she knew I belonged to her."

"She used those words?"

Annabeth nodded. "She said that over and over when I kept asking who I was. It took me a while to remember the new stuff. But at least that went away. Then the surgeries started. Four in all, and this is the best they could do." She smacked her uneven left cheek.

"Those first days in the hospital, did you have any flashes of memory you couldn't explain?"

She picked at her tattoo. "My brain's shit. The neurologist

wanted me to do all sorts of therapy, but Gran didn't have a lot of money, and I needed to learn how to deal with everything else."

"Like what?"

"Like not being a pain in the ass for no reason. I used to rage at the smallest things. I broke dozens of glasses. I had to get that under control." She studied him, suspicion lighting her eyes.

Cage scooted closer. He'd have to have these pants dry-cleaned.

"I was like a baby," she continued. "It was months before I could do basic things like feed myself and wipe my ass. I couldn't talk because my jaw was wired shut. You want to know what's humiliating, even if you're a smush-face? Having someone wipe your ass after you crap in a bedpan. You wanna hear more?" Her tired voice had turned sharp, the shame in her eyes replaced by shining anger.

"I get the picture. I'm sorry we even have to discuss it."

Her shoulders inched down from her ears. "Whatever."

"What about school?"

"She said I'd already graduated." Annabeth had been weeks away from her senior year, taking AP classes at the local college.

"Did she have pictures of you around the house?"

"As a little kid, yeah. But she lost a lot of the others in Katrina. I always wondered if she was lying, because she lived in the French Quarter. Her house made it through just fine. I figured I must have been really pretty before, and she didn't want to make me feel bad that this is the face I'm stuck with."

Yet another mood swing, but this time she curled her body into a ball, defeated. Cage waited.

Finally, she took a long, ragged breath. "I knew I wasn't Lyric when you showed me that picture."

He kept his expression neutral, but his heart raced. "You

recognized her?"

"I've been dreaming about her ever since I found out Gran was dying. The girl tells me to run like I'm racing for the state championship, whatever that means. She says, 'Never look back,' and then I'm running. Then everything goes blank."

Lyric had known Annabeth was a track star. Had she helped stalk her and then reconsidered? Or had Lyric been a victim herself?

"I think you and the real Lyric were kidnapped by the same person, and she was still alive when he kidnapped you and Mickie. Thanks to the chaos of Hurricane Katrina, no one followed up on her missing persons report. Does the Lyric in your dreams say anything else?"

"Nope."

"She must have told you her name and her grandmother's phone number before she helped you escape. She knew your speed gave you a fighting chance."

Annabeth stilled. Her slack face hardened, her glare sending chills down his spine.

"And I messed it up. They're probably dead because of me."

"That's not what I'm saying."

She jumped to her feet, her fists against her head. "It's the truth."

Cage slowly stood, giving her space.

Annabeth glared at him, unintimidated by his height. He braced for another attack.

Instead, she whirled around and started banging her head against the bars. "I let them die. It's my fault. It's all my fault."

Cage seized her, pinning her arms against her chest. "You're going to hurt yourself. Calm down."

She slammed the back of her head against him, but he was bigger and stronger. He held her still. "Annabeth, just breathe."

The name seemed to douse her anger. She stopped fighting him and burst into sobs.

"I'm not her anymore. I'm not anybody."

5

THE DOOR TO the holding area slammed open, nearly hitting Cage in the face. "Sorry, didn't see you there." The pock-faced officer Bonin had called Pietry smirked.

"No problem. Can I help you?"

Pietry cocked his head. "'Scuse me?"

"You're out of uniform and off duty. I assume you're here to talk to me when Bonin's not around."

"Smart guy. I just wanted to finish our conversation from earlier. Ninety-nine percent of the cops you'll be working with don't want you, and we ain't gonna let you make us look like dumbasses to the big boys."

"Pretty sure you can do that all on your own."

"Cute," Pietry said. "My point is, don't expect anyone besides Bonin to work with you. Rest of us have it our way, you'll be out of here before Christmas."

"Point taken." Cage stepped around the wide man and jogged up the old stairs, taking them two at a time. He'd expected the NOPD detectives to have issues with him, but he'd hoped the uniforms would be easier to get along with.

He slipped out the substation's side door and walked across the small courtyard to the café. Iron tables and chairs filled the space between the station and café, and most of the seats were taken, despite the heat. Inside, the exposed brick and arched ceiling made the narrow café seem more like a tunnel with tables and chairs. The tiny black and white tiles made him dizzy.

Bonin waved to him from a corner table near the kitchen.

"Café keeps a table for the NOPD," she said as he sat down. "Nothing goes together better than cops and donuts."

She tossed a paper-clipped stack of papers on the table. "Medical records. And the Jasper County Sheriff sent over the accident folders. Hope you like your coffee black."

Cage savored the first few bites of the warm beignet and then dug into the records. "She's telling the truth."

Bonin nodded. "August 15, 2011, she climbs from a deep ditch and steps in front of a car on a desolate county road near Jasper, Texas. The only thing that saved her is the car's slow speed. The driver had some time to brake."

Annabeth's head had slammed into the windshield, and her face had been a bloody pulp and unrecognizable. Even the mole on her lip wasn't visible. "Broken eye socket, fractured jaw, skull fracture, broken nose. Face initially unrecognizable from swelling. Fractured clavicle. How the hell was she even able to give them Lyric's name?"

"The county sheriff said she told the driver before the paramedics arrived." Bonin licked the powdered sugar off her fork. "Out of sheer will, probably."

"Grandma's desperate to believe, and the girl's face is messed up. Charlotte Gaudet takes her home and pawns her off as Lyric."

"I thought I recognized the family name. Charlotte was a well-known Voodoo priestess—her family dates back to the city's early days. She lived in the French Quarter until she died a couple of weeks ago."

"A priestess?"

A half-smile played on Bonin's lips. "We take our traditions and ghosts seriously."

New Orleans's history of Voodoo and all things supernatural made for a hell of a marketing strategy. "Touristy stuff, right?"

"Some of it. But plenty of people practice Voodoo as their religion." She held up a clear evidence bag containing the tarnished ring. "Voodoo explains why she was so desperate for this. It's an antique mourning ring. My grandmother had one and kept a lock of her firstborn's hair in it. See the glass face?"

She pointed to the delicate center of the ring. "That looks like dirt, but my bet's on ashes. Charlotte's, to be specific."

"And why would she carry around her grandmother's ashes?" The coffee would make him sweat even more, but he needed the caffeine.

"Probably a protection spell," Bonin said. "If they're Charlotte's ashes, another priestess would have had to perform the spell before she died. Did she mention anyone else, someone she'd ask for help?"

"She said Miss Alexandrine was coming to fix things."

Bonin's eyes widened, her face paling to something that looked a lot like fear. "Miss Alexandrine lives a few blocks from where Annabeth was arrested. She's a very powerful and well-respected priestess."

"Will she curse me to die in twenty-four hours or something?" He couldn't keep the sarcasm out of his voice.

"First off, Voodoo isn't about curses; it's about love and light and living a better life, just like any religion," Bonin said. "Secondly, you need to drop that attitude. You might not believe, but this is New Orleans, and spirits and magic are part of our history and culture. You want to be successful here, don't disrespect it. Let me talk to her when she shows up."

"I'm good with that." Cage wasn't worried about the Voodoo woman hexing him, but he didn't want to lose her as a potential witness. He thumbed through the medical records. "Violent multiple sexual assaults. How far did the Jasper sheriff take the investigation?"

"His theory is she was dumped and left for dead. She was barefoot and had external injuries that probably came before the accident. Bruises around wrists and ankles indicated she'd been bound. No hit in CODIS from the rape kit. Soil and trace was taken from her fingertips. I'm trying to track down the original samples."

CODIS was the FBI's national DNA index system. But it only worked if the offender had been caught and his DNA entered into the system.

"Listen, there's a reason I brought you here."

"Besides the sugar high?"

"That's just a bonus," she said. "My lieutenant at Major Crimes won't be an issue, but the Quarter's district commander is a by-the-book guy. He's at a conference today, but he'll find out you're here. Patrol guys already talking about you—and Annabeth."

"Guess I should let the LBI know."

"You think? Look, I'm sure you know the NOPD and city government have a long history of corruption. I'll stand up for every cop I've worked with, but plenty of people still have their hands in the wrong cookie jar. And most of them think the LBI's new division is really about having an inside narc."

"That's not what I signed up for," Cage said. "The LBI wants to take some of the load off NOPD's major crime so the police can allocate more resources to drug and gang control."

"And you can bet that if you see something unethical, the LBI will expect you to report it to them. People are afraid the state wants to clean house."

"Is that what you think?"

"About the state? Absolutely."

Dani had suggested the same thing, calling Cage a Pollyanna if he really believed the state didn't have ulterior motives. "I'm here to help with the NOPD's major crimes. Period."

Bonin smiled. "I know. But I wanted you to understand what you're up against. My advice is to call the LBI as soon as we're finished here. They can deal with the district commander and smooth things over."

"Yeah, I will." A line in the medical report had caught his attention. "Annabeth said her feet felt like she'd stepped on a hairbrush. How far from the accident scene did they search?"

"That's when the sheriff got defensive," Bonin said. "He claims they searched a five-mile radius but found nothing. He insisted she was dumped, naked and barefoot."

Cage turned the report and pointed to the scribbled note in the margins. An overwhelmed hospital with little experience in major crimes had likely written it as an afterthought. "She had lesions on her feet. They removed longleaf pine needles."

"Lots of pine trees in that part of Texas."

"Look at the accident scene pictures. This is a clearing. Gravel on the side of the road. No pine trees in sight." He pulled up Google Maps on his phone. Annabeth had been hit on a county road, but a main highway was only a few hundred feet away. He soon had an aerial view of what he was looking for. "You only see the pine trees when you see the whole picture. I suck at figuring out distance on a map, but I'm guessing there's at least a couple of football fields' worth of clearing before any of the pine trees."

"How did she escape?"

"Lyric helped her," Cage said. "That's the only explanation. It's why Annabeth had Charlotte's phone number. That means he kept Lyric for nearly six years."

"She's special to him. The first victim," Bonin said, "or an accomplice. You can't rule that out."

"Either way, we start with Lyric. And there's only one person who can help us do that. How well do you know the officer she assaulted last night?"

CAGE STEPPED OUTSIDE to make the call, crouched beneath the eaves of the Eighth District Police Station. Like everything else in the French Quarter, the building was well over a hundred years old. Its stately columns and ornate entrance resembled the plantations Cage had grown up around.

Sweltering August heat snatched his breath away. He opened his top button, loosened his tie, and hit send.

"Finally," Dani answered on the second ring. "Is it really her?" They'd met long after the girls disappeared, but Dani knew the case haunted him.

The knots in Cage's stomach loosened at the comforting sound of her voice. He missed her already. "I think so," he said. "She had a head injury and has no memory of Roselea."

"That makes no sense."

"I know, and I can't go into details. You haven't told anyone, have you? Not even Jaymee?"

"No," Dani said. A faint hint of defensiveness crept into her tone. "You're not coming home tonight, are you?"

"I can't," he said. "Not until I get this straightened out."

Dani's tired sigh tweaked Cage's nerves. "You're supposed to be here, helping me pack. I understand why you rushed to New Orleans today, but you promised you'd be home tonight."

"I'm sorry," he said. "It's a lot more complicated than just bringing her home."

"Guess you were overconfident. What did Rogers say?"

"I haven't told him yet." So much for his promise to Bonin.

Calling his boss was a straight shot to the Georges. Cage might be an ass, but he needed more time to get through to Annabeth.

"He's going to be pissed that you're running around his turf going cowboy before the new division is launched."

"I'll deal with him. How's Emma?"

The baby had a nasty summer cold, and from the rough sound of Dani's voice, she'd caught it as well.

"Sleeping, finally." Dani coughed. "We're both exhausted. Did you even bring an overnight bag and change of clothes?"

"Shit." Add shopping to his list.

"I'm pretty sure I suggested that before you left. Her being booked under a different identity made it pretty clear this wouldn't be the open and shut deal you said it would."

He didn't want to fight. They'd been arguing too much since Cage took the new position. He hadn't sought it out. The Louisiana Bureau of Investigation had come to him on a recommendation from his superior. Dani initially supported him, saying Ironwood was too much for her now with the baby to care for. The restoration was taking longer than they'd planned, and Dani couldn't be as hands-on as she wanted.

He changed the subject. "Did you hear from the committee?"

"We got the grant. The historic society will use the money to finish the restorations and then open it up for tourists."

"It's still ours, Dee. We can go back anytime, especially when the town's not full of tourists."

"I know." Sadness layered her voice. She loved the old home as much as she loved her family. "Downsizing is the right thing. But moving out of town, to New Orleans … It's just so much."

Cage tried to keep the irritation out of his voice. "We talked about this. And I needed a change of scenery. There's too many memories."

His mother had succumbed to Alzheimer's nearly a year ago. His father was too heartbroken to stay in the house Cage grew up in, so Dani and Cage had planned to move in while his father holed up in a retirement community outside of town. Then the LBI called.

"I worry about your dad."

"He's made friends. Jaymee and Nick can keep an eye on him. And it's not like we won't be back to visit. We're not talking about the other side of the country."

"Yeah, I know. It's just all happened so quickly".

"We close on the house in two weeks. We're committed to this thing now."

"Unless the LBI fires you for waltzing into the NOPD as an agent before you even start. Why can't you just let the police handle this? She's their responsibility now."

"You know why."

"How long are you going to blame yourself for being human?" Dani said.

He didn't have the energy for the same old argument. "I have to go. I'll call you later."

6

"WALKING WOULD HAVE been faster." Cage fought the urge to start blaring his horn. Everything about the French Quarter was compact except for the traffic, which moved at snail speed.

"It's hot as balls," Annabeth said. "I still don't see why we're going to Gran's house. She's dead."

"Lyric disappeared years before you did, and she was still alive when you were taken. That means she's either important, or she's involved. We need to search the house, and I'm hoping you'll tell the whole story."

"I have."

"No, you're not."

She crossed her arms and huffed, turning to look out her window. "Did you really get that fat cop to drop the charges?"

"That was all Detective Bonin." He hoped the patrol officer kept his mouth shut about Annabeth's case.

"That hot, light-skinned woman?"

"That's her." He'd yet to tell Annabeth she wouldn't be staying home tonight. Cage couldn't risk letting her out of his sight. "Just promise you'll stick with us. If I lose you, I'm out of a job."

"Okay." She ran her finger over the antique ring. "Thanks for giving this back."

"Why's it so important to you?"

"You wouldn't understand."

Traffic inched forward. Someone in front of Cage blared their horn. A bicycle cart with two tourists holding giant fish bowls filled with a red liquid sliced around the cars. A group of college-aged kids tromped down the sidewalk, slurping from tall tubes filled with something green and frothy.

Historic Creole townhouses flashed by, the lower-level shops open for business. Above were the famous iron balconies and coveted French Quarter residences. Every building seemed to be built on top of the next structure, jammed together like an accordion. Here, the influence of the past overpowered the present.

"Do I have to go back to Mississippi?"

"I haven't told your parents yet."

"Couldn't that get you in big shit trouble?"

He laughed. "Definitely, and I can't put it off forever. As for going back, you're a legal adult. No one can make you."

"What are they like?"

"Who?"

"The Georges," Annabeth said. "My parents, I guess."

Sam George wasn't a bad person, but he liked to call the shots and get his own way. The captain in charge had patiently listened to George every time he stormed in, demanding answers. He refused to accept the lack of evidence, despite numerous searches with multiple crime-scene technicians and volunteers. George's denial had been understandable, and Cage's captain allowed the man to vent countless times, often at any hour of the night. But the Adams County Sheriff had drawn the line when Sam George publicly accused the sheriff's office of not taking his daughter's disappearance seriously because Annabeth was a person of color.

Racism still dirtied the south, but the captain and her deputies had worked long hours—often off the clock—to bring Annabeth and Mickie home. The only role Annabeth's skin played in their investigation was in her physical description in the state and national databases.

"They're good people. She's a teacher. He works for the county prosecutor." And used his position every chance he got.

"Do I have any brothers or sisters?"

"No."

"Did they think about having another kid? You know, as a replacement?"

Cage tried not to let his mouth drop open.

"Was that a bad question?" Annabeth watched him, almost childlike.

"An unusual one."

She nodded. "Sorry. I do that sometimes, especially sexual stuff. My brain thing."

"Is that what your neurologist said?" Bonin had left another message with the Tulane specialist. If he didn't return her call soon, Cage would outsource.

Annabeth stuck out her tongue. "Dr. Douchey? He's always got plenty to blab. Focal retrograde amnesia is the fancy name he sort of diagnosed me with. He says I'm lucky I didn't lose my working memory."

"What makes him a douche?"

"He says I don't want to remember—even if my brain is capable—so I don't try."

"You think that's true?" He squinted to read the street sign. *St. Peter.* At this rate, they'd never get to the Gaudet house.

"I do try." Her voice was sharp. "And Gran didn't like him, either. She said the therapy was too stressful, and I didn't have to go."

He left that one alone. "Charlotte was a Creole Voodoo priestess, right?"

Annabeth's face brightened, and she twisted in her seat to face him. "She could trace her ancestors back to Haiti. They came during the Revolution. Voodoo is in her blood. She said it was in mine too. But so much for that."

She scrubbed at the tattoo. "This was her idea. The scar was ugly and a reminder of what happened. Now I feel stupid."

Cage pressed on before her mood shifted again. "Is there some sort of protection spell on the ring?"

She looked at him, wide-eyed. "What do you know about protection spells?"

"Nothing. But I spoke with someone who does. She knows Miss Alexandrine too."

"Everyone knows Miss Alexandrine," she said. "She'll fix things when she comes for me."

"How does the ring protect you?" He hadn't meant to sound sarcastic, but the clogged street and honking horns were getting to him.

Annabeth covered the scar with her opposite hand and turned away. "You don't believe in it, so don't worry about it. Turn right here." Annabeth didn't speak again except to give him directions.

He pulled in the alley next to a faded brick townhouse. A rusting iron fence protected a small patch of untended flowers.

"The house is over one hundred years old, and it shows. With my medical bills, Gran never had much money for repairs." Annabeth looked at Cage. "Why do you think she did that when she knew I wasn't Lyric?"

"My guess is you were the next best thing and all she had."

They stepped into the sweltering heat, and Cage tried to get his bearings. The high peak of St. Louis Cathedral was visible to his right, and he knew Jackson Square and the famed Café Du Monde were just a few blocks away.

Annabeth lingered in the alley. "It was bad enough living here after she died, but now …"

A black car squeezed in behind Cage's, and Bonin stepped out to join them. She offered her hand. "We haven't been formally introduced. Detective Myra Bonin. I'm working with Agent Foster."

"You're wearing the wrong shade of lipstick for your skin." Annabeth turned and headed toward the front door.

"Nice kid," Bonin said.

"You talked to the neighbors?"

Bonin shaded her eyes to look up at him. "Lyric and Charlotte fought all the time over Lyric's hard partying and friends. Charlotte couldn't control her. Most people believed she ran away. They steered clear when she came back home, mostly because Charlotte ran them off."

Annabeth had left the front door open, and they stepped into a small entryway. Thank God Annabeth had left the air on.

"Charlotte started her own investigation," Bonin said in a low voice. "She tracked down and hounded Lyric's friends, blamed them for not protecting her, and got pissed off when none of them knew anything. After a couple of years, everyone's empathy was gone. No one wanted to deal with her. I'm sure she cursed every one of them."

"That answers the question about why everyone accepted Annabeth was the missing granddaughter. Easier to believe than deal with her wrath."

"This is New Orleans. Everyone in the neighborhood knew Charlotte as a Voodoo priestess. They wouldn't question her word."

Claustrophobia rushed through him. The cottage may be

historical, but like everything else in the Quarter, it felt compressed and secretive. Annabeth sat on the floor in the front room, holding a framed photo with a vacant expression on her face.

The picture had faded, but the smiling girl in the pretty yellow shirt was missing two front teeth and clinging to a middle-aged, light-skinned woman with a beautiful smile. "She said this was me when I was six."

Annabeth traced the picture with her fingertips. "She told me all about my growing up. Her stories were so vivid I sometimes thought I might actually remember it."

"Did she mention that she and you—Lyric—weren't getting along before she disappeared?" Cage asked.

"That's not true. They were best friends." Annabeth said this fervently, an edge in her voice. It didn't surprise him that Charlotte had made up her own narrative. But it seriously hindered their chances of figuring out what happened to Lyric.

"Have you gone through Charlotte's things yet?" Bonin asked.

"I couldn't deal with it."

"Will you give us permission to search the house?" Cage asked.

"Whatever." She sat down in the threadbare recliner and put her head in her hands.

Cage hesitated as Bonin headed for the next room. "I know you're hurt by Charlotte's dishonesty. But I don't think she knew who you were. She didn't know Annabeth was missing or that her fingerprints and dental records were on file. She just knew you were lost, and she needed her granddaughter."

"You don't have to make me feel better."

"I'm just giving you my opinion. You can take it or leave it."

Annabeth traced her fingers over the picture. "She made me

feel loved."

"That's more than a lot of people can say."

"You should check her closet first. That was the only place off limits to me. It's the back bedroom on the left." She closed her eyes and tucked her knees under her chin. "There's a box of pictures and keepsakes in my room. They're supposed to be Lyric's. I'll get them and meet you upstairs."

CHARLOTTE GAUDET'S RECORDS of her search for Lyric consisted of a thick, spiral-bound notebook and roughly nine hundred sticky notes. She had considered every person in her granddaughter's life a potential suspect. Countless sticky notes were devoted to specific people in Lyric's inner circle. Some had alibis. Others had angered Charlotte with their lack of information, and she'd labeled them worthless.

"This is a mess." Bonin gathered up the unattached sticky notes. "I can't read half of them."

A wrinkled piece of brown paper slipped from the notebook. Cut in a perfect square, one side bore the Rouses Grocery logo. The other side contained a long paragraph written in another language with a fine-point blue marker. Candle wax had splattered the paper, along with some other residue that smelled like Dani's herb garden. Rosemary? Thyme?

Bonin snatched it off the floor and donned a pair of tortoise-shell reading glasses. "This is a spell. It's in Creole. *'Sean Andrews, I command you cast away all lies and speak only the truth to me. In the name of the Father, the son, and the Holy Ghost, I compel you. Tell me the truth!'*"

"A spell?" Cage was already sick of the word.

Bonin glared at him over the top of her glasses. "Yes, a spell. She used blue ink because that's the color of truth. Looks like she used an orange candle and specific herbs that would give her power over him. That's why she wrote her name over his. But the targeted person has to touch the paper in order for a spell like this to work. Their skin needs to come into contact with the herb oil on the paper."

Cage skimmed back through notebook pages until he found the list of names. "Sean Andrews's name isn't crossed off. Guess her spell didn't work."

"Or she wasn't satisfied with his answers—if she even gave it to him," Bonin said. "It took four months for the original investigators to find him after Katrina. He was evacuated to Ohio, and he'd only just arrived when the original detective found him."

"If I didn't know you were a rational, decorated investigator," Cage said, "I might think you believed these spells work."

"People only need to believe to make the spell work. Growing up here around Voodoo and conjure, you see enough to believe." Bonin smiled. "Spend enough time in New Orleans, and you might too. This city does that to a person, but that's something you have to experience to really understand."

Cage turned the page and his heart stopped.

Blue pickup.

A door slammed shut downstairs.

Cage barreled down the stairs as Bonin ran to the window. "She's cutting through the back alley."

7

I RACE TOWARD the sound of squealing trumpets and bumping tubas. A second line parade is strutting down Decatur Street, and I slip into the throng of marchers.

Cage is going to be mad, but I need time to think without his constant questions. I'm not really doing anything wrong—Bonin got the charges dropped.

I can't get my breath. What if Cage catches me?

A buzzing sound tears through my head, drowning out the band. My heart keeps racing. Someone brushes my arm, and I twist around in panic. Has he found me?

"Sorry, girl!" One of the costumed dancers bopping between the second line and the brass band tips his hat and smiles.

Running, running, running. Don't look back. Pain in my shins. I need my track shoes. Stupid—you're naked.

"Shit." My knees hit the pavement first, and the dancer grabs my arm before I face-plant. People prance on, but the dancer helps me stand.

"You can't walk with your eyes closed 'round here," he says. "Especially in the second line. You gonna need to clean that."

Blood trickles from my knee. The dancer's too close. I back away, pain shooting through my arms.

"You all right?" Most of the second line's moved on, and I'm exposed.

"I have to get out of here." I turn and run, dodging the stragglers. My heart's pounding too fast.

The band cuts left, but I sprint ahead until I burst into the French Market. This time of day, with the summer heat on full blast, the market's not too crowded with shoppers. But there's about a million people trying to sell their crap. A couple of ladies selling overpriced silver jewelry stare at me.

I find the ladies' room, and it's about fifty degrees hotter. I splash water on my face and then take a long drink from the faucet. I wet a paper towel and clean my knee the best I can. My head feels heavy. I glare at my smushed-face reflection. The cracks in the mirror make my face even more distorted.

"You're ugly. And it's your fault."

I plop down on one of the benches near the restrooms. My shirt's drenched with sweat and water, and the wet paper towel is stuck to my bleeding knee.

Cage thinks I can tell him something about the real Lyric that will magically lead him to the kidnapper, but I got nothing. Gran always said "we" were best friends, but that was another lie. All the other so-called stories and memories she told me probably were too.

I told Cage the truth. I have been dreaming about the girl—the real Lyric—telling me to run. But other memories seeped through, and they won't stop.

This is your fault. Why? Why?

I didn't know who screamed that until today. Now I can't get her out of my mind, and I don't know what any of it means. The only person who might be able to help me is Miss Alexandrine, and her house is the first place Bonin will look.

I clutch the protected ring and hope Charlotte's spirit is still tethered to me. "Tell me what to do."

A woman with albino skin is suddenly standing in front of

me. "Faith" is tattooed on her chunky arm with a cross as the "t." A tiny handmade juju doll hangs on a chain around her neck.

"I'm not interested in buying dolls or a reading."

She smiles. "I don't need to read you. Your energy is blasting across the aisle."

Or she can tell by looking I'm in deep shit. Plenty of charlatans around, especially in the market. Tourists are suckers.

"I'm cool." Hopefully she gets the point.

"I also can't ignore someone in such need."

"Lady, I'm fine."

She hands me a bottle of water. "You look dehydrated."

"I don't have any money."

"That's all right." She starts to walk back to her booth and then stops and gives me another weird smile. "Perhaps a priest could help you."

Confession? No way. I don't even know what the hell I should confess to. If I had a way to get inside my head and …

I nearly drop the water. She's right. I do need a priest.

8

CAGE LOST HER. Annabeth had locked the courtyard gate, and by the time he ran around the front of the house and through the alleys, she was long gone. They'd driven up and down the streets for three hours, stopping to check in various pubs and stores. The priestess everyone was supposed to be afraid of wasn't home. With dusk moving in, they'd gone back to Charlotte's house.

Cage let Bonin search Annabeth's room—she could deal with it if anyone tried to say the girl's verbal consent to search had passed.

He'd screwed up this time. The new job would be toast, and Sam George would never allow the Adams County Sheriff to take him back. He and Dani had some money in savings, and the grant would take care of Ironwood. She'd have to go back to work full time, and they wouldn't be able to live at Ironwood during tourist season.

What about the house in New Orleans? They closed in two weeks.

He sat down on the front step, sick from the heat and from his stupidity. Had Annabeth been playing him the whole time? How much of her memories was she holding back?

Blue pickup. Jesus Christ. Everything about Annabeth came back to bite him in the ass.

If his instincts had been so wrong about her, then maybe he needed to find a new profession.

The front door banged shut behind him. Bonin handed him a glass of water and sat down on the step next to him.

"I screwed up."

"We screwed up," she said. "I'm just as responsible. I bought her act too."

"Maybe it's not an act," Cage said. "The brain injury causes mood swings and aggression, makes her impulsive."

Bonin handed him a thick, short black candle with his name carved into the wax. Tiny black crystals were stuck in some kind of oil oozing around the burnt wick.

"What the hell is this?"

"It's a crossing spell," Bonin said. "A pretty sloppy one but still effective."

He stared at her.

"Voodoo isn't black magic, but there are tricks. This spell is meant to create confusion."

"That's why my name's carved in it?"

"Yep," she said. "And before you start talking about black magic, that's Hollywood bullshit. Many of our Loa are associated with Catholic saints."

"Loa? As in L-o-a?"

"In Voodoo, the supreme creator is distanced. We pray to the Loa—the spirits of Haitian and Louisiana Voodoo. There's a Loa for just about everything, including ancestral Loa. We make offerings to them in exchange for help and guidance. Black magic is only done by outliers."

Cage came from a Mississippi small town that embraced its antebellum homes and Civil War heritage. Cultural traditions lasting for generations made sense to him—those customs represented everything that made the southern states unique. "I grew up in southern Mississippi. Voodoo, hoodoo, root doctors—I know black magic isn't accepted by most practitioners. But for the love of God, please tell me you don't believe this spell shit works?"

"You realize you just mentioned God like he's the only sentient being who could actually exist. Like all religion isn't ultimately leading to the same thing."

"That's not what I'm saying. I don't care what God you pray to or how many or if you do at all," Cage said. "But you're saying this girl put a spell on me? That's why I lost her? It couldn't possibly be because she locked the gate and had a head start."

Bonin's mouth tightened into a straight line. Her eyes blazed. "I never said that's why you were confused. Whether or not I believe the spell can work isn't the point."

"Then what is?"

"You want to believe this was an impulsive decision; I'm telling you it took some planning and thought. She broke into a locked cabinet downstairs where Charlotte kept much of her supplies. She found the oil and the black salt and took the time to carve your name and then lit the candle and let it burn long enough for some of the oil to melt into the wax."

Bonin snatched the candle from him. "We weren't upstairs more than ten minutes. And she didn't know the spell by heart. She had to search through one of Charlotte's books."

Cage leaned against the iron railing. "She planned it."

"Not an impulsive move. Which means she has zero credibility as far as I'm concerned."

A text chimed on his phone. He lazily held it out in front of him instead of protecting his privacy and immediately regretted it.

FaceTime so I can stare at your handsome face.

"Your wife's sweet. Take the time to call her."

He flushed. "It's not my wife."

9

HE STARED AT the sleeping woman. She'd been nothing but trouble from the start, but her hold on him seemed to get worse every time he tried to get rid of her. He slipped out of the room and sat down at the table, reading the text again.

The phone rang five times before his cousin answered, grouchy with sleep and probably fucked up on something. "What?"

"You sure?"

"Yeah man," was the reply.

The girl's body had shattered on impact with the car. He'd witnessed the scene with his own eyes. What a damned waste. She was a fine piece and a fighter. He would have thoroughly enjoyed playing with her.

"The old lady really believed she was her granddaughter?"

"Uh, that's the big question, but I can't get much information. We got a fucking small-town deputy working for the LBI's new department. Supposedly, he's to assist with big cases, since we got so much street crime down here. It's all bullshit. They want to put a handsome, white face in homicide to make the press happy. Makes 'em more confident we're doing things right. Like white people can't be corrupt."

He rolled his eyes. He'd listened to this argument a hundred times already. "And this girl doesn't remember anything?"

"Nothing. She's still wrapping her mind around the whole thing. Brain damaged, you know. Screwed up her face too. Damn shame."

Sure as hell was. "Why you telling me all this? I haven't seen her in years. Didn't even know she was missing."

"Thought you ought to know, I guess. It's a crazy mess. How's things?"

His cousin droned on for another thirty minutes, and he supplied the necessary answers until he finally managed to end the phone call.

Only two women had ever escaped him, and the loss haunted him. He wasn't worried about her identifying him. She'd gone this long with her head screwed up, she probably wasn't going to have some big revelation. And the other had her chance a long time ago and blew it. Stupid.

He scrubbed the graying stubble on his cheeks. Staying put was the smart thing to do. He was safe here. His routine was perfected. He had a steady job and his fun on the side.

But she's alive. I never had the chance to break her.

He shuffled to the bedroom, fumbling in the dark for his keys. The woman in the bed rolled over, her dark hair spilling on the pillow. Still pretty, even if the drugs and alcohol had taken their toll on her skin.

And she enjoyed the game. Sometimes she got more into it than he did. She'd be pissed when she found out he'd played without her.

Keys in hand, he slipped out of the trailer and headed for his sacred place.

A little stress relief would help him decide what to do.

10

"SPECIAL AGENT FOSTER." Summer Jordan's throaty greeting belonged on a phone sex line. She lifted the plastic face shield and grinned. "I'm honored you're still willing to consult with country doctors like me."

"Are you seriously doing an autopsy right now?" Cage wanted to sink into the stairs.

"Shh," she said. "As long as you can only see me, it's not a privacy violation." She rubbed her forehead with crimson latex gloves.

"Christ, Summer."

"You said looking at the girl's medical records was urgent, and I've got a full plate today. Who's that with you?"

"Detective Myra Bonin." Her voice was sharp. "I'm working with Cage, and I wasn't aware he sent a copy of Annabeth's medical records to you."

"I wouldn't call them a copy. He takes shitty cell phone pictures." Summer wrinkled her forehead and stuck out her chin—her telltale expression for breaking open the ribcage. "A doctor's handwriting's hard enough to read as it is, and you're sending me crooked pictures with shadows."

"Sorry," Cage said. "I was in a hurry, and I need to upgrade my phone."

Snap-snap-snap.

"Seriously? The Louisiana Bureau of Investigation didn't get its hotshot a shiny, new phone?"

"You realize how much trouble we could get in, right?" Bonin looked ready to punch him. "It's bad enough I convinced the arresting officer to trust me in dropping the charges. Now we've lost her and broken privacy laws so that some county coroner—"

"Regional Medical Examiner," Summer said. "Six counties. I attended one of the country's top medical schools, and before I decided dead people were better, I studied neuroscience."

Snap-snap-snap.

"I'm sorry," Bonin said. "I know better than to make assumptions. But I'm still not happy about him sending you her records."

"Apology accepted. Cage, the rest is on you."

"Summer's being modest," Cage said. "She spent a year working as a surgical intern specializing in brain injuries."

"Fine," Bonin said. "She's probably qualified, but you still haven't given a decent reason for ignoring a major privacy law."

"We both think Annabeth's hiding something, right?"

"I'm starting to think she's a fraud, yeah."

"I'd like to have a medical opinion before we hit her with that."

Summer's tongue peeked out from the corner of her mouth. Cutting away the heart, for sure. "You need to talk to her current neurologist."

"We're trying to reach him," Cage snapped. "I need answers, and you're the only option right now."

Summer wielded the bloody forceps like a laser pointer. "Good Lord, you're stressed. When was the last time you got laid?"

Bonin choked back a laugh.

Mockery was an essential part of his friendship with Summer, and he usually enjoyed trying to one-up her. But he was short on time, and he could do without the morbid sounds of her yanking out internal organs. "None of your business. Just give me your opinion on her diagnosis."

"First off, in her most recent records—which are still from Tulane and not her current neurologist—she isn't diagnosed with focal retrograde memory loss," Summer said. "She spent several months in their therapy program, and both the hospital neurologist and psychologist note her long-term memory loss shouldn't be permanent."

"So she's faking," Bonin said.

He didn't want to believe it. The fear and confusion in her eyes had been too raw to be an act.

"That's not what I'm saying." Summer gritted her teeth and twisted hard. "This guy's heart's a tricky bastard. Did you read how badly Annabeth was injured?"

He'd skimmed over the details. "I got the gist."

"Let me give you the specifics: severe tearing, signs of healing and tearing again, both vaginally and anally. Slivers of a foreign object embedded into her vaginal wall. Would you want to remember?"

"Repressed memories?" Bonin asked. "I thought that wasn't a real thing."

"You're confusing repressing with recovered memories, usually severe childhood sexual abuse—that's a whole other debate," Summer said. "We're capable of blocking out things we don't want to deal with—and that's without a traumatic brain injury. And don't forget the trauma she must have gone through during the initial days of her recovery. To be honest, I'd be more surprised if she *did* remember."

"Is she making the conscious choice not to remember?"

Cage asked.

"Got it." She held up the oozing heart. "Look at the size of this thing. This is what obesity does. Every school kid should have to see something like this."

He started to explain that Summer spent too much time in the morgue to have any real social skills, but Bonin stared in fascination. "That's incredible."

"Her repression probably isn't a conscious choice," Summer said. "The brain is extremely complex, and we don't fully understand it, but the body in general goes to great lengths to heal itself. This is the same idea. Think of it as psychological scar tissue. Speaking of scar tissue, you should see the—"

"I don't care! Thanks for your help, Summer."

She laughed. "Good luck, you big pansy."

His screen went black.

"I'm still pissed you went behind my back with this," Bonin said. "But everything she said adds up."

"To what? She's hiding stuff, but you didn't see her reaction. She didn't know about Lyric."

Bonin pulled a document from her bag. "This is a copy of Charlotte Gaudet's will. It leaves everything to her granddaughter, specifically describing Annabeth without giving a legal name."

"She believed Annabeth was the only family she had."

Bonin slipped on her sunglasses. "French Quarter real estate's extremely valuable, even if it's in subpar condition. This house is worth over a million dollars."

11

IT'S DARK BY the time I get to The Conjure Shop on Rue Domaine. The priest usually doesn't come to the shop until evening, so I've been stuck in the heat. I suck in the shop's wonderful cool air. "I need to speak with Sen Michel."

The big girl behind the desk looks bored. "Who're you?"

"Tell him it's Charlotte Gaudet's granddaughter."

She jumps at Gran's name and scurries between the silky curtains that lead to the back room.

Most of the Voodoo shops in the Quarter cater to tourists—lots of junk and watered-down spells, if that. The Conjure Shop's off the main path, and High Priest Michel knows his stuff. He should, since Miss Alexandrine taught him.

"Lyric." He comes through the curtains, barefoot, wearing white pants and a thin white dress shirt. Gran always said his dark skin glowed because of the spirit within him, but I swear it fades as soon as he sees me.

"How can I help you?" Sen Michel's not looking me in the eye. Sweat pops in the crook of his neck.

"I need you to look into your crystal ball."

It sounds ridiculous to say it. Crystal balls are for sorcerers and frauds. But a real Voodoo priest knows how to use the crystal to enhance his powers.

He purses his beautiful lips, still not quite looking at me.

"What's wrong? Why have you been running?"

"I'm in a hurry," I say. "Some things have come up, and I need answers. About me. My past and my future."

"The crystal doesn't tell your future," he says. "It shows your intentions, your inner reality."

"That's what I need." Tell me what the memories mean. Can I trust Cage Foster? What should I do?

Sen Michel stares at me for too long, his dark eyes hypnotizing … and sad.

He knows. He's always known.

The reality nearly knocks me onto my ass. I've spent time with Sen Michel, learning rituals and discussing my eventual initiation as Gran's successor.

He knew, and he never said a word.

I know better than to go after a high priest, but all I see is red. I charge toward him, knocking over a tray of juju dolls. He catches my wrists. I try to jerk away, but he's damn strong.

"Rete," he whispers.

"Settle?" I'm screaming. "You knew all this time, and you're telling me to settle?"

The girl at the counter is reaching for the phone.

"Don't," Sen Michel says gently. "Ché, come into the back. We need to talk."

Sen Michel's private space is small and sweet smelling, and a massive altar takes up half the room. The altar is loaded with offerings like cash, wine, and dozens of other bits and pieces.

"How could you?" I turn on him.

He holds up his hand, his expression so fierce I shut up. "Listen to me. A shadow is over you."

"A spirit?"

"It's too vague," he says. "It may be your ancestor trying to warn you."

"Not my ancestor," I snap. "Remember?"

"You have much to learn," Sen Michel says. "Voodoo is family. You don't have to be blood for an ancestor to accept you. And Charlotte must have prayed for them to watch over you."

I don't know if I believe that. I'm not sure I believe in anything right now, but I'm not going to tell him.

"Whatever surrounds you is impossible to fully read," Sen Michel says. "But it fears for you. It wants you to trust the man you're running from."

The hairs on the back of my neck stand up. After I came home from the hospital, I accepted the Voodoo faith and Gran's teachings without question. On my worst days, when my temper's out of control and I start wishing I'd died on that road, Voodoo calms me down. The Loa don't care about my face or my missing teeth, and they forgive me when I lose my shit. I don't care if the spirits really exist or if the spells work. I believe in the religion because it's all I have—real evidence of the magic doesn't matter.

Maybe the shadow Sen Michel's seeing is just my own energy, or it's really a Loa watching over me—or he's being a melodramatic actor. I wouldn't be the first person to accuse him.

But how does Sen Michel know about Cage?

"Everything is changing for you," Sen Michel says. "You must decide what path to follow. Trust the people who are trying to help." He stops and yanks the white scarf off his head. "I can't blaspheme Voodoo like this. Myra Bonin called me ten minutes ago. She said you'd probably show up here and that I should convince you to trust her and the cop she's working with."

12

CAGE DUCKED HIS head and followed Bonin into the small store on Dumaine Street. Located on the bottom floor of an ancient brick townhouse and away from the main tourist traps, The Conjure Shop had only a discreet wooden sign above its entrance.

"You're sure she'll be here?"

"I found handwritten rituals in her room from the High Priest who runs this shop," Bonin said. "He works at night, and there's a good chance she'll show up, especially since Miss Alexandrine is MIA. I don't think she has anywhere else to go."

Tables loaded with candles, statues of saints and Voodoo dolls took up much of the small store. Various herbs and oils lined the back wall, along with baskets of multi-colored baggies tied with thick string.

"What's a gris gris bag?"

"Like a mojo bag," Bonin said. "Blessed by the priest for whatever you need it to do. And it's pronounced gree-gree."

Cage picked up one of the little bags. It felt like a hacky sack. "This one is for money and good luck. Does that mean I'll win the lottery if I carry it around?"

"Can I help you?" The woman at the counter looked unimpressed with his question.

Bonin held up her badge. "We're looking for a girl who—"

"With the weird face? She's in the back with Sen Michel."

The metallic purple curtains behind the front counter snapped open, and Annabeth marched out. The rage in her eyes reminded Cage of his mother during the end stage of Alzheimer's. Her anger erupted out of nowhere, her punches somehow landing like a prize fighter's despite her weak body.

"You bitch."

Cage stepped around Bonin and caught Annabeth in mid-lunge. She screamed and twisted, beating him with her fists.

"Let her go," a tall black man dressed in flimsy white linen came through the curtains. "You'll only make it worse. She needs space and calm."

"She'll need a lot more than that if she attacks a cop." Cage locked the fighting girl against him, her hands pinned to his chest, her body heat burning rage and sweat. She tossed her head back and glared up at him.

"So much for being able to trust you. I bet it was your idea to have him trick me and make me think the spirits wanted me to trust you."

"I have no idea what you're talking about."

She stomped on his foot. "Liar."

"Cage didn't know anything about my calling Sen Michel," Bonin said. "I told him I'd found stuff from Michel in your room."

"I'm sorry, Myra," Michel said. "I couldn't do it."

"Damn, Michel. I told you it was important."

"Bitch," Annabeth said. "What do you think Miss Alexandrine's going to do when she finds out about this? She'll fix you good." She struggled against Cage. "Let me go, asshole."

"Not until you calm down."

"I'll say you attacked me."

"In a room full of witnesses to claim otherwise," Bonin said.

Annabeth slammed her head against his collarbone. "I trusted you."

"Is that why you set a spell on me?" Cage gritted his teeth. That would leave a mark.

"Set a spell on you? You sound like a dumbass when you say it that way. And you don't believe, so what difference does it make?"

"You're right." His arms ached from struggling with her, and he was fed up with her distrust. He put her first, risking his job. "I think it's all a bunch of made-up crap to make New Orleans mysterious for the tourists, and you're the one who looks like a dumbass when you carve my name into a candle."

She spit on him.

"Enough." Bonin yanked a pair of handcuffs off her belt. "That's a second assault charge."

Annabeth's face turned milk-white. She stared at the cuffs, gasping for air. "No one's handcuffing me." She looked back up at him. "Please, please don't put those things on me."

Her angry tone had evaporated to childish, uncontrollable fear. She trembled against him, tears in her eyes.

He kept one arm locked around her while he wiped the saliva off his neck. "Your kidnapper handcuffed you."

She stilled. "I don't remember. Just please, don't."

"I think you do," Bonin said. "You've remembered for quite a while, but you stuck with Charlotte Gaudet to make sure you inherited her house. It's worth a lot of money."

Charlotte's will confirmed that she knew Annabeth wasn't her biological granddaughter, but she loved her, listing 'the woman living with her as Lyric for the past seven years' as her only living family member and sole heir. Alexandrine Dupree was named executor, with the specific instructions not to reveal the truth to the girl unless her safety depended on it.

Annabeth's head whipped back and forth. "Miss Alexandrine's supposed to take care of her will."

"I think you're lying. Maybe you didn't know at first, but you found out the truth at some point. Charlotte was dying. You didn't know your real identity, so why not stick around?"

The priest seemed to come out of a shocked trance. "Myra, she wanted me to look into the crystal ball and essentially tell her who she was. If you saw the look on her face when she realized that I knew the truth, you'd understand."

"She's a good actress," Bonin said. "She fooled us with her meek act all the way here just so she could take off, even though I did her a favor and got her assault charge dropped."

"That's not true." Annabeth looked up at him, her chin digging into his chest. "You believe me, don't you?"

His muscles ached from struggling with her. "I told you my job was at stake. You promised not to take off. Why should I trust you now?"

"Because I need you to." Her voice wavered with panic.

"You found out about Charlotte's lie and decided she owed you," Bonin said. "I bet you conned her into the protection ritual too. The ultimate punishment—her soul bound to you instead of joining her ancestors."

"Fuck you." Annabeth's scream seemed to amplify her body strength. She slammed her head into his chest and then planted her knee into his groin.

He dropped his arms and staggered back until he hip-checked the table of Voodoo dolls, knocking a doll onto the floor. Its painted open mouth mirrored Cage's shock.

Sen Michel and Bonin had Annabeth pinned to the floor, one handcuff already on her wrist.

"Don't cuff her." Cage barely mustered the words.

Bonin jammed her knee into Annabeth's back and yanked her other arm behind her, snapping the cuffs tight.

"She didn't give me a choice."

13

BITCH BONIN SAID I could get sedated at the hospital or come back to the cell. The hell if I'm going to the hospital again. I tried to apologize to Cage, to explain how I had my anger issues under control for a while, but now it's like someone's lit me up from the inside.

He put an icepack on his nuts and told me he didn't want to hear it.

Bonin did this. If she hadn't asked Sen Michel to lie to me, I would have been cool when they showed up. I might have even told them about the images that keep exploding in my head.

I'll find a way to get her back for what she said about Gran's spirit. I would never do that, even if I had known the truth.

My hands reach for the ring. Cage took if off the chain, but he said I could keep the ring if that meant I'd stay calm and get some rest. "Maybe your head will be right tomorrow."

Right. My head's never going to be right.

I sense her immediately. It's her perfume—always jasmine. She walks so softly I don't see her until she arrives at my holding cell. She's wearing her pretty white sundress, which makes her dark skin shine.

"Where have you been?"

Miss Alexandrine sighs and looks down at me with her dark, knowing eyes. "I'm sorry. I was speaking at the Preservation

Society. You knew that, remember? That's why I told you to come by last night."

"But I didn't show up. And I called you at 3:00 a.m."

"Child, I have other commitments, and you got yourself into this mess. And old man Hastie at the front desk said last night's charges were dropped. You went and got yourself arrested again?"

I'm too tired to do anything but squeeze my face between the bars and whine. "I lost my temper. I tried to apologize."

Gran used to say that Alexandrine's eyes were the source of her power. They scare the hell out of me, especially when she's glaring at me like she is now. "You kicked a man in his privates. What did you think would happen?"

"I didn't. I was too busy thinking about how everyone lied to me. Gran, Sen Michel. And you, right? You lied just like the rest of them, you old bat."

Her expression flashes to hurt, and that makes me want to bawl.

"I'm sorry. I just want to go home."

Miss Alexandrine clears her throat. "You're supposed to go before the judge in the morning before bail is set."

I drop my forehead against the bars.

"Lucky for you, old man Hastie and I go way back."

14

THE MAISON DUPREY sat on the north end of the Quarter, nearer to Rampart Street than Bourbon. Bonin's sister had Cage's room ready, and he was so drained he barely raised an eyebrow when the front desk clerk warned him about the ghosts known to harass tourists.

He still hurt like hell. After calling Dani, more ice, food and sleep were his only concerns. To hell with Annabeth for tonight.

His suite was on the top floor, and as soon as he cranked the air conditioning, he took a quick shower and then fell into the double bed, ice pack in place. He found his phone and called his wife.

Four rings, and her voicemail picked up. Even sick, the baby woke up at the crack of dawn, and Dani was usually asleep by now.

"Hey Dee-Dee. I'm sorry I haven't called back. Things have been crazy here. Anyway, I'm sorry about earlier. Give Emma a kiss for me, and call when you can. I love you."

He tossed the phone aside and let his eyes close, but his mind refused to quit.

Blue pickup. Skinny white guy. Gross, slicked-back hair. I'm telling the truth! Please, just let me go. I won't do it again, I promise.

He flicked on the television. The weather channel meteorologist warned of record-breaking heat and the possibility of strong storms.

A violent thunderstorm and a small tornado had blown through Roselea the same day Annabeth and Mickie disappeared. They'd gone to the lake for their picnic, thinking the storm would hold off until evening. It struck much sooner, the F1 tornado touching down less than a mile from the lake. Six crucial hours passed before anyone realized the girls were missing. Initially, the scattered contents of their picnic basket along with the girls' toppled bikes suggested they might have been victims of the storm. But the tornado had missed the lake, and the area around the lake showed signs of struggle. All water searches came up empty. If the storm had taken the girls, their bodies would have shown up somewhere. Just like Katrina, the storm had provided the perfect diversion.

The rapid knock on his door nearly made him fall off the bed. He winced as he shuffled to the door and squinted through the peephole. He didn't see anyone, but the persistent knock came again. He locked the security latch and cracked the door a couple of inches. No one was there. The hall appeared empty, but a kid giggled from her hiding spot.

"I'm a cop. Don't bother me again." Cage slammed the door.

The little girl pounded on the door again, giggling hysterically. Cage would ground Emma for a week if she ever pulled a stunt like this.

He jumped off the bed and yanked open the door. The girl had already vanished.

"Kid, I'm going to call the manager if you don't knock it off."

"Who are you talking to?" Bonin came down the hall carrying something that smelled heavenly. "Nice abs."

He crossed his arms over his bare chest. "Just got out of the shower. Did you see the little girl running around? She keeps knocking and taking off."

"That's just Izora. She likes to play." Bonin looked him up and down.

"One of her parents works here? They need to teach her some manners."

"No, no, no." Bonin's shoulders shook with her laughter. "Izora's one of the ghosts that haunts the hotel. She's just a little girl, and she's lonely. Most of the other ghosts are older."

Cage stared at her. "A ghost was ding dong ditching me?"

"I thought you were used to ghosts, living in an old plantation house."

He held the door open for her. "How do you know this ghost's name? Did she tell you?"

"Cute," Bonin said. "When the hotel opened in the '70s, the spirits started bugging the guests, probably because they were pissed about the months of construction—the hotel used to be five different townhouses. Anyway, the owner brought in a medium, and she said the little girl bugging the guests up here was named Izora, and she died in one of the yellow fever epidemics. No one's been able to find an actual record of her, but the name and story stuck."

Cage tore open the pack of white T-shirts and slipped one over his head. "She better let me sleep tonight."

"Here," Bonin handed him the bag. "Best Po-Boys in the city."

Cage was so hungry a dirt sandwich would have tasted wonderful. "I think this guy uses severe weather or some kind of chaotic event as a distraction. He does his scouting, and then he waits for something to happen or even causes it. By the time police start searching, he's long gone. Maybe we can use that to find other victims."

"That's a pretty big net, but worth a try," Bonin said. "We've got the weather and his preference for café au lait."

"Bi-racial women," Cage clarified.

"In New Orleans, we say café au lait. Usually Creole, but not always. Before the United States bought Louisiana, that skin color was held in high regard. Chased after, even. Still is, to some extent."

Bonin leaned back in the chair, stretching her long legs. "How are your nuts?"

"Sore."

"I know a great healing spell." Bonin grinned. "Family legend says it came over with the slaves."

"No thanks." He wadded up the sandwich wrapper and tossed it in the trash. "Spirits and ghosts, I get. But the whole magic thing—I can't get my head around that."

"Eventually enough strange things will happen that you'll start to understand the real heart of New Orleans. I'm sorry I had to cuff her. But she gets super strength when she's like that."

"I know. She reminded me of my mom, toward the end of her Alzheimer's." Cage's throat knotted. Most days, he felt relief his mother wasn't suffering anymore. But every once in a while, an acute sadness sucked the energy out of him. "She had these violent outbursts and had to be sedated."

"Annabeth is scary. Either she's an exceptional actress or extremely dangerous."

"It's not her, it's her TBI." Images of his poor mother, out of her mind and attacking anyone who tried to help her, cascaded over him. He didn't want to remember her that way. "I know you think she's faking."

"Honestly, I don't know what to think of her anymore. I'm just hoping she'll tell us everything tomorrow. Because she's definitely holding something back. By the way, I booked her in as Lyric Gaudet and skipped the fingerprints for now. We've kept a lid on the match so far, but it's not going to last for long. My boss will know before noon tomorrow." Bonin dug into her bag and tossed a gris gris bag at him.

He caught it and smiled. "Money and massive success?"

"It's not from the store. I made it myself. For clarity and good luck. You're going to need it when you explain this shitstorm to Agent Rogers at the LBI. Pick you up at 8:00 a.m."

She started to shut the door and then poked her head back inside. "Hold the bag in your right hand and ask for clarity and good luck. Explain why you need it. Keep it with you—always on your right side. That's the power side for men."

Cage waited until the door shut and then picked up the bag.

Never hurt to try.

15

CAGE LET BONIN drive while he sat in the passenger seat and fumed. "How did this happen?"

"Miss Alexandrine's got a big reputation," Bonin said. "And she knows just about everybody. Probably performed rituals for them. She convinced the desk sergeant to let her go ahead and post bail."

"Without talking to the judge?"

"She knows the judge too."

Cage dragged his hand over his stubble. He hadn't had time to shave this morning. "If she doesn't let us see Annabeth, I'll arrest her."

"No, you won't." Bonin slowed at an intersection for pedestrians. Tourists swarmed around artists hawking their creations. Two boys had commandeered a prime spot on the corner and rapped away on their bucket-drums. "Trust me, the last thing you want to do is piss Miss Alexandrine off."

BONIN CUT A left onto St. Ann, and they drove past Bourbon. "A little New Orleans history for you: Marie Laveau's first house was on St. Ann Street, near Congo Park. It's Louis Armstrong Park now. Miss Alexandrine lives just down the street."

"Wasn't everybody afraid of Marie Laveau?"

"More Hollywood crap," Bonin said. "The Rue St. Ann

house was a sanctuary for the poor and sick, especially children. Marie performed charms and rituals, yes, but she was good. People who know the real history call her an angel of mercy." The car slowed. "She was pretty much confined to the Rue St. Ann house at the end of her life. The original house is gone, but people see her spirit walking through here all the time." Bonin parked in front of a modest, yellow cottage with green plantation shutters.

"Please let me do the talking."

"No problem." Cage followed her up the short walk.

A woman dressed in white answered the weathered door. She couldn't have been more than five feet, but her age was impossible to tell. Her startling eyes held him in a trance, her high cheekbones and gleaming skin reminiscent of an Egyptian queen.

"Myra Bonin. I've been expecting you. How's your grandmother? She feelin' better?"

"Yes, ma'am," Bonin said. "That herb you gave her did the trick."

"I knew it would." Her gaze landed on Cage. "My Lord, you're a tall man. And as handsome as Ly—sorry, Annabeth—says you are. I'm still getting used to using her real name."

He flushed. "Thank you. Is she here?"

Bonin elbowed him, but Miss Alexandrine only smiled sadly. "She is. We all need to talk. Come inside."

Annabeth stared at them defiantly as Cage and Bonin sat down. "Told you she'd fix everything."

"Hush," Miss Alexandrine said, handing him the sweet tea she'd insisted on serving. Cage took a long drink to keep his mouth shut.

"Apologize for the way you behaved last night," Alexandrine said.

Annabeth crossed her arms and stuck out her lower lip.

"Ti fi, pa anbarase m." The priestess pointed her finger. "Mwen pa pral disrespeted nan pwòp lakay mwen."

"What is she saying?" Cage whispered to Bonin.

"Not to embarrass and disrespect her."

"Good luck with that."

Annabeth's middle finger shot up.

Alexandrine pinched the girl's arm. "I promised your Gran that I'd take care of you, but I won't hesitate to fix your attitude real quick."

"How about this bitch trying to get Sen Michel to trick me?" Annabeth said. "Or what she said about Gran?"

"I did what I had to. She ran off." Bonin side-eyed Annabeth. "By the way, you need to practice your spell work."

"Fuck you."

"I won't have another word like that," Alexandrine said. "Apologize. Now."

"Whatever. Sorry I ran off." Annabeth curled into the chair, refusing to look at all of them.

Cage took another drink of tea and wished he'd remembered aspirin. A headache nagged at his temples. "Why didn't Charlotte come forward?"

"You have to understand that Lyric was her whole world," Alexandrine said. "Even though they fought constantly. Lyric had a group of friends in the Ninth Ward—one supposedly her boyfriend—who partied hard and didn't take their future seriously. Charlotte prayed for Lyric to turn her life around before she went down the same path as her mother."

"Charlotte said in the original police report that she and Lyric had a fight the day she disappeared," Bonin said.

"Over that boy, mostly. Lyric wanted to ride out the storm at his house in the Ninth Ward. Charlotte said no, the Ninth was always too close to ground zero. Lyric finally gave in and promised to stay. She left to get supplies around an hour before the curfew started."

Alexandrine reached for Bonin's hand. "You remember how bad it was, don't you? Chaos and death everywhere."

"I'll never forget it," Bonin said. "I was a patrol officer. After the levees broke, we got on boats and tried to help people, even though we were told not to. Everyone was too busy arguing over who was in charge to actually do anything. When we were finally allowed to search houses … God Almighty, I'll never get those images out of my head."

"I stayed right here," Alexandrine said. "And so did Charlotte. That house has been in her family for nearly three hundred years. If it was destroyed, she'd just go right along with it. Praise God, the Quarter was spared. But Lyric didn't come back, and people said the Ninth was gone. Charlotte marched to Rouse's as soon as it reopened. The manager said Lyric had bought $100 worth of supplies—just like she'd told Charlotte she would."

"Grocery store on Royal Street," Bonin clarified. "It's been there forever. Was the power out by the time Lyric went to Rouse's?"

"Security footage?" Cage asked.

"Hurricane, dumbass," Annabeth said. "No power."

Alexandrine stood up to tower over Annabeth, spewing Creole so fast the words ran together.

He nudged Bonin.

"Disrespectful, foolish, something about a curse that'll make her break out in hives, I think."

Annabeth shrank against the priestess's wrath. "Okay."

Cage's phone vibrated; Agent Roger's office number flashed on the screen. He sent it to voicemail.

"Why was Charlotte so certain Lyric ended up in the Ninth,

especially after she bought supplies?" Bonin asked as Alexandrine sat back down.

"Because Lyric didn't always tell the truth, and that wasn't the first time she stole from Charlotte. Telling her to not to do something was as good as any spell, especially when it came to Sean Andrews."

Cage and Bonin shared a glance. "We found Charlotte's notes about her search for Lyric. Do you know why she put a truth spell on Sean?"

"She blamed him, even though he went with his family to the Superdome and never saw Lyric that day. Charlotte never accepted that." Alexandrine sighed. "She was convinced Lyric ended up taking up with some other friend in the Ninth and figured Sean was covering for him. That never made sense to me, but Charlotte was damn near out of her mind. I always thought Lyric must have drowned and been washed away, but Charlotte never gave up hope."

Alexandrine's strange eyes clouded. "She was relentless with the spirits. We conjured, worked the rituals, but the Loa were silent, no matter how generous our offerings. Divination produced nothing but bleakness."

"You're losing me." Cage's phone vibrated again. He should have called his boss first thing this morning, but news of Annabeth's being bailed out had distracted him. He'd welcomed the opportunity to put it off a little bit longer.

Bonin elbowed Cage as Alexandrine's gaze swept over him. Her mesmerizing eyes locked with his, and he had the sensation of being questioned by a relentless investigator. She gave him a tiny nod.

"Divination is a practice for learning about the future," she said. "We ask the Loa—our Voodoo spirits—for guidance in all things. None were able to help, until finally her ancestor,

Dayana, appeared."

"Dayana." Cage tried to be polite. "Is that a spirit? Or an ancestor? Sorry, I'm confused."

"Many ancestors rise to the position of family Loa—spirit," Alexandrine said. "Dayana's father came from Haiti during the revolution. He was a very powerful priest, and he passed those powers to Dayana. Every generation of Charlotte's family had someone who possessed the power, right down to Lyric. But she rejected our faith."

"And this Dayana said Lyric was alive?"

"Trapped and praying for help," Alexandrine said. "Dayana promised to find a way to bring Lyric home. Not six weeks later, Charlotte receives the call that Lyric is in a Jasper hospital."

"She should have told the Jasper police when she realized the truth." His phone vibrated a third time, his headache flared. The frustration leaked into his voice. The police might have mobilized a better search. Even if the kidnapper had already taken off, he'd likely left evidence behind. Seven years ago, the cops had a real chance at catching him.

Cage ignored Bonin's dirty look. He didn't care how powerful the priestess was—her friend's silence had probably cost other girls their lives.

"She considered it, but the Jasper Police were more concerned about the rich, white citizens who hit her with their car," Alexandrine said. "She fell in love with Annabeth. She couldn't risk losing her."

Cage downed the rest of his tea. Rogers was definitely going to fire him before he officially started—and probably find a way to permanently destroy his career. He rubbed his temples—ignoring Bonin's questioning look—and tried to pretend he still had a job. "She risked other girls' lives in keeping silent."

Alexandrine's eyes turned to ice. "Charlotte didn't make the decision lightly. She made sure there wasn't any dental work or anything else to use for identification."

"But not her fingerprints," Cage said. "Those prints are the reason we're sitting here."

"I assume she didn't consider a teenaged girl would have fingerprints on file," Alexandrine said. "I can't blame her for that."

Or she didn't look into fingerprints because she'd known they were the best shot at identification. "Annabeth's grandfather worked for the prosecutor's office during the Atlanta Child Murders case," Cage said. "Her father grew up paranoid about unidentified kids. He had Annabeth fingerprinted when she turned twelve. If she'd told the police, they would have identified her."

"Charlotte believed she'd tried her best," Alexandrine said firmly. "She decided Lyric had given her life for this girl, and her ancestor had brought Charlotte to care for her."

The pain wrapped around his skull. "Did she realize that Lyric must have been in the same place as Annabeth? She had Charlotte's phone number. Her ancestor's ghost didn't make those things happen."

The priestess stared him down, her disconcerting eyes amused. "Her jaw was broken, her brain bleeding. The brain surgeon told Charlotte it was a miracle that she communicated the number. How do you think that miracle occurred?"

He didn't care. But he sure as hell didn't believe some ancestral spirit had anything to do with it. "Ma'am, I respect your faith in your friend, but whoever took Annabeth and Lyric may still be out there."

"That's why Charlotte did the ritual." Alexandrine refilled his glass, and he drank greedily. Too much salt in his breakfast. Bonin nudged him again, and he scooted away. She'd told him to be polite. And the tea was delicious.

His cell again, but this time a text from Rogers flashed on the screen.

'You have ten minutes to call me back or don't bother showing up for work next week.'

Cage barely heard Alexandrine's explanation of the spell performed over Charlotte before she died so that her ashes would protect the girl. Rogers wasn't ready to fire him. Maybe Cage could spin the situation to make Rogers see it as a publicity win for him.

"Charlotte's whole being is in that spell. As long as Annabeth wears the ring, she's safe."

"It's going to take more than a spell to protect her." He set the glass down hard, splashing some of the tea onto the coffee table. "It's only a matter of time before the media finds out. If he's still alive, he'll come for her. Her memory loss won't matter."

"Then I entrust that duty to you." Alexandrine reached over and took his hand in her warm one. "She must face who she really is now. Keep her safe and bring this person to justice."

He couldn't look away from her powerful eyes. "I can't do that unless she tells us everything."

She turned to Annabeth and said something in Creole. Annabeth's chin trembled, and she shook her head. Alexandrine spoke again, 'Charlotte' the only word Cage could make out.

"Mwen pral nan pwoblèm. Mwen ta dwe te di li anvan."

"Yes, you should have told us everything from the start," Bonin said. "Now's your chance to make it right. You won't be in trouble if you just come clean."

"Like I can trust you."

"I trust her," Alexandrine said. "Go on."

"If it's about your abduction, something you remember,

you're not going to be in trouble," Cage said.

"Even for keeping important information from the cops?"

"Why would you do that in the first place?" Bonin asked. "Didn't you want them to find the person who hurt you?"

Annabeth's eyes turned murderous. "Don't you dare judge me, especially after what you did."

"You're comparing me trying to keep your foolish ass safe to your withholding information?"

Instead of bursting into another verbal tirade, Annabeth wilted. "You have no idea what it's like to wake up and not remember existing."

"You're right," Bonin said. "But we're just trying to help you. We can't do that if you're not straight with us."

"It's only a little snippet. And until today, I wasn't sure it was even real. Like maybe I hallucinated it. I knew the cops would want me to take them back there. I couldn't remember, and I didn't want to." Annabeth's fingers dug into her tattoo again. "There were graves. And Mickie was in one."

16

"SIR, PLEASE HEAR me out."

"Not until I'm done chewing you a new asshole, Foster." His soon-to-be supervisory agent Mark Rogers reamed Cage for five minutes straight. Rogers was an LBI star, and the new unit was his brainchild. He'd made it clear that tarnishing his image would be the fastest way out the door.

"It's bad enough that you're acting as an LBI Agent without having the credentials," Rogers said. "But now you're telling me you can't inform this girl's parents, even though the fingerprint evidence is solid?"

The old pavers in Alexandrine's small courtyard seemed to suck up the sun. Cage felt dizzy from the heat. "Sir, there are extenuating circumstances."

"Like what? Has she been held captive for seven years? Are we looking at some kind of trafficking ring?" Rogers sounded too excited at the prospect.

"No, sir." He quickly explained Annabeth's condition and his theory on her disappearance. "She's already remembered bits and pieces of what's happened, including seeing the other missing girl in a grave." Graves. Plural. Annabeth was sure of it, even if the image was murky at best.

"How do you know she's not putting on an act?"

He couldn't offer any proof other than gut instinct. Even

Annabeth's story about not knowing Mickie's name until today could have been made up. "Why would she do that? She was captive less than a month, sir."

"Jesus Christ, Foster. Why didn't you just let the NOPD handle this?"

"I worked her disappearance as a rookie, sir, and I knew Annabeth as a kid. My former captain and I both believed Annabeth would recognize me and realize she was safe."

"And now you think the smoking gun to this whole thing is locked inside her head?"

"Lyric and Annabeth were taken by the same person, nearly six years apart. That's a long dormant period. There's a good chance he took other girls in between."

"He kept Lyric alive, according to your theory," Rogers said. "Lyric's getting old. He replaced her with a similar looking girl."

"And then he had to replace Annabeth seven years ago."

Rogers sighed. "Foster, what do you want from me?"

"Time," Cage said. "Not informing her parents is a risk, and I'll take the blame for that. If I can just have a couple of days, she might—"

"Seven years, and she's remembered a handful of things. What makes you think that's going to change now?"

"The pressure. Whatever wall she's built around her memory is cracking. I don't think she can stop it. I just need time."

"This family has suffered enough," Rogers said. "And if word gets out that we located her and didn't inform them immediately, the unit is screwed before we get started."

Selfish media-whoring asshole. "And what happens when the media finds out we took her home against her will?"

Rogers grunted. "Is she refusing to cooperate?"

"She wants nothing to do with going back to Mississippi," Cage said. "But she's willing to work with a hypnotist to see what else she might remember."

His hole kept getting deeper. Cage hadn't even brought the idea up to Annabeth.

Rogers was silent.

"If we bring her parents before she's ready, she'll never trust us. We have one chance."

"Keeping this from her parents is a big risk for the unit. And by unit, I mean you. I just can't sign off on it. Make the call."

"Sir—"

"It's not open for debate. Call the Georges."

The screen door slammed, and déjà vu washed over him. Annabeth, wringing her hands and gnawing her lip, silently imploring him. Altered face, but the same soulful, pleading eyes. She'd just been a kid, and he'd made the wrong decision out of selfishness.

Not this time. "There's only one problem with that, sir."

"And what would that be?"

Dani would kill him if she ever discovered what he was about to do. "She ran off. I don't know where she is, and I need time to find her."

17

BONIN DROVE WHILE Cage sucked down a big bottle of water and swallowed two aspirin. He wasn't sure Agent Rogers actually believed him, but his lie had worked. He'd given Cage two days, and then her parents had to be informed.

"You're nuts," she said. "That had to be the bourbon talking."

"What bourbon?"

Annabeth snickered. "Miss Alexandrine's tea is the best."

"Sweet tea and bourbon is a Creole favorite," Bonin said. "Why do you think I kept giving you dirty looks?"

Sean Andrews worked at a body shop in Metarie. By the time Bonin pulled into the parking lot, Cage's head had almost quit throbbing.

"You are to remain silent," Bonin told Annabeth as they entered the loud body shop. "Got it?"

Annabeth ignored her and poked Cage in the ribs. "The dude at the counter is hot. Not as hot as you—you're ridiculously good looking, and it kind of freaks me out. Cops shouldn't be able to use their hotness to entice suspects."

Cage's face burned. "Shh."

He and Bonin showed their badges to the twenty-something man at the dirty counter.

"We need to talk to Sean Andrews," Cage said.

The kid paged Sean over the intercom.

Annabeth flipped through the magazines on the single table in the congested lobby. "Dude, these are like a year old. You can't get current ones?"

"Uh ..." the man behind the counter looked at Cage.

They were saved by a tall African-American man coming through the "Employees Only" door. Wiping his hands on a blue towel that looked too dirty to do much good, he glanced at Annabeth and stopped short. "I heard you were back. That you had surgery and looked different." He shuffled his feet, rubbing his hand on the back of his head. "I should've called."

Annabeth spoke before Cage could explain. "I'm not Lyric, but I thought I was for a long time. Gran lied to me. Charlotte, remember her? She died last week. I stole something and got fingerprinted. Turns out, I'm some missing girl from Mississippi and whoever took me stole Lyric too." She jerked her thumb over her shoulder. "That's why they're here."

Sean blinked, his mouth open.

Bonin grabbed Annabeth's elbow. "I told you to be quiet."

Annabeth jerked away. "Touch me again, and we'll have a big problem."

"What happened to your face?" Sean asked as they sat down in a small, cluttered office that smelled of oil and dust.

Annabeth chose to lean against the door. She narrowed her eyes. "What's wrong with my face?"

"Uh," Sean glanced at Cage and Bonin. "It's just ... you still look like her. Or like you might be her."

"You can say it," Annabeth said. "One side of my face is saggy, and my eyes don't match up. It's not like I don't have a mirror."

"I'm sorry," Sean said. "I just really thought you were Lyric."

"She suffered a brain injury that removed all tact," Bonin

said dryly.

"But she's definitely not Lyric? Why's she got the tattoo? Lyric used that phrase all the time. Helped her get past her mom dying."

"Charlotte said I should get it to remind me to breathe when I start to freak out." Annabeth's strained voice was no more than a whisper.

Cage jumped out of his chair and stood in front of the girl, blocking her view of everyone else. He gently touched the tattoo, its surface still rough from her scratching. "This helps you. That's what matters. Breathe."

She obeyed, taking large breaths. "I'm okay."

Cage ignored Bonin's raised eyebrow. He sat back down and focused on Sean. "This is Annabeth. We believe Lyric was still alive and with her before she helped her escape. A car accident that same night caused the head injury, and she was able to tell the responders Lyric's name and grandmother's phone number."

Sean stared. "And Charlotte said this was Lyric?"

"The point is," Bonin said, "Lyric must have been alive then. Charlotte said you had a story about the person you believed took Lyric. The original investigator never followed through."

"Imagine that," Sean scowled. "A cop not doing his job."

"We're here now," Cage said. "And we're listening."

"That was a long time ago." Sean crossed his arms across his thick chest. "I was a dumb kid."

"We don't care about whatever you were in to," Bonin said. "We just want to hear your story."

"We partied a lot," Sean said. "Sometimes just a few of us at someone's house, other times we'd find an abandoned house and kick it for a few hours before the cops rolled by. Wild times."

"When did the strange guy show up?" Cage prompted.

"Summer, 2005. Only to the big parties. Hung out on the fringe—never told anyone his name. He was older, kind of creepy. But he had good shit, so I let him in. Few days before she disappeared, we were at this big party in a warehouse down by the water. Near the levees. Katrina flattened that sucker. Anyway, Lyric went to the bathroom and then outside for a breather. Next thing I know, she's yelling at him and telling him to take off before she calls the cops. Even said she'd curse him." Sean grinned. "She never was too devoted to the family religion, no matter how much her grandma taught her."

"This man tried to attack her?" Bonin asked.

"She said he offered her coke if she came to his car. Got pissed when she said no. He took off when I came out."

"You get a license plate?"

Sean shook his head. "I was too screwed up. All I know is that he was driving a blue pickup truck. Real redneck."

Sonofabitch.

"You said this wasn't the first party he came to," Bonin asked. "Is this the first time Lyric saw him?"

"She said it was, but I didn't believe her. She was mad as a cat that night. Guys came on to her all the time, creepier than him. You think she might still be alive?"

"Chances are pretty slim." Cage managed to gather his thoughts. "You have a description of this guy?"

"Normal looking white guy. Probably tall as me, maybe six feet. Always wore a dark T-shirt and jeans. Slicked back his hair. I think he had a beard, but I can't swear to that. Parties were always dark, you know?"

The liquor turned in his stomach. Annabeth had given him the same description seven years ago before she disappeared.

18

GOD, I HATE Dr. Douche. I wanted to cry when he called Bonin back. Now we're all sitting in his office, and Douche is giving me that fake smile. It's pity, and I don't like it.

His skinny hands match his skinny face. The man needs a pizza or something.

He opens a file, and my heart thuds. I know it's mine.

Mickie's dead face flashes in my head. Her eyes were open, just staring at me. Why did you let this happen?

I didn't know. I never have.

Everyone's looking at me.

"What did you just say, dear?" Dr. Douche asks.

"Uh, nothing. Just thinking out loud." Evidently.

"She's starting to remember things," Cage says. "She recognized a couple of women we believe may be tied to her disappearance."

I roll my eyes. He makes it sound like they helped kidnap me.

Who killed Mickie?

I'm thinking about it again. Blood everywhere. Screams. I think those are mine. It's been the same dream for years, but now I know her name and I'm afraid.

"Her TBI occurred mostly in her frontal lobe," Douche says. "That's the cause of her disinhibition. That's also why she has impulse control issues and a quick fuse."

"We've noticed," Cage says.

I stick my tongue out at him. Bonin kicks my shin. I'm not sure if I like her or not.

"Here's the fascinating thing about her case. The frontal lobe doesn't have much to do with memory. The hippocampus, the amygdala—those regulate memory, and they're in the temporal lobe. The damage to this patient's is minor." Douche smiles at me.

"Is she capable of remembering a significant amount?" Bonin asks.

"My predecessor diagnosed her with focal retrograde amnesia based more on the symptoms she presented with rather than her brain scans." Douche talks slowly, like he thinks we're too dumb to understand him. "Because of the minor damage to her temporal lobe, she should have recovered at least a portion of those memories by now. I've worked with patients with significantly more damage to their temporal lobes who were able to recover fifty percent or more of their memories."

"Given her minor temporal lobe trauma and the knowledge that this girl did experience severe sexual trauma, is it possible her amnesia is more of a blackout?" Cage's voice is nice. I think it's a tenor. "Can that be reversed?"

"In her case," Douche says, "my professional opinion is that it's a combination of both. She suffered immensely, and her TBI provided the perfect opportunity to block it out."

"I'm not blocking it out. I can't remember!"

"Not on purpose, dear." Douche smiles at me. "It's a coping mechanism, and a very good one. But it's likely a lot of information is still locked inside your head and accessible."

"Accessible how?" Cage asks, and I know what he's thinking.

"She's a good candidate for hypnosis."

I get up and walk out.

Cage runs after me like I'm going to disappear. I guess that's fair.

"What are you doing?"

"I'm done with him."

"Didn't you hear anything he said?" Cage's forehead wrinkles are getting deeper. He's pissed. "You could remember who took you. Maybe even where you were. If you can remember burying Mickie, the rest is there."

I know it is, and I don't want to see it. I can't. There's got to be another way.

My nails dig into my palms. "I'm not being hypnotized. And if you try to make me, I'm out."

He's put his job on the line for me. I heard him lie to his boss, and I don't get it. But I can't go back there. I won't.

"ARE YOU SERIOUSLY using a paper map?" Annabeth tossed her backpack on the floor and plopped down on his bed without any hesitation. She leaned back on her elbows. "You know about the internet, right?"

"I'm a visual person," Cage said. "And yes, I know about the internet."

"Duh, that was a joke." She scooted to the center and lay down, stretching her legs and arms out as far as possible. "Comfy."

Cage's neck burned. Having her in his hotel room was inappropriate enough, but Annabeth lounging on the bed with her shorts hiked up her thighs was plain wrong. He'd be fired on the spot if his boss found out.

"Why am I here again?"

"Because I put my neck on the line for you, and I'm not letting you out of my sight." Cage mentally crossed his fingers and hoped he wasn't about to launch another tantrum. "I want to talk to you about hypnosis again."

"No."

"We need you to remember," Cage said. "And once your parents show up, you'll be too stressed out to focus."

"No, I won't, because I'm not meeting them."

"Annabeth, I have to call them. It's bad enough waiting."

"Call them," she said. "That doesn't mean I'm going to meet them. I'm an adult, remember?"

Sam George wouldn't be able to handle this new version of his daughter. She'd always been a daddy's girl, the good child who did as she was told and didn't question her parents.

Except that one night that changed everything. He was going to have to tell her eventually.

"Hypnosis," he tried again.

"I said no. If I'm going to remember, it's going to be my way. No one else is going to have that kind of control of me. Got it?"

"Fine." He snapped open his laptop and logged into NamUs. Their national database utilized multiple resources for each missing persons entry, but slogging through the mounds of data would take more time than he had.

Annabeth had been found in Jasper, Texas—237 miles from home. He was searching in the dark, but he had a gut feeling the kidnappers stayed in a specific region. He narrowed his search to Texas, Arkansas, Mississippi, Louisiana, and Alabama. Might as well go in alphabetical order. He dug out his newly acquired black-framed reading glasses—an unexpected deficiency of hitting his mid-thirties.

"Holy shit. The glasses make you look even hotter." Annabeth openly stared. "Like, 'I want to jump you' hot. Have you ever thought about modeling? I bet you've got chicks chasing you all over the place."

Cage almost knocked his laptop off the small desk. "Christ. Really?"

"Was that out of line?" Annabeth asked. "I was giving you a compliment."

This was going to backfire on him, big time. "You don't say things like that to someone in a position of authority."

"Are you in a position of authority right now? 'Cause you took off your gun, and you're sitting at a desk with a computer. You look more like an accountant. A smoking hot one, but still. I don't feel like you have authority over me."

"I'm still in charge of keeping you safe."

"But you're not holding me against my will. I think that gives me the authority." She licked her bottom lip and grinned.

"I'm a cop." He willed his flushed cheeks to fade. "By definition that puts me in an authoritative position. That's all I meant. You don't go around telling people they're hot at random. Especially me. Got it?"

She shrugged. "You get really deep lines between your eyes when you're pissed. That's going to cause wrinkles. And I don't think you'll look as hot with wrinkles."

He gritted his teeth and turned back to the laptop.

"How long is this going to take?" Annabeth asked. "Can we get room service? Ooh, better, there's a really good restaurant around the corner."

"In a while. I have to search state by state and try to come up with similar cases."

"Come on," she said. "Doesn't the program have like, a match feature?"

"It's not that sophisticated. Why don't you watch TV for a little bit?"

"Gives me a headache." She settled into the pillows and

closed her eyes.

He started searching Alabama missing girls from 2005 to present between the ages of fourteen and twenty, with biracial heritage. The results came back with too many names. Both Lyric and Annabeth were around five-five and 150 pounds when they disappeared. He narrowed his parameters accordingly. Still twenty-seven results, just in Alabama. This would take him all night.

Annabeth sat up and started digging in her backpack. Cage tried to ignore her, but he couldn't block out his peripheral vision.

She set a white tea light candle on the nightstand, along with a chipped, white coffee cup. She lit the candle and then slid off the bed, heading for the bathroom, cup in hand. The faucet ran for a few seconds, and she returned, placing the cup next to the candle. Annabeth sat back down and closed her eyes.

Cage twisted around for a better view.

Annabeth began to whisper the Lord's Prayer, followed by a Hail Mary. "I believe in God the Father Almighty, Creator of Heaven and Earth." She poured three drops of water in front of the candle as she spoke, confident in her movements.

"Papa Legba, Open the gate for me
Atibon Legba, Open the gate for me
Open the gate for me Papa that I may pass
When I return I will thank the Loa."

He wanted to ask who she was praying to, but Cage didn't dare disturb her. Annabeth bowed her head and continued.

"Dayana, ancestor of Charlotte and Lyric, I pray to you for guidance. I know you brought me to Charlotte, who loved me. But now we need to know the truth. Please guide us to the person who stole me, and who stole Lyric, and probably other girls. Give us the power and strength to know the way. Dayana, keep us safe as we search for this monster—even those who don't believe in you."

Annabeth's face changed as she prayed, her tense expression becoming serene. Her body relaxed, her voice soft and calm.

She was staring at him now. "What?"

"Nothing, sorry."

Annabeth blew out the candle. "Aren't you going to ask questions or make fun of me?"

"It's none of my business," Cage said. "And I would never make fun of someone's faith, even if I don't understand it."

She lay back down and turned on her side, away from him, breaking the spell. Her prayer wasn't all that different from the ones he learned as a child. He knew Catholics lit candles and prayed to the saints; Voodoo incorporated that. It wasn't the prayer itself that hypnotized Cage, but Annabeth. She'd been through so much—yet she still believed in the mythology she'd been taught under false pretenses. Her faith hadn't wavered.

Cage had been raised to believe in God, but he'd never been much for any ritual prayers or Bible stories. After his sister's murder, he questioned God's existence. His still questioned it some days, but Cage refused to completely abandon the idea. Something larger had to be at work in the universe, even if humans had all the details wrong.

A soft snore interrupted his thoughts. Annabeth had stretched out, her dark hair falling around her face.

Might as well tell Dani he had a twenty-something woman in his hotel room.

19

"YOU TOLD AGENT Rogers what?" Dani's shock resonated over the speaker. "You could get fired."

"I know," Cage said. "But pushing her to meet her parents is the absolute wrong thing for her."

"Still so chivalrous."

He cleared his throat, glancing over at Annabeth. "You might not think that much longer. She's currently asleep on my hotel bed. And she says I'm hot."

A beat of silence, and then she burst into laughter. "Thank God you're keeping close tabs on her. I take it her brain injury makes her blurt out the truth? Or should I be worried?"

"The doctor called it, 'disinhibition.' She just blurts shit out."

Dani giggled. "I bet your face turned all shades of red, and you got those little lines between your eyes. I'm kind of jealous, actually. Saying what you're thinking without consequences? I'd never shut up."

The tension drained out of him. He'd been afraid she was still angry. "I think I might have discovered a pattern, but if I want to figure it out this decade, I need your help." He explained the missing persons database and what he was searching for.

"Don't the NOPD and LBI have people who do this sort of thing for a living, and much faster?"

"That makes it hard to keep her a secret. Plus, I'm not technically on the job."

"Right. What do you need me to do?"

"Take Texas and Mississippi," Cage said. "Go into both NamUs and the individual state databases. We're looking for girls similar in age and appearance to Lyric and Annabeth who disappeared during some kind of chaotic event, but not necessarily weather-related. Anything that had the police's and media's attention."

"Got it," she said. "Emma should sleep another hour. I'll call you back when I have something. If I find anything at all."

"You will," Cage said. "He—or they—have done this more than once. Oh, and make sure you check the input information for any sort of vehicle that might have been seen. Specifically, a blue pickup with a white camper top."

"What if you don't find anything?"

"I'll figure that out later. Listen, I'm sorry about yesterday. I know things are hard for you right now, and you're sacrificing a lot for me."

She sighed. "It's okay. I love you, and that's all that matters."

"I love you too."

20

CAGE SPENT THE next hour searching and cross-referencing missing girls in a tri-state area and logging the pattern on a map. Annabeth huffed in her sleep and rolled to her side.

His phone buzzed with Dani's call.

"You find anything?"

"I think so," she said. "No girls from Texas that really match. But in Mississippi, Shauna Lane, aged fourteen, disappeared from Meehan in 2014 during Fourth of July fireworks."

Cage pulled up Shauna Lane's information. Like the other girls, she was mixed race with an athletic build. She'd been walking home from a friend's when she disappeared. People had been too focused on the neighborhood fireworks show to notice her getting into any vehicle.

He marked it down on the map and stepped back.

"What do you have?" Dani said.

Cage said. "In May 2008, a fifteen-year-old went missing from a truck stop in Hampton, Arkansas during a torrential rainstorm. Biracial, athletic—he definitely has a specific type. So, starting with Lyric, you have five girls."

"Disappearing every three years or so. Always one girl, except for Mickie. I think she was just in the wrong place at the wrong time. Or maybe she looked enough like his type he decided to treat himself to two."

"It's all circumstantial, but when you stand back and look at it . . ." Cage did just that and studied his map. "It's pretty hard to ignore."

"And Annabeth turned up in Jasper. But there are no missing girls in Texas that match. Not in the last fifteen years. You can double check, but—"

"I think Texas might be a safe zone," Cage said. "Jasper could even be his hometown. I need to get her back there. If she remembers seeing graves, there's no telling what else she could remember once she's there."

"I'm not going back." Annabeth sat up on the bed, her hair tousled. "And I'm done discussing it. Figure something else out."

"Hypnosis."

She flipped him off.

"Do you see this?" Cage pointed to the map. "He might have taken at least three more girls. You're the only link we have to him."

"I'm not a link," she snapped. "The road took care of that."

"Be careful." He'd almost forgotten Dani was still on the line. "Doesn't sound like getting pissed off at her is going to work. Use your Southern charm. God knows you're oozing it."

He dragged his hand over his face and tried to calm down. "Thanks for your help, Dee. I'll call you later."

Annabeth glared at him as he hung up the phone. "Is that the little wifey?"

"Please don't be mean," Cage said. "When you have your memory flashes, what causes them? Do they happen at any specific time?"

She shook her head. "I told you, they're random."

He took off his glasses and set them on the desk. "You don't want to be hypnotized, fine. But there's a sliver of hope that you might remember something by going back. Lyric helped save you because she wanted a chance to be rescued."

"And I owe her?"

"That's for you to decide. But now that you know who you really are and what she did for you, don't you want to be able to say you did everything you could?"

She slammed her fists against the bed. "Fine. I think I killed Mickie. Are you happy now?"

21

HE'S STARING AT me with those eyes and lips, and the lines are back between his eyes. His short, brown hair is standing on end from running his hands through it. He drags his hand over his trimmed beard. There's like, three gray hairs on his chin, and they make me kind of nuts. I want to name them. "I need you to tell me everything."

"I just did."

Cage purses his lips. His shoulders tense, and his collarbone peeks out from his white shirt. "Why do you think you killed Mickie?"

My stomach turns. "I dream about her too. Only her throat's being slashed, and there's blood everywhere. Like pouring out." My guts feel like I've chewed up a rock. "The way I see it, I'm the one with the knife. And then I'm burying her. I dug her grave."

There. Now he knows. I'm a murderer. I must be.

"Have you always had this dream?"

"Not at first. It started out with her in the grave. Gran said they were just bad dreams. I wanted to believe her."

I see the spark in his eyes. He can't understand why Gran didn't tell someone about me. Sometimes I don't either. But I loved her. "I don't care that she wasn't my blood. I still miss her."

His expression softens. He strokes his scruff, a habit I totally dig.

"How did it start?"

"I told you, back in the hospital, I remembered seeing another girl in a grave. But that was it. Once Gran got sick, I started dreaming more. Sometimes I was awake."

"Did you remember anything about the place you were held?"

"Just that I was trapped. It was totally dark, but it's like I could feel the walls close. And it stinks like a dirty toilet. I'm staggering around, reaching out, and then she's in front of me. She's got a flashlight. I see her face—Lyric. She's terrified. That's when she grabs my shoulders and tells me to run and not to look back. To get help. That's the first one. Then I'm killing that girl, Mickie. I'm killing Mickie."

Cage exhales a hard breath and leans back in the chair. He's thinking about what to say to me, chewing on his bottom lip. He seems to analyze every word before he speaks. "Have you finally told me everything?"

I nod.

"Can you see the doctor is right, and those memories are right here." He taps his forehead. "He's taken more girls. You could be the one who brings him down."

"Why don't you just ask me to negotiate world peace while I'm at it?" My nerves feel stretched and hot. I'm supposed to count to ten and take deep breaths. The shrink says my anger is really fear. I don't care what it is. I just want it to stop.

"Annabeth—"

"Don't call me that." My bare feet hit the carpeted floor. "I'm not her."

And I'm not Lyric. I'm just a girl stealing someone else's life.

The pressure works its way down my throat and into my

chest until I feel my ribs ache. I'm breathing too fast, but I can't slow it down. "I've told you everything now, and that's all I can do. Leave me alone."

I rip several strands of my hair out, hoping the pain would settle me. When it doesn't work, I dig my fingernails into my tattoo.

Cage stands up and reaches me in one long stride. He grabs my wrists, his big hands easily fitting around them. "Stop."

I crane my neck to look into his eyes. This close, he smells like lavender and cedar.

"I know you're scared. But this isn't going to help you."

I inhale his sweet scent, and the pressure ebbs and evolves into something even more unstable. I know I shouldn't. But I can't help myself. I grab his shirt collar and pull his face to mine.

22

HE COULDN'T STOP thinking about her. So many plans just gone to waste. And she was in New Orleans, ripe for the taking again.

Did he dare go back?

His girl would be against it. But he could convince her.

Still, was it safe? He needed more of an insider's information than his dumbass cousin.

He lit a cigarette and then checked to make sure the shower was still running. She'd be in there forever.

Inside the closet, he dug beneath dirty clothes until he found his lockbox. She knew better than to try to spy on him, but he still took precaution.

He thumbed the combination and popped the lid open. His old cellphone sat on top of his many souvenirs. He powered it on and dialed the special number.

"Hello?"

"Hey." He blew out a ring of smoke. "You see this shit?"

23

"WHOA." CAGE PULLED back, releasing her hands. "What are you doing?"

Annabeth's face reddened, and her hands snatched at her hair again. "I'm sorry. Sometimes I get an urge I can't stop. It's part of the whole filter thing."

He tried to downplay his shock. "You need to find a way, at least with me. I'm married."

"I know." She turned away, shaking her head. "I feel so stupid."

Cage didn't know what to say that wouldn't encourage her. He shouldn't have had her stay here.

"There's a bar downstairs," Annabeth said. "It's probably way overpriced, but I need a drink."

He was shaking his head before she finished her sentence. "I can't let you out of my sight, and I'm not finished here."

"I'm trusting you," Annabeth said. "So, you have to trust me. I'll be downstairs in the bar. Come have a drink after you're off the phone. I promise I won't make it awkward."

She wasn't backing down. If she took off, she'd likely go straight to Alexandrine's or Charlotte's house. Cage said a silent prayer he wasn't making a mistake.

"I'll be down in fifteen minutes."

Annabeth let the door slam behind her, and Cage sank onto

the bed. His insides turned, the back of his neck hot. He hadn't been tempted to cheat. Risking his marriage was out of the question. But Annabeth's warm body pressed up against his had set his pulse into overdrive.

"Visceral reaction," he said to the silent room. "It's been a while, and my emotions are all twisted because of screwing up before she was kidnapped."

The tension drained from his shoulders. He was drawn to her out of duty and guilt. That wouldn't change until he saw her kidnapper in cuffs or in the grave—and he told Annabeth the truth.

BY THE TIME he arrived at the hotel bar, fifteen minutes had turned into thirty. He needed to take a shower and get his head straight. Most of the tables were full of chatting guests. Cage's eyes swept the bar. His stomach plummeted.

Annabeth wasn't there.

"Sonofabitch." So stupid. If she wasn't with Alexandrine or at her old house, Cage wouldn't be worrying about moving his family—he'd be begging for his old job back.

"Excuse me." A smiling, middle-aged woman touched his shoulder. She wore a hotel nametag. "You're looking for Annabeth?"

"You know her?"

"No," she laughed. "But she told me a handsome, tall white cop was going to be down here lookin' for her. My money's on you."

"Yes, ma'am. Where is she?"

"In the courtyard," the employee said. "You want a drink?"

Cage ordered a beer and headed to the courtyard. Humidity still hung like a soaked mop, but the night air was cooler. Clear lights strung across the courtyard illuminated the uneven stones and white wicker tables. A bubbling, three-tiered marble foundation almost blocked his view of Annabeth. She was tucked away in the far corner, near the old iron gates leading onto the street.

She raised her glass. "I was starting to think you ditched me."

Cage sat down in the chair across from her. "What are you drinking?"

"Champagne," she said. "Cost ten bucks. You can get a grenade for that, and you're drunk before you're half finished."

"A grenade?"

"All I know is that it's bright green and loaded with alcohol. It's served in a tall tube thingy. I've seen grown men pass out from drinking just one."

"You worked at a bar?"

"I was a bar back," she said. "And bussed the tables. They didn't trust me to take orders. Can't blame them. I had to quit after Gran got sick." She drained the plastic glass and tossed it into a nearby trash bin. "What do you think? Feel like you're back in time?"

"Every time I come to New Orleans," he said. "Starting with driving in and seeing the big cemeteries. Even the newer ones—there's something about the above-ground vaults that make this whole place feel like it's stuck in time. Then you get down here, and it's crazy."

"Like no other place in the world," Annabeth said. "I always think of it like putting a full-color picture of the French Quarter today on top of an old tintype from two hundred years ago."

That's exactly how it felt to him. Two different moments in time existing in a weird harmony. "That's one of the best analogies I've ever heard."

She snorted. "Sometimes my brain works really fucking

awesomely."

He took a long pull from his beer, nerves heating him from the inside. Might as well get it over with. Hopefully she didn't cause a big scene. "I need to tell you something."

"If it's about earlier, I'm really sorry. Yeah, you're hot as hell, but I'd never hit on a married man if I could control my brain."

"It's not that. It's about the blue pickup truck."

"You already told me about that."

"There's more to it." The beer soured in his stomach. "It's my fault you were kidnapped."

24

HIS HEART POUNDED in his ears as he waited for her temper to explode. She breathed deeply, trembling with the effort to stay calm. "I think I'm going to need another drink." She flagged down the server and ordered more champagne.

"On your room?" the server asked.

Annabeth smiled sweetly at Cage. "Yes, just like the first one."

He waited until the server was out of earshot and plunged ahead. "I became a cop because of my sister's murder. I was a rookie then and angry at the world. Being a cop made me feel powerful."

"You were an asshole," Annabeth said.

"Pretty much. You were a track star, like I said. Colleges were scouting you. Unless you were injured, an athletic scholarship was a real possibility."

Annabeth glanced down at her legs. "My thighs rub together when I walk. You sure you're talking about me?"

"Yes, you were thinner and in great shape." He clamped his mouth shut. "Not that you're fat now. Not at all. But you were younger and trained all—"

"Please shut up about my weight," Annabeth said.

"Right. A couple of days before you disappeared, I pulled you over for erratic driving. The car reeked of pot." Given the late hour, he hadn't been surprised. Kids partied. He'd done plenty of stupid things when he was her age.

"You begged me to let you off," Cage said. "You had a big meet coming up, and the college recruiters were going to be there. I let you go. Never even told your parents."

"Is that all?" Annabeth asked. "Sounds like you were a cool guy."

"That's not all. At the time, we didn't know who killed my sister. She lived in Jackson, but she came home a lot. She was a social worker, a big advocate for kids. One weekend she came home on a mission. She managed to have a dealer's kid taken out of his house—for abuse, not drugs. She was killed a couple of weeks later. Everyone thought her murder was revenge."

"Where do I come in? I'm totally confused."

"I was sure you bought from him. If you gave him up, then I could get a warrant and bring his ass down. Maybe he'd cop to murdering my sister. But you kept telling me it wasn't him. It was some skinny white guy with greased back hair who drove a blue pickup with a rusty white camper that smelled like filth."

She sat her empty glass down. "You didn't believe me."

"It was too detailed. I assumed you didn't want to be a narc." A bitter laugh bubbled out of him. "All these years, I blamed myself for not arresting you that night. You would have been grounded and not out at the lake. But the thing is, you bought the dope less than an hour before. The guy was headed toward Natchez, and you said I could still find him if I hurried. You told me he creeped you out. I told you to get home and to come see me the next day if you wanted to admit the truth. I never looked for that truck until it was too late."

The beer tasted hot and gross, but he slugged it anyway. She watched him, her expression blank.

"I'm sorry, Annabeth. But I'm going to make it right. Don't

you see? We have a real shot at finding him now."

"Let's walk. Bring your beer." She marched toward the street.

Cage didn't want her running into a big crowd, especially with alcohol in her system. He caught up with her at the open gate and followed her out. The crowds had thinned, but plenty of people still roamed, drinks in hand. "What're you thinking?"

She had to take two steps to his one, but she somehow made him feel like she was in charge, and he had to work to keep up with her. "Annabeth?"

"Right now I'm thinking about food. Let's head toward St. Peter Street. It's pretty much a straight shot to the grocery."

"We're going grocery shopping?" Now he was really confused.

"Rouse's," she said. "Isn't that where Lyric went the night she disappeared? Maybe someone there saw the blue pickup."

"Detective Bonin and I planned to go there tomorrow."

Annabeth drained her glass and picked up her pace. "You and I can go tonight instead. They have a yummy deli."

He wished he'd ordered another beer and then immediately felt foolish. This was the French Quarter. Bars on every corner and in between.

"You know you're walking over dead bodies?" Annabeth spoke loudly enough two women passing by turned and stared.

Cage decided to play along. She'd let him have it eventually. "Let me guess. A crime discovered during renovations?"

She rolled her eyes. "Nothing that interesting. The hotel's built over the city's first cemetery. So are a ton of other buildings in this area. Hundreds of bodies underneath. Here's St. Peter Street."

Cage fell into step next to her. "So, the cemetery?"

"Back in the early 1700s, this area was out of city limits. It became St. Peter Cemetery. Don't ask me the exact area, but we're on top of it now, and it's several blocks. Anyway, it took them a while to figure out people were going to float up because of the whole sea level and water thing. The above-ground burials came later. The cemetery got full, the city grew, and the Spanish created St. Louis No. 1. And they built right over the top of St. Peter Cemetery."

"They didn't move the bodies?" He should have a more compartmentalized view of death, but his mother's grave flashed in his head. If people built over her, Cage would tear them apart. "Didn't the families care?"

She shrugged. "Some did. The rich people moved some of their family members. But a whole shit-ton stayed, and now they pop up all the time. Some dude went to build a swimming pool in his backyard a few years ago and wound up finding, like, fifteen coffins."

She scowled as they passed Bourbon Street. "I hate that place. The whole of it. Crowded and full of pushy drunks. Plenty of locals and horny college kids. And not a damn one appreciates the history they're partying on top of."

"At least this isn't peak tourist season," Cage said. "It's too damned hot."

Annabeth pulled her dark hair back into a loose ponytail. "Hot as balls, for sure."

They walked in silence for a few minutes. At the late hour, past the bars, the crowd seemed to thin out. But the streets felt even more narrow and claustrophobic to Cage. He wanted to talk about the blue pickup, but he wasn't sure how far he could push her.

"I thought I was a native Creole." Annabeth broke the silence. "That my ancestors helped settle this city. Even though I couldn't remember, that was my identity, and I was proud of it."

She rubbed her eyes. "Gran said I'd just forgotten, thanks to my head injury. So she taught me the history of the city and our—her—family. Now I don't know who I am."

"Your past is different, but the last seven years are still the same," Cage said. "That's who you are."

"But that's all Gran, isn't it?" She craned her head up at him. "She taught me what to believe, so I could be Lyric."

He couldn't argue with that. "She loved you, and she made choices to protect you. And you may not be Creole, but you're biracial. Your grandfather marched with Martin Luther King. You did a project on it in high school."

"*I* didn't," she said. "The other me did. She's gone, and I'm this … enfimyè."

In the distance, lights illuminated the St. Louis Cathedral. Another place he'd have to take Dani. "What?"

"An imposter."

Cage stuffed his hands in his pockets. "I'm real damned sorry about what happened to you."

Annabeth stopped in the middle of the sidewalk and stared up at him. "What do you want from me? Am I supposed to tell you it's all good? That you didn't make a mistake? Well, I'm not going to say that because you did. So did I by even associating with the guy. And probably being stupid enough to trust him. Stop being all drama queen about the past. At least you remember. And we're doing something about it."

Pain shone in her dark eyes, her uneven face more pronounced when she was upset. Cage cleared his throat. "I'll stop being all drama queen if you stop pretending the last seven years weren't real."

"I'll think about it." She pointed across the street. "There's the grocery."

25

LIKE EVERYTHING ELSE in the French Quarter, Rouse's occupied the lower level of a three-hundred-year-old-plus building. Vines and hanging plants decorated the wrought-iron balcony above, likely a residential space. A four-man jazz band sat out front, their horns blaring.

Cool air and the scent of fresh-baked bread greeted them. Annabeth skipped the crowded liquor aisle and headed for the fresh food market. "I'm starving. Feed me. Ooh, po' boys. Probably not as good as Johnny's, but I'm not picky."

The curvy African-American woman behind the counter scowled. "Our po' boys are just fine."

"Is your owner here, by chance?" Cage asked.

Her eyebrows knitted together. "He's always here. Somethin' wrong?"

"No ma'am." Cage showed her his badge. "I'm investigating a cold case and had a few questions for him."

She sent the bored-looking kid working with her to fetch the manager while Annabeth ordered a club sandwich po' boy.

"Can you double the meat?"

"Gotta charge extra for that."

"He's paying." Annabeth smirked at Cage. "And I see you checking us out. He's got a ring, I don't. We're not like, together-together. He's married, with a kid. Yuck on that. And we're not having an affair. Which kind of sucks because he's hot."

The woman stared. Cage's skin burned. "She has a problem with filtering her thoughts."

"I'd say so."

A man in a crisp white short-sleeved dress shirt bustling down the aisle from their left saved Cage from further embarrassment. "Lyric Gaudet? Is that you? After all this time?"

Annabeth turned to face him, and the pudgy man skidded to a stop. "Sorry. My mistake. But damn if you don't look like her, at least from the side." His gaze seemed to deliberately avoid her face and landed on the tattoo. He looked confused. "Wait."

"I'm not her," Annabeth said. "I thought I was. Charlotte had me get the tattoo. Lyric and me were kidnapped by the same person, a few years apart. I've got a traumatic brain injury that screwed up my memory."

Both the owner and the deli worker stared.

Cage put his hand on Annabeth's arm and squeezed it, hoping she'd get the hint. She shoved his arm away and glared at him.

"I'm Cage Foster, with the LBI. We're looking into Lyric's disappearance. This is Annabeth."

"Guy's got a type, then." The manager adjusted his belt and puffed his chest. "I watch crime shows."

The woman behind the deli rolled her eyes. Annabeth burst out laughing, and the woman winked.

The manager kept talking. "'Course, NCIS New Orleans is my favorite. You know they film here? Close by too. I think it's a lot of outside shots but still, pretty cool."

Wonderful. Another person without a clue how the system really worked, thanks to television.

"I know it's been a while, but do you remember telling Charlotte Gaudet that Lyric came in for supplies right before Katrina hit?" Cage asked.

"Sure do. Lyric and me had a whole conversation about whether we should evacuate. We figured the weather people were overreacting, like usual. And the Quarter's the highest ground. I told Charlotte all that. How's she doing, anyway?"

"She's dead," Annabeth said. "Cancer."

The manager blanched. "I'm sorry."

"Until she spoke with you," Cage said, "Charlotte believed that Lyric decided to try to leave and drowned. But your story convinced her something else happened." He glanced at Annabeth. "Now we know for sure it did. Can you remember anything from that day?"

The man's eyebrows knitted together. "Boy, I remember everything from Katrina. August 28th, day before she hit, we had a mandatory evacuation. Most people in the Quarter were like me and Charlotte—they weren't leaving. Store was busy. I thought when the storm was downgraded to a Category Three that New Orleans got lucky. You know the levees were supposed to withstand up to a Category Three?" Bitterness crept into his tone. "Bunch of lies that killed a lot of people."

One of the reasons Dani had initially hesitated about moving here. Their house was in Uptown—a good distance from the water. But with Katrina, it didn't matter. Who knew if the levees were secure now?

"I'm sorry to bring it up," Cage said. "When did Lyric come in that day?"

"She came in around five-thirty. Half an hour before the curfew. I told her to get home so she didn't get in trouble."

"You're certain she was going home?"

"She bought Charlotte's favorite candy. Said she hoped it would keep her calm during the storm."

"Peanut brittle," Annabeth said. "Not pralines. She joked

that made her less New Orlenean."

The manager nodded. "Let me tell you, it was raining hard and getting dangerous. I told her get on home and stay safe. She walked out the door and turned left. Headed home."

"That's St. Peter Street," Annabeth said. "It's the shortest route to Charlotte's house. St. Peter to Chartres, then on to her house on Madison. Fifteen minutes on a hot day."

"You've made the walk?"

"I used to work right around the corner."

The manager stared at Annabeth, his forehead wrinkling. "You know that place is one of the oldest homes in the area and probably worth a mint. Lyric was Charlotte's only heir. What's going to happen to it?"

"We're figuring all of that out," Cage said before Annabeth could blurt something else out. "Was Lyric alone that night?"

"Far as I could tell."

"And you didn't see anyone suspicious?"

"Man, it was chaos. I didn't pay attention."

"What about a blue pickup?" Annabeth beat Cage to the punch. "He let a guy with a blue pickup go before I got taken. We think it's the same guy."

"Hell, I can't remember that kind of detail, especially from a night like that one."

The deli worker handed Annabeth her overflowing po' boy. "Well I can, because the guy was rude and pissed me off. Skinny, white dude parked his damned truck in the no-parking area, right where the band plays. Even if they weren't out that night, there's a rule. He came in like he owned the place, still smoking his cigarette. I told him to get out, that we was closed. He grabbed a box of condoms and sauntered out. I hollered that I was calling the police, but he flipped me off and told me they had more important things to do right now. Now who the hell's going to be worried about condoms in a damned hurricane?"

26

ANNABETH CHOWED THROUGH the rest of her sandwich as they headed toward Chartres Street. Cage was grateful for the silence. Rouse's didn't have the security footage from Lyric's visit twelve years ago, and the deli worker could only remember the man being "plain, skinny, white, and rude." Not much help, but essentially the same description as Sean Andrew's.

"It's the night before, the Quarter's creepily quiet, probably boarded up. Maybe it's raining." Working through things out loud helped Cage see the bigger picture—and sometimes the tiny, crucial details. "She's carrying groceries and..." He checked his notes from the owner. "Two gallons of water. The man she knows offers her a ride home. She doesn't like him, but the hurricane is coming in and she's desperate. Sonofa*bitch*."

"You say that a lot." Annabeth finished her sandwich and took a long drink of water. "He takes advantage of bad situations. Fucking bastard." She spit the last two words. "He killed us both."

He stopped in front of the Cathedral, the historic landmark illuminated by floodlights, and leaned against the wrought-iron fence surrounding it. Calculating bastard was more like it. He watched, waited, and knew enough about his victims to know when to strike. Organized, careful planners like him terrified Cage. How many like this guy were out there, skillfully moving in plain sight?

"I think the Cathedral's closed," Annabeth said. "It's pretty late for priests and nuns. They get up at the ass crack of dawn."

He turned to admire Jackson Square. The gates were closed, but the blooming flowers shined beneath the moon, along with the big statue of Andrew Jackson. Horse-drawn carriages waited on the other side of the park.

"Do you think he's still alive?"

"He could be. But even if he isn't, he took other girls. And he may have one now. Or be on the hunt for one." He'd gone over the map at least ten times before even trying to go to bed. "Looks like he takes a girl around every three years, and usually in warm weather. It's already August." Cage wasn't backing down on retracing her steps. If she wouldn't consider hypnosis, then maybe the stress of being back at the accident site would force her to face her memories. Cheap shots, but he was getting desperate. "That's why I want to take you back to Jasper."

Shaking her head, Annabeth charged down the alley between Jackson Square and the shops. "I want to see the horses."

He followed her around the historic square, keeping an eye out for horse crap. A large crowd swarmed the famous Café Du Monde, and the smell of the beignets made Cage's stomach grumble.

Several artists displayed their work on the iron gate surrounding the historic square. Some things weren't much better than the average find at a touristy gift shop, but others were truly incredible. Cage made a note to come back with Dani and buy a painting for the new house.

A woman wearing a long purple scarf sat at a table advertising psychic readings, while the wheelchair-bound man next to her played his guitar. Cage dropped a five into the man's plastic cup and ducked his head before the woman could offer to tell his fortune. The guitar player nodded his thanks and launched into a blues riff.

Carriages waited along Decatur Street at the entrance of the park. A group of tourists climbed into a large white carriage and the mule strutted off, his big hooves echoing against the street.

Annabeth strode right up to a large bay mule with dark, shining eyes. "Okay if I pet him, Rick?"

The driver grinned. "Wondered when I'd see you again. Course you can. He loves you."

"I take it you're a regular?" Cage asked as she stroked the animal's soft coat, leaning into the crook of the mule's neck.

"Since Gran died, yeah. I like to come out here some nights and see the horses. They make me feel like I'm not going to explode." She patted the bay's nose. "He's my favorite. I've wanted a horse for as long as I can remember."

It was a long shot, but Cage had to take it. "What would you name him?"

Annabeth didn't pause to consider the question. "Charlie. That's a good name for a horse, right?"

The air left Cage's lungs. His jaw went slack.

"Dude, now your face kind of looks like mine," Annabeth said. "What's your problem?"

He glanced at the driver, whose nose was buried in his phone. Now probably wasn't the best time to tell her, but she wouldn't give up until he answered. "Annabeth's family owns horses. Her horse is named Charlie."

27

AFTER HE TOLD her about the horse, Annabeth walked silently to Charlotte's empty house and then back to the hotel. This had been the route Lyric likely would have taken in the storm, but Cage doubted she made it more than a block or two from the store. The man in the blue pickup had been waiting.

Annabeth turned her back to him as the elevator ascended. She stalked to the door and waited for him to swipe his keycard. "You sure I get the bed?"

"Yes." Cage held the door for her and tried one last time. "Please consider hypnosis. If you can come up with that name—"

"I'll think about it. But I'm not making any promises."

CAGE ALMOST CRIED with happiness when Bonin arrived with the giant cup of caffeine. Between worrying about Annabeth taking off and the miserable couch, he'd only slept a couple of hours.

"It's probably the only good thing that's going to happen today," Bonin said. "My boss found out and immediately called the Georges. They're due at the station in an hour, and he says if I have any idea of her whereabouts, I'm to bring her in. Unless I want to get fired."

Cage's stomach dropped. He'd been hoping for another day before the shitstorm erupted. And Rogers would be livid the NOPD got the jump on his glory. He no doubt had an entire press conference planned.

"Shit." Cage didn't want Bonin to take the heat for him. "This was my decision. Not yours."

"You can tell my boss that. And her parents."

"She's not ready to see her parents. Shouldn't she have some say in that decision?"

"It's not up to us. What if this were your daughter? Can you imagine what they're going through?"

The idea of something happening to Emma—of never knowing what happened to her or if she was even still alive—made him physically ill. "I'm just trying to put her first. Someone should."

Bonin drained her cup and tossed it in the wastebasket. "I'm going to tell my boss I spoke to you in person this morning and relayed the message, but I didn't see the girl. As long as that door doesn't open," she glanced at the bathroom, "I'm not lying. You do what you have to."

As soon as Bonin left, the bathroom door swung open. Annabeth stood there, wide-eyed and wearing a hotel towel that barely covered her.

"My God." Cage turned his back. "Coming out in a towel crosses that line we talked about."

"I heard what you said. What're you going to do?"

Cage put his hands on his hips and rolled his neck. His old boss at the Adams County Sheriff had promised he always had a place there. "That's up to you."

"If you don't bring me in, won't you be fired?"

"Probably."

"You'd do that for me?" Her voice trembled.

He exhaled. "It's the right thing."

She rushed up behind him and threw her damp arms around his waist. "I'll talk to them, and then we'll go to Jasper."

28

SAM GEORGE LOOKED ready to throw Cage to the floor. His wife kept her hand on his arm, probably holding him back. "Where is our daughter?" Sam demanded. "You should've called us immediately."

Bonin shot Cage a look. She'd escorted them from the lobby and looked like she'd already had her fill of Sam. He had an air-tight alibi on the day the girls disappeared, but he was controlling and alpha male. Cage always had the impression things were Sam's way or no way.

"Please, let me explain." After seeing her dry heave into the wastebasket, Cage decided he would speak to the Georges first and try to make them understand how fragile Annabeth was. "You're aware of her memory loss and that she's been living as someone else?"

"Because some woman identified her as her granddaughter," Sam said. "She had to know she wasn't. I want her brought up on charges."

"She's dead, remember?" Krista George finally spoke. "That's the only reason we found out."

"That's all part of the case we'll discuss," Cage said. "But understand that Annabeth didn't know. She believed Charlotte Gaudet was her grandmother, and she loved her. She's mourning for her as the only family she had."

Krista George looked stricken. Sam swelled up as though he were insulted by his daughter's memory issues.

"The extensive trauma to her face—"

"Detective Bonin showed us a picture," Krista George said. "We know what she looks like. She's still beautiful."

"Did she tell you anything more?"

Bonin shook her head. "Thought I'd leave that to you."

"We spoke with her neurologist yesterday," Cage said. "Her brain injury affected her vision but also her filter. Sometimes she says things she shouldn't. Embarrassing things. It's not really something she can help. She also deals with anger and mood swings. She's not the same girl you remember, and she's terrified to meet you. That's why I waited."

"Once she sees us, her memory will come back," her father said. "It's in there."

This was going to be a disaster. Sam didn't have the patience to deal with Annabeth's condition, and she would sense that the minute he walked in the door. He almost suggested Krista go in first, alone, but Cage knew it was a waste of breath. "Don't expect it to come quickly. She's been through more than we can imagine, and she's afraid of the memories. You have to be patient, and you have to abide by her wishes. She's not ready to go back to Mississippi."

Krista nodded, but Sam shook his head. "I'm done talking with you, Foster. She'll come with us. Period."

"She's a legal adult. If she refuses, then she doesn't go."

"How dare you? She's our child."

"Who doesn't remember you and is trying wrap her head around all this," Cage said. "If you try to force her, Sam, I'll arrest you."

"I'd like to see you try, Foster." Sam puffed out his chest. "I know what's best for her."

"No, you don't," Cage said. "And if you love her, you'll put her first."

29

I'M GOING TO throw up for real this time.

The room is hot and small. My face feels like I've stuck it inside a blazing oven. I can't catch a full breath. My head throbs, and my vision keeps streaking. I don't want to lose it in front of these people, but I'm about to panic.

These people. My parents, who love me and never gave up hope. And I can't remember anything about my life with them. It's bad enough for me—at least I don't know what I've lost. But what about the Georges? Wouldn't it be better if they thought I was dead?

The door handle is moving.

My vision completely blurs, and all I see is the mix of shapes and colors in front of me. I scoot away from the table and rub my eyes. That's when I see the woman moving toward me. Her arms are open. Does she think I'm going to hug her? Am I supposed to?

Tears are in her eyes, and her pretty face is twisted as she fights back tears. I step back, feeling nothing but fear. She stops, suddenly realizing that I'm scared. A man stands beside her. Dark skinned, well-built, his short black hair speckled with gray.

"We've missed you so much." The woman is talking now, her voice barely above a whisper. I wish something about it was familiar. But I've got nothing.

"You must recognize us," the man said. My father, I remind myself. And this is my mother. They raised me, apparently loved me, and I don't know them from a stranger on the street.

Cage appears behind them and silently crosses the room and stands next to me. Some of the tension between my shoulders melts.

"It's okay," the woman says. "We always believed we would find you one day. We know everything's turned upside down for you—"

"Which is why you'll be coming home," the man says. He's used to calling the shots, and he doesn't look like he takes no for an answer. "Once you're in familiar surroundings, you'll remember."

I shrink against Cage. He's warm and strong and smells like sandalwood. I try to say something, but all I can manage is to shake my head back and forth.

Cage speaks for me. "She's not ready to come home and pushing her against her will isn't going to work."

Mr. George steps forward, his big body just a few feet from mine. "This is our child, and you won't tell us what we can and can't do. You didn't find her seven years ago, and you didn't call us when she showed up here. If I have it my way, you'll be looking for a job by tomorrow."

Something inside me snaps. I push away from Cage, the room suddenly shimmering in a familiar red aura. The pressure's building in my chest and pounding against my skull.

"If you do that, you will never see me again."

The man stares at me. I stare back, the red threatening to completely take over. "Cage is only doing what he thinks is right for me. My memory might be all kinds of screwed up, but I'm an adult. I'll decide when or if I go back to Mississippi."

My mother starts to cry. The man's jaw tightens, and I know

he's not backing down.

"I know this city. I can disappear real quick," I say. "If you can't respect that, then we have nothing more to say."

My mother buries her face in her hands. I feel bad for her, but her wailing is scratching my nerves. I rub my temples and then the tattoo. Inhale, exhale.

"Are we just supposed to leave you here? What are you going to do here now that that woman's dead?" Mr. George's voice cracks. He jams his hands in his pockets. His neck muscles strain.

Is he trying not to cry or not to yell? Is that the kind of parent he was? Did he yell a lot? What if he hit me? He doesn't seem like he's patient or tolerant. Maybe he's the reason I'm blocking out my past.

"I'm going to try to recover my memories. I'm the only person who can stop my kidnapper." As the words tumble out, I know they're true.

"There are some good hypnotists at Tulane," Cage says. "I'm sure her neurosurgeon could help us get in quickly."

I face Bonin for the first time. We share a long look and finally she nods. To hell with my genetic background. This is the only world I know.

"No hypnotist," I say. "I'm going to have Miss Alexandrine perform a ritual. The spirits will guide me."

30

CAGE'S HEAD FELL back against the door. He should have seen this coming.

Sam's neck swelled like a balloon. "A ritual? Are you talking that foolish Voodoo witchcraft?"

Annabeth's shoulders hiked up to her ears. I squeezed her arm, willing her not to explode. She'd managed to hold it in this far, but I felt the pot boiling.

"Voodoo is not witchcraft." Bonin spoke up. "That's all Hollywood storytelling. Voodoo is a religion. Rituals are about love and light and clearing one's spirit."

"She needs a doctor," Sam said. "Not some back-alley, French Quarter pothead looking to make a buck off a sucker."

Annabeth moved too quickly for Cage; her hand connected with her father's cheek, the slap loud as a detonated bomb. "You do not talk about my Gran and Miss Alexandrine like that. Or Miss Alexandrine will hex your ass."

Cage grabbed her arms before she could take a second swing, pinning her against his chest. Annabeth's nails dug into his arms, and she jammed her right foot between his ankles and tried to sweep his leg. He held his ground, and she slammed her head against his chest.

Sam rubbed his cheek, staring at his daughter like she was poison. "They've made her crazy."

"This is the brain injury," Cage said. "She's kept her cool longer than I thought she would. But once she loses it, someone's got to help calm her down."

Krista stepped around her husband. She'd stopped crying, her fair skin ghostly pale. "She's not crazy. She's different. And we can't change that. If she believes this Miss Alexandrine can help her, then she has to try." She slowly lifted her hand to touch Annabeth's clenched fist. "Whatever your mind needs to heal, I support it." Her voice caught, but she didn't cry. "Cage, please take care of her until she's ready to give us a chance."

HE DIDN'T RELEASE Annabeth until he'd pulled her out of the room and shut the door. She yanked her hands free and pulled at her hair.

"Stop." Cage grabbed her wrists. "You made your point. Did you hear what your mother said? Take a deep breath and think about how hard that had to be."

She glared at him, but she stopped pulling her hair. Bonin stepped out of the room. "Your boss at the LBI is trying to get a hold of you. He sounds pissed."

"I need something to eat." Annabeth had caught her breath. "I think freaking out drops my blood sugar or something."

Bonin handed her four dollars. "The vending machine is down the hall, around the corner. Don't try to take off. Everyone knows to watch for you."

"She won't." Cage prayed he was right as Annabeth stomped down the hall and out of sight. His chest hurt where she'd slammed her head against it. Kid was a lot stronger than she looked. "A Voodoo ritual. Christ. You think if we support that she'll see a hypnotist?"

"You should open your mind," Bonin said. "The ritual isn't much different than being hypnotized. It just isn't mainstream and backed up with a medical degree.

"Well, I hope Miss Alexandrine can work her magic and get through to her."

"Look, I like you," Bonin said. "I think you'll be good for the city."

Cage waited for the caveat.

"But you have to be careful with this girl," Bonin said. "She's got a huge crush on you, and she's unstable."

"I can handle her." His phone shrilled Dani's ringtone. "I'll meet you at the back entrance in five minutes."

Dani wasted no time. "Annabeth's story is on the national news, and she's the talk of Roselea. Actually, the two of you are the talk of Roselea. Someone told a reporter about her staying in your hotel room."

Who the hell knew about that? Bonin wouldn't have put Annabeth in jeopardy like that, and Cage's failure would be a direct reflection on her. "Dee, you know the deal about that."

"Of course I do," she snapped. "But the neighbors don't. Her old friends and track coach don't. You know how many questions I've dealt with in the last hour?"

"I'm sorry," Cage said. "Don't answer the phone anymore."

"They're showing up here," Dani said. "The entire county already knows where Ironwood is."

He didn't know what else to say, and he needed to get moving. "Don't answer the door. Tell them all you know is that I am protecting her until the investigation is finished. If they won't leave, call the sheriff."

"I can handle the questions," she said. "But the way you're being talked about, the innuendos and assumptions people are making …"

"Because she's young and …" Still attractive, even with her facial trauma. "You know I'd never—"

"I'm not worried about that," she said. "I just hate to see your name smeared like that, especially when you're so clueless."

Cage shoved the back door open and stomped down the old steps. "What the hell does that mean?"

"Seriously? The would-be hero trying to make things right with the damsel in distress? You've carried so much guilt around since she disappeared, and you don't owe her anything, Cage. Trying to be her knight in armor to the point of destroying your career is going too far."

Bonin honked her horn. Annabeth waved impatiently from the backseat.

"I've got it under control, Dani. I have to go."

31

CAGE TRIED TO blend into the pearl-colored walls of Miss Alexandrine's kitchen, but the compact old house made him feel like a giant. He'd already smacked his head against the doorframe twice. Rogers laid into him about the delay, but Cage argued that allowing Annabeth to try the ritual would extend an olive branch. When this didn't work, he'd convince her to see the hypnotist.

"Funny how quickly you wrangled this girl up once her parents were on the way," Rogers said. "Was that magic too?"

"Just luck, sir."

Afternoon sun glinted off the candles in the altar beneath the center window. Cage recognized a Catholic saint, but the rest of the faces painted on various cards and glass squares were a mystery to him.

Miss Alexandrine surprised him by allowing the sunlight to stream into the room. He'd imagined the ritual taking place in a dark room full of candle smoke.

Wearing a flowing, white sundress, the priestess spread a lacey, white tablecloth over her kitchen table. She opened a bottle of oil and smeared it over two white candles.

"Holy oil," Bonin whispered reverently.

Alexandrine lit a smudge stick of some sort of plant and placed it carefully in a glass dish. The room quickly smelled like a fall wildfire.

"What's that?" Cage mumbled.

"Mugwort," Bonin said. "Shh."

Annabeth sat in front of the candles. Her hair was still wet from the bath that was supposed to be an important part of the ritual. The white dress she'd borrowed from the priestess drooped off her shoulders. Apparently white was a vital part of the whole deal. Purifying, Bonin said.

"What's the bath do again?"

"Helps to cleanse her spirit," Bonin said. "And relax her."

"And that helps the magic work?"

Alexandrine looked up from lighting the candles and gave him a soft smile. "Not magic. Faith. A person must believe for the rituals to work."

"So, you're saying believing in the spell opens your mind?"

"Something like that. And this isn't a spell. It's a ritual."

Whatever the hell it was, she needed to get on with it. They'd snuck out the Eighth District's back door, but two reporters had been waiting. Annabeth covered her face as Cage rushed her to the car amid the shouted questions.

And the mugwort stink was making his eyes burn.

"I'm ready," Annabeth said. "Let's fix my brain."

Alexandrine placed a white cloth doll between the candles. Annabeth's name had been written on a delicate piece of white paper that had been pinned to the doll. She quickly yanked a hair from her head. The priestess draped it around the doll's neck like a scarf.

Alexandrine took the opposite chair and softly began chanting in Creole.

Cage nudged Bonin, who stood on tiptoes to whisper. "She's asking Damballah, the symbolic father, to heal and open Annabeth's mind."

The priestess instructed Annabeth to close her eyes and then drew smoke from the reeking mugwort stick to Annabeth and then the doll.

"Give your mind to Damballah," Alexandrine said. "Allow him to heal your wounds so that you may remember."

Annabeth nodded, her eyes still closed. A smile played on her lips, her expression serene. With the tension washed away, her face seemed less uneven. She swayed back and forth in time with the prayer, Miss Alexandrine's gentle voice somehow becoming a roar in Cage's head.

"Open your eyes."

Annabeth obeyed, her face hardening. She looked across the table expectantly. "I don't feel any different."

"You will," Miss Alexandrine said. "Keep the doll with you so it can help you heal."

"My brain is still broken."

Miss Alexandrine laughed and blew out the candles. "Child, it's not a magic switch. Give your mind time to open."

Annabeth slammed her hands down on the table, sending its contents flying. "What the fuck do I have to do to get my life back?" She jumped to her feet, grabbed the woman's thin shoulders and shook her. "You said this would work!"

Bonin stepped forward, but the older woman held up her hand, her steady gaze on Annabeth. "This is the injury."

She wrenched Annabeth's hands off her shoulders and held them tightly. "Damballah doesn't like violence. This won't help you."

"I don't care!" Annabeth's scream pierced Cage's ears. "You're a liar. Damballah's not real. None of the Loa are." She shoved Alexandrine out of her way and stalked into the entryway, grabbing her backpack. "I'm done with this shit." She slammed the door.

Stunned, Cage moved to follow her, but the priestess held up her hand. "Give her a few minutes."

"How often does that happen?" Bonin asked.

"It's become more frequent since Charlotte got sick," Miss Alexandrine said. "She helped her recognize the signs of an outburst. And she isn't normally so physically violent. All of the stress is tearing her apart, poor child."

"Are you going after her?" Cage asked.

Alexandrine's eyes settled on him, and the sensation of being completely exposed washed over him. "I think you should. She admires you. She's probably halfway to the cemetery by now. It's where she goes when she's upset." She pointed at Bonin. "Take her with you, or you won't be allowed in."

HEAT BLISTERED CAGE'S scalp as he waited for Bonin to find a place to park. Thirty minutes to closing, in the heat of the day, and tourist groups still littered St. Louis No. 1. He wiped the sweat off his forehead and glanced at the guard at the main entrance. The Archdiocese no longer allowed tourists to wander freely in the city's oldest cemetery—only family members and guided tour groups were allowed in. Cage debated flashing his badge, but since it still said Mississippi, he knew it would be worthless to the gatekeeper.

"Had to park a block away. We should have walked, but it's too damned hot." She held up the pass allowing her to visit her relatives' tomb along with her badge and marched past the security guard.

Claustrophobia set in as soon as Cage stepped past the tent at the entrance. Tombs of all sizes and styles clogged the cemetery, with only inches between many of the above-ground vaults. Footpaths zigzagged in no particular pattern, destroying his sense of direction.

"Do you have any idea where we're going?" he asked Bonin.

"Alexandrine said the family tomb is in the middle of the cemetery, just off the main alley. If she's there, we should see her."

She pointed to the white, pyramid-shaped tomb near the front entrance. "That's the Varney tomb. Used to be the center of the cemetery before the city expanded in the 1800s. We follow the path to the tomb's right."

The wall vaults surrounding the cemetery's perimeter made the place feel cut off from the rest of the world, and Cage felt insignificant amid the sea of congested vaults filled with generations of people who helped create New Orleans.

Decay was everywhere he looked. Aging tombs, some of the brick ones so degraded only small sections of the base remained. Dried up weeds tangled through many, and some were no more than a pile of rubble. Wilting flowers rested in front of the iron gate of a double-tiered, marble tomb.

"Where's the Voodoo queen?"

Bonin smiled. "There are many Voodoo queens buried here. But Marie Laveau's tomb is that way." She hooked her thumb over her left shoulder, but he couldn't get his bearings. The maze-like layout put him in a trance.

Or maybe it was the heat. "Christ. It's got to be twenty degrees hotter in here."

The alley snaked to the right, the heat intensifying. His sunglasses did little to detract from the hazy sun.

Ahead, a figure dressed in white crouched in front of a granite tomb.

"You go ahead," Bonin said. "She doesn't trust me. And I should visit my grandparents while I'm here." She headed down the path to their left, quickly disappearing among the giant stone monuments.

Cage hovered a few feet from Annabeth, sweat stinging his eyes. Tourists filed past him, some looking dangerously close to heat stroke. No one seemed to notice the girl in the white dress sitting on the ground.

It was too damned hot to mess around.

Cage sat down next to her. She didn't flinch, her eyes barely drifting in his direction. He focused on the tomb. Like so many of the tombs, a black iron gate surrounded the marble, part of its fleur-de-lis ornaments rusting. The vault had two levels, the bottom section much larger than the top. Most of the exterior was in good shape, although some of the marble had eroded from the extreme weather, and black mold had worked its way into some of the nooks and crannies.

"Sanité." Cage read the name on the front. "Your Gran's family tomb, right?"

"Charlotte Gaudet's family tomb, yes. She would have been the seventh generation of a prominent Voodoo family buried here."

"Really?" Cage wiped the sweat from his eyes.

Annabeth appeared unbothered by the heat, although her dark hair stuck to the back of her neck and a fine sheen of moisture covered her face. "Her ancestor, Jean Henri Sanité, fled Haiti during the Revolution and brought his Voodoo with him. Handed it down for generations. Long before any famous Voodoo queens, people came to the Sanité family for prayer and ritual and to learn how to connect with Spirit. It's an honor to be interred here."

"But Charlotte chose to be cremated so you'd be protected."

Annabeth nodded. "The last person to be buried in this tomb was Charlotte's grandmother—the one who witnessed one of Marie Laveau's last rituals as a little girl."

"That's got to be at least a hundred years ago." Cage studied the fading granite tablet on the front of the tomb, counting eleven family members. "What about Charlotte's mother?"

Cage chewed on the question he probably shouldn't ask.

"You're wondering how so many people could fit into the thing, right?" Annabeth said. "After a year, the remains can be taken out and pushed to the back of the tomb to make room for new. They burn the coffins." A wistful smile spread over Annabeth's face. "Only those who learned the ways and prayed to the Loa rest with Sanité. Charlotte learned the ways from her grandmother, but her own mother shunned everything. So did Lyric's mother. But Charlotte embraced it, and she taught it to Lyric before she disappeared. She started teaching it to me once I was able to keep things straight—re-teaching, she said. Passing down the knowledge to her last descendent meant everything to her. Lyric, I mean."

Cage finally understood. "It wasn't just about wanting her granddaughter back. She knew Lyric was gone, and she didn't have anyone to carry on her family legacy."

"It was everything to her. Sanité and the ancestors would never allow me to pray to them or to act as family, especially with Charlotte sacrificing her Spirit to protect me. I can't carry on her family legacy."

"Charlotte disagreed," Cage said. "Maybe it's less about blood and more about devotion. Honor her wishes and set her free."

She finally looked at him with watering eyes. "How?"

"We find the kidnapper. You can put her ashes in with her family, and her spirit can join the ancestors."

"The ritual didn't work."

"Didn't Miss Alexandrine say to give it time and have faith?" He smiled and nudged her shoulder. "Besides, since when is any prayer automatically answered?"

She rolled her eyes. "You don't even believe in Voodoo. And now I don't know if I do, either."

"Yes, you do. You're just impatient and exhausted." Cage shifted around to kneel in front of her. "You're a lot stronger than you give yourself credit for. The only way for you and Charlotte to find peace is to bring this bastard in, so I'll support whatever you need to believe for that to happen." He pulled the white doll out of his back pocket. "I think you'll need this."

She slowly reached for the doll.

He stood and offered his hand. "Let's go back to Miss Angeline's. It's too damned hot here."

32

I STROKE THE soft feathers in the white doll's crown, staring into her black, stitched eyes. Where's her power? Why is the ritual taking so long?

Cage says he wants to take me to a hypnotist in Tulane tomorrow before we go to Jasper. I don't want to go under, but Cage is stressing about the news people finding out. Some reporter already tried to talk to Miss Alexandrine, and she scared him off by chanting some spell nonsense.

He says we don't have time to just rely on the ritual. Hypnosis might speed it up.

Poor guy. He's trying so hard to respect Voodoo when it's obvious he thinks it's all a crock.

But Cage is worried about my kidnapper going back and covering my tracks. I'm not worried about him coming after me. Cage will keep me safe. But I don't want to be hypnotized. The idea of being totally powerless like that makes me want to puke.

Believe, believe, believe.

At least Cage trusted me enough to let me stay with Miss Alexandrine. Bonin looked at him like he'd lost his mind, but Cage said I'd be better off here. I promised him I wouldn't take off. I won't let him down.

I rub my hands across my face and trace the scar that runs along my hairline to my saggy jaw. I reach into my mouth and fish out the partial denture. Six teeth shattered when my face slammed the pavement.

I don't want to look at the pictures Annabeth's—my—parents gave me, but I reach for them anyway. That pretty girl smiling at the camera isn't me. I'll never remember all of her life, and I sure as hell won't look like her again.

"Stop that now." Miss Alexandrine was in the doorway, wearing a pink nightgown that didn't fit.

"Your gown is too short. Bend over and I'll see your hoo-ha."

She burst out laughing. "You're the only person I'd ever allow to speak to me that way."

"Only 'cause you feel sorry for me."

"Feeling sorry for someone's a waste of time," Alexandrine said. "So is feeling sorry for yourself. Doesn't change anything. Faith and doing what needs to be done is the only way to make life better."

"So why do you let me talk to you that way?"

"Because that's who you are, and I love you for that." She comes over to smooth my hair and sits down beside me. "The ritual isn't some magic spell that will bring everything back. It might come in pieces over time. But if you believe it will, if you leave your heart open, I promise it will work." She takes the pictures and flips through them. "You look like your mama. Even though your skin is closer to your dad's coloring."

"*She* looks like her mother." I point at the droopy side of my face. "I look like this. And no ritual's going to fix that. I need more surgery, and I don't even know if they'll help."

Alexandrine sighed. "You had so many surgeries when you first came home. I think once Charlotte got you out of that hospital, she never wanted to go back. And the medical bills ..." She shook her head. "Charlotte was thinking about selling the family home in the French Quarter to pay them off."

"She did all of that for me just to save her family legacy? She knew she couldn't fool the Loa."

"Is that what you think?" Miss Alexandrine looks at me with watery eyes. I've never seen her cry, not even when Gran died. "Maybe at the very beginning, in the hospital, she considered that. But she loved you. She wanted you to get better and live your life."

My throat knots. "I miss her."

"Me too." Miss Alexandrine clears her throat. "You going to Texas with Cage tomorrow?"

"I told him I would. He thinks I can help."

"So do I, but he's a married man. With a baby."

"I know that!"

"I see the way you look at him."

"He's gorgeous," I say. "I saw you checking him out too."

She grins. "At my age, that's called admirin.' You look like you want to jump him."

"I already told him I would if he wasn't married."

Miss Alexandrine laughed. "It's not the wanting to jump his bones that worries me. Don't be falling for a man you can't have." She pushed to her feet and stretched. "Rest. Let your mind start to heal."

Right.

I wish I'd grabbed my sleeping pills from Gran's house.

I SHOOT OFF the pillow. Sweat soaks the back of my neck. My chest feels like it's going to explode.

I fumble for my cell phone and Cage's business card. Hopefully he's not a heavy sleeper.

"Yeah?" He sounds groggy and confused. It's almost three a.m.

"I need you to meet me at Charlotte's house."

33

CAGE KILLED THE engine in front of the small cottage on Madison Street. The lights streaming from the windows flashed off, and Annabeth burst out the front entrance holding a set of keys and a small box. She locked the door and ran to his car, jumping into the passenger seat.

"I dreamed about Lyric again," she said. "And she talked to me."

"What'd she say?"

Annabeth pushed her hair off her face, still clutching the box. "It was hard to hear her, like we were underwater or something. But she told me to get this. It was in her room, hidden in the back of her closet. I guess Gran didn't know about it."

"She told you this in the dream?"

Annabeth shook her head. "No. Maybe. I just knew when I got here that I needed to search her room. Her spirit must have come to me."

"Or your memories are starting to surface."

"Because of the ritual."

"And your open mind." Cage didn't care how she remembered as long as he had a trail to follow. "Tell me more about the dream."

She closed her eyes. "We were somewhere dark and smelly.

In a big, black space, and then I saw a wooden door. Lyric opened the door and told me to run."

Cage's head spun as he tried to piece together what she'd told him. If Lyric was a victim, why was she able to unlock the door? Why didn't she leave with Annabeth? "You were locked in a smelly, dark place with a wooden door. Maybe a shed, or a barn."

Annabeth gently lifted the lid. "This is the real Lyric. The one she kept from everybody but herself." She held up two dried, white roses that were tied together with a string. A small, square pamphlet was tucked between the delicate stems.

"Her mother's funeral program," Annabeth said. "I always felt guilty for not remembering my own mother. But now ..."

"You have a mother who loves you deeply," Cage said.

"I'll talk to her again after we solve this case." She grinned, her emotions changing with whiplash-like speed. "Guess I'm a detective now too."

"No," Cage said. "You're just the informant."

She rolled her eyes and lifted a picture out of the box. Someone had clumsily cut the right side of the photo off. "This is Lyric's mom. She was light-skinned, just like Lyric and me. Gran used to say that every man in New Orleans wanted a light-skinned Creole like us."

Annabeth kept digging through the small box, commenting on each trinket Lyric had kept. She stopped mid-sentence.

"What's wrong?" Cage asked.

She stared straight ahead, a torn and faded card gripped tightly in her right hand.

"Shit." Cage stopped the car and grabbed her chin. A chill burst through him.

Annabeth's dark eyes appeared vacant and fixed.

He checked her pulse; it was fast, but not crazy fast. Her

breathing seemed to be normal, and she held on to the painted card like her life depended on it.

"Annabeth." Cage took her face in his hands. "Look at me. Snap out of it."

Finally, she blinked.

"Say something," Cage said. "Let me know you're okay."

"Purple flowers," she whispered.

God, did she have a stroke? How much more misery did this girl have to deal with?

Annabeth exhaled and leaned limply against the seat. She held up the card. It had been ripped down the center, showing only part of the black queen cradling a child. "This was Lyric's."

Cage reached for it; her left hand snapped up to block him. "Don't touch it."

"Okay." He backed off, keeping his hands where she could see them. "What is it?"

She caressed the ripped card the same way a mother gently handles a newborn infant. "It's a Tarot card for the Loa Ezili Dantò."

Of course it was. "And the Loa are again?"

"The spirits we pray to. God is worship, but we can't really talk to him. Instead we pray to the Loa. We give them offerings in exchange for their help." She held up the card. "This Loa is one of the most powerful. It makes sense why Lyric would have this, although I don't know why it's torn in half."

"So this … E-zily—"

"Ezili," Annabeth corrected him.

"Right. What's so special about her?"

"She is many things," Annabeth said, "but a mother above all. She can be tough and wild, but she will love and defend her child until the end. She doesn't take anyone's shit, and she tells things straight up. She fights for anyone who's been beaten down and mistreated but especially for women and children." She looked at him, her eyes wide and shining now. "Lyric's emotions imprinted on this card. It has a psychic connection to her."

Cage could guess where this was going, but he didn't interrupt.

"I had a vision." Her eyes seemed to become alert. "Lyric."

"A vision?" Or her memories had started to filter through because she was ready to accept them. If Lyric had this half of the card in her box, maybe she had the other half with her. Annabeth could have seen it at some point during her captivity. "What did you see?"

"Lyric. Not like her pictures, but older. Her face wasn't totally clear, but it was her."

"Annabeth—"

"Lyric is alive." She held the card to her lips. "And she told me to look for the purple flowers."

34

HE STARED AT the TV. The same gray-haired anchor who'd been sitting at the front desk since as long as he could remember told the story.

The neurologist said she might remember. That she might be able to bring a terrible person to justice.

He drained his beer and threw the bottle at the trash can. Bring him to justice. After so many playthings, blending in was his specialty.

"What do we do?"

He turned to the chain-smoking woman next to him. "We find her. And we take care of her."

35

CAGE PULLED THE cap over his head, shielding his eyes from the morning sun. He leaned against the hot metal of the car while the gas slowly pumped.

"You're sure?"

Bonin nodded. "Don't say anything to her about it."

After Annabeth's dream and "vision," Cage decided to forgo the hypnotist and stay ahead of the impending media storm. Twenty miles outside of Jasper, Texas, Bonin got word the press had published photos and significant facts about the investigation.

"Whoever did this had access to a lot of details." Someone had leaked both before and after pictures, along with the information about Annabeth's TBI and more about her life as Lyric Gaudet. The media had already made the obvious leap: a serial predator had been on the loose for more than a decade.

Cage's bet was on Sam George tipping off the media. The two of them had never clicked, and the Georges had been through hell. Sam was rightfully pissed off at his daughter not coming home. He'd likely considered leaking the story a chess move instead of a dangerous risk for Annabeth.

"The Girl Who Lived," Bonin said. "Like she's got a scar on her forehead and a magic wand. They could have come up with something more original."

"Don't bring it up," Cage said. "I've already warned her it's going to happen. She needs to stay calm."

"She's wearing the mourning ring," Bonin said. "She believes it will keep her safe."

Cage shoved the nozzle back into the pump. Bonin was a good cop, but he could use a more narrow-minded partner right now. "Surely you don't think that's all she needs."

"I support whatever she needs to feel safe. We can't risk her taking off again. And after what you described last night, I'd think your mind would be a little more open."

Her vision, some kind of psychic connection from an old Tarot card. Alexandrine supported the theory. Lyric had learned the Tarot from her mother. At least she'd been more practical about the chances of Lyric still being alive.

"I don't think so," Alexandrine had said. "The mind and psychic connection are unexplainable things. It's more likely that Lyric's spirit has returned to this card because a part of it is tethered here. Her spirit is telling you to look for the flowers. You see her as her spirit wishes you to."

Annabeth didn't argue, but her body language said enough: a vision sent from a living, breathing Lyric was the only option. Cage hadn't bothered to argue. If she wouldn't listen to Alexandrine, she wasn't going to buy his logical explanation of her memory coming back.

Still, after he'd gone back to the hotel and tried to grab another hour of sleep, Annabeth's blank face and empty eyes haunted him. Whatever had happened to her was neurological and not a vision or communication from a spirit.

But what if it was? He'd listened to footsteps in the empty halls of Ironwood, heard doors slam, and watched things fly off counters. Dani swore she saw a woman in a vintage gown walking through the servants' quarters. Cage accepted these things without question. Most of the South was haunted. Why couldn't he consider this?

Annabeth emerged from the gas station carrying a giant soda and a bag of chips. She waved at them, and Bonin nudged Cage. "She also thinks Agent Sexy will keep her safe."

Cage ignored her and snapped the nozzle back into the pump.

"I was about to starve to death." Annabeth pulled a Starburst package from her back pocket and grinned. She flapped the candy back and forth. "Want some?"

"No, thanks," Cage said. "We need to get back on the road."

"You're the boss. By the way, did I tell you the whole gun belt thing is really sexy? Like, could you be any hotter?"

Bonin choked a laugh. Cage rolled his eyes to the sweltering sky. "Inappropriate."

CAGE EASED THE car onto the shoulder of the dusty county road. Annabeth had been hit approximately five-hundred yards from the intersection of State Route 2800 and the county road. "This should be damned near the spot."

Annabeth stepped out of the car.

"I ran through the woods."

"You remember?"

"You told me I must have, because of the pine needles in my feet." She turned in a circle. "There's trees on both sides."

"The couple who hit you said you'd come from the west." Cage said. "The local police searched a full mile radius, but they were operating on the assumption you'd been dumped in the woods nearby. They never made the connection with the pine needles."

"There's pine needles in the clearing," Bonin said. "Scattered everywhere. Wind blows them. She might have been dumped."

"She had lacerations on her feet," Cage said, "from the needles, suggesting she stepped on them. Some were deeply imbedded, so it didn't happen when she stood up and walked to the road."

Annabeth rubbed her temples and clicked her teeth. "I don't remember anything about this place. We need to look for the purple flowers. That's what Lyric said in my vision."

"Relax," Cage said. "This is just a starting point. Bonin, you have the map?"

Bonin spread a Texas DOT map across the hood of the car. Every county road was marked, and Cage had already compared it to his Google Earth results. Farms and communities dotted the area he wanted to search. "We're not looking at people who still live here," Cage said. "Even if he thought she died, he would have fled. Probably as soon as he found out she escaped."

"But someone else might be living there now," Bonin said. "We should start with the properties that have a decent amount of land. The farms with barns."

Cage agreed. "Let's just drive around and look first. I don't want to knock on any doors unless we have to. The less the local police know, the better."

Annabeth had wandered across the clearing of dried-up grass and hovered near the edge of the woods. She rubbed her temples again. "Why aren't we looking for the flowers?"

"What is it?" Cage quickly joined her. Her skin had paled, making the spattering of freckles stand out.

Cage touched her shoulder. "Do you remember something?"

She shook her head, but her hands trembled. She rocked back and forth on her heels.

"Annabeth, talk to me," Cage said. "Take a deep breath. Don't let your emotions take over."

"She looks like she's in shock." Bonin had joined them.

"Talk to us," Cage begged. "What is it?"

Annabeth's head whipped back and forth, her breathing short. "No, no, no."

"Annabeth, you're safe." Cage gently took her quaking hands. Despite the heat, her skin felt like ice. "Look at me."

She finally made eye contact, her pupils dilated.

"Good," Cage said. He hated putting her through this. Pandora's box could explode at any moment, and he and Bonin weren't equipped to deal with the emotional fallout. "Tell me what you remembered."

"Not a memory." Her voice sounded weak as a newborn kitten's. "Terror. I can't remember what happened, but I know I was scared out of my mind, waiting for him to find me before a car came by. I can't see it, but I feel it. Does that make sense?"

Cage nodded. "We're on the right track. You definitely came from the west."

"How do you know for sure?" Annabeth asked.

"Because I watched you look at the entire area when we got out of the car. Nothing bothered you until you came over here."

She nodded. "I feel dizzy."

"Go back to the car and get a drink," Bonin said. "There's water in the cooler in the back."

Annabeth surprisingly obeyed, moving slowly to the car.

Bonin and Cage trailed behind. "I know what you're going to say," he said. "But her reaction's all we have."

"That's what worries me."

THEY SPENT THE next hour driving the county roads and dirt paths. A few big farms had large barns, but Bonin's quick public record search showed they'd all been owned by the same people for more than a decade. And this time during the Texas summer, purple wildflowers grew in abundance.

Annabeth wasn't deterred. "Those aren't the right flowers. I'll know when I see them."

"We're nearly four miles from where she was hit," Bonin said. "That's at least an hour walking. Given her injuries, I doubt she ran very long."

Cage turned left onto a raggedy, narrow dirt path that cut through the patchy woods. It looked like it hadn't been used in a while.

"This isn't on the map," Bonin said. "No clue where it goes."

Cage eased ahead. "That's why I'm taking it." He glanced in the rearview mirror at Annabeth. She hadn't reacted to any of the farms or barns they passed. She was laser-focused on the purple flowers. Her mind had probably invented the whole "vision" to give her something to concentrate on.

The long path opened into a large, circular clearing pocketed with weeds. Beyond the clearing were fields of natural grass and heavy thickets of weeds.

Thirty feet from the empty clearing sat a decaying barn.

"STAY IN THE car." He left the engine running while he and Bonin crossed the clearing and took a mangled path toward the barn. Weathered from the blistering Texas sun and rotting with age, the barn leaned dangerously to one side. "A good wind would knock this thing down."

"Be careful," Bonin said as Cage forced the wide front door to slide open. He covered his face and tried not to gag at the stench of rotted earth and decaying manure.

"Looks like an old horse barn," Cage said.

They walked toward the two stalls. The door to the larger one had disintegrated off its hinges and lay on the ground.

"I've never seen a horse make those marks." Bonin trained

her light on the jagged punctures in the wood.

Fingernail scratches.

"There's no mention of wood beneath her nails," Cage said. "But that doesn't mean this isn't the right place."

Across from the stalls, bags of oats and flower seeds rotted, adding to the putrid smell.

"We need to find out who owns this property, who lived here seven years ago. And we need crime scene techs to search for blood and trace," Cage said.

"After all this time?" Bonin said. "And I doubt Jasper County's going to cooperate."

A shrill scream tore through the air. Cage and Bonin bolted outside.

Annabeth wasn't in the car.

"Cage!" she screamed.

He and Bonin raced through the weeds to the other side of the barn. He breathed a sigh of relief at the sight of Annabeth standing a few feet into the field, unharmed.

She pointed to a large swath of blooming purple coneflowers.

36

"HER SNIPPETS OF memory won't be enough." Bonin glanced at Annabeth, who stood silent, staring at the coneflowers. "You need the Texas Rangers and the FBI, and you need to sweet-talk the Jasper County Sheriff into thinking he's the one asking for their help. None of that's going to happen based on flowers."

Annabeth turned her dark eyes on Bonin. "I'm not making this up. Lyric told me to look for the flowers."

"I believe you," Bonin said. "But it's not enough."

"If the flowers come from the seeds in the barn, they were planted the previous fall, if not earlier. Annabeth escaped in the spring," Cage said. "Lyric told you about the flowers as a point of reference because they were blooming."

His instincts churned as he walked around the flowers. They had multiplied over the years, but the side-by-side rows were too uniform. No one randomly planted a garden like this in the middle of a field, and there was no sign of any other plants or vegetables. This wasn't some leftover flower garden.

"We have to dig up the flowers."

THEY RETURNED AT dusk with shovels and flashlights. With no visible address, Bonin had been unable to find out if the land belonged to someone or was state property. Cage figured finding the remains trumped asking nicely.

Annabeth clutched the mourning ring, her skin flushed and sweaty.

"You can wait in the car," Cage said. "Sit in the A/C."

"I don't want to be left alone." She stared into the patch of trees bordering the open field—the woods she likely sprinted through that fatal night. "Maybe it's my broken brain messing with me, but this place feels familiar. I keep smelling wet ground—like after a rain. But this place is dry as a popcorn fart."

It had rained the night Annabeth escaped.

"And Lyric saved my life. If she's buried here, I should stay." She held up the large flashlight. "You dig. I'll shine."

The setting sun had incited the katydids and cicadas to kick off their nightly song.

"I hate bugs," Annabeth said as Cage started to dig around the perimeter of the flowers. "The singing ones creep me the hell out."

"Reminds me of home," Cage said. "We used to sit out and listen to them for hours when I was kid."

"My granddaddy cooked up the grasshoppers." Bonin drove her shovel into the ground opposite him. "Cicadas too. Everyone loved them. I never had the stomach to try."

Annabeth made a gagging sound. "Old people are weird. Charlotte talked about cooking bugs too. Nasty."

Cage's shoulders already throbbed. Sweat soaked his shirt. If it weren't for Annabeth's uncontrollable mind, he'd strip off his shirt. But after the claustrophobic atmosphere of New Orleans, the wide-open lands of Texas felt like heaven and reminded him of home. He would miss nights on Ironwood's restored back sunroom, looking over the grounds that once held so many secrets.

"Shit!" Bonin dropped her shovel, stumbling backwards and

landing hard on her butt. "Is that a copperhead? I just scooped it up with the damn shovel by accident."

"Get back." Cage snatched the light from Annabeth and trained it on the tangled pit of flowers.

Red-brown cross bands, copper-colored head, and a vibrating yellow-tipped tale. Cage's insides turned cold.

"What's that awful smell?" Annabeth pinched her nose.

"Copperheads give off a musky scent when they're pissed off," Cage said. "They're venomous and mean."

This time of night, the snake's food coma made him less threatening—unless someone pissed him off by accidentally shoveling up his hiding spot. A man needed to steer clear of a threatened copperhead—"turn and haul ass" as Cage's father always said when he told the story of a friend getting bit on the toe by a baby copperhead. The boy was too far from the hospital, and by the time he received treatment, his toe had swollen to bursting.

The nearest hospital was almost thirty minutes away.

"Their bites usually aren't fatal," Cage said. "But I'd rather not test that theory."

This snake was less than two feet from him. Its strike distance was probably eight inches, maybe ten. Figure three feet to be safe. The shovel was four feet long, plus the length of the blade. Should be fine.

"Annabeth, keep the light on it and stay still. You too," he said to Bonin.

"Don't kill it!" Annabeth said.

"I'm not planning to."

He blinked against the sweat stinging his eyes. His heart hammered in his ears as he edged forward. The copperhead's tail vibrated faster.

Cage slipped the shovel blade underneath the angry snake.

He saw a brief glimpse of fangs before the snake struck, its venomous bite coming within inches of Cage's hand. He threw the shovel as hard as he could. It landed with a thud several feet away.

Annabeth trained the flashlight on the shovel as the snake hissed and lurched, slowly uncoiling and slithering away.

"Christ," Bonin said. "I thought it was going to nail you."

"Me too." Cage took the light from Annabeth and retrieved his shovel. Hands still unsteady, he carefully checked the flower patch for more snakes.

"Looks clear," he said. "Just be careful."

They resumed digging, fighting with the dry ground. Annabeth's light flashed left to right as she patrolled for more snakes.

"How far down do you think we need to go?" Bonin huffed. "I don't want to shatter a skull and ruin evidence."

They'd already dug at least three feet and a good distance into the flowerbed. "This is far enough. Let's switch to spades."

Bugs swarmed his face. His back ached, and he needed a shower. Bonin looked ready to call it a night. Behind them, Annabeth paced. They dug in silence until something shiny caught Cage's eye.

"Focus the light here."

Annabeth knelt beside him and pointed her light at the long, glittering object.

Cage snapped on latex gloves and slowly began sifting through the dirt, easing the gold chain from the earth. A delicate, dirt-crusted heart dangled from the chain.

He gently rubbed off the dirt, the hair on the back of his neck standing up.

A small 'M' was engraved on the heart.

"This belonged to Mickie," Cage said. "She was wearing it when she disappeared."

37

I CAN'T SLEEP.

I wanted to stay with Cage, but he says I need rest. How am I supposed to sleep knowing what's coming tomorrow?

Maybe Lyric really is dead and Miss Alexandrine is right. Her spirit is leading me. She wants me to find her body and bring her home.

She's not supposed to go in the family tomb, but maybe if I pray to the ancestors to make an exception since she saved my life, they'll listen. I'll worry about it later.

Cage says the identification process will take a while—and he said it may just be Mickie's body buried out there, but I know he just doesn't want me to get my hopes up.

He stayed out to watch the area. The killer is probably long gone, but just in case, Cage wanted to stand guard.

I'm scared he's out there all alone.

I roll over in the lumpiest bed on earth. Bonin checked us in to some motel on the outskirts of Jasper, and my air conditioner is wheezing. It's at least eighty degrees in here.

I run my fingers over the ring, memories of Gran—Charlotte—coming fast. Tears well in my eyes. She deserved better than cancer.

I deserve better than this. So did Lyric and Mickie and the others he stole.

My chest burns. My muscles feel stretched and thin. I'm breathing too fast.

I will not freak out.

Deep breaths. Close your eyes. Visualize something that makes you feel calm.

I have to keep my cool, or Cage won't let me near the burial site tomorrow. I need to be there.

Sunday dinners with Charlotte and Miss Alexandrine. Watching the little kids play in the sprinkler.

I grab the white doll and the torn Tarot card and press them to my chest. I count to one hundred, the anxiety easing enough my lungs no longer hurt.

I think we were kept in the barn. In the horse stalls, probably. Were we chained? Or did he use rope or twine? Did he rape us in the barn? It seemed too dirty.

But there's no house. He wouldn't just stick us in the barn and leave us, would he? Go back to town?

Maybe he camped out. The doll seemed to shiver.

Sweat broke out over my upper lip. The blue pickup's rusty hitch.

My feet dragging across the dry, dusty clearing. Staring at the back of his head and wondering what sort of weapon would knock him out.

The squeak of a door opening.

Metal steps descending.

I sat up in bed. "He had an RV."

38

MOBILIZING RESOURCES TOOK too damned long. Out of respect, Cage notified the Jasper County Sheriff first, but let him know the nature of the case meant his next call would be to the Texas Rangers. His belief the victims crossed state lines meant informing the FBI.

Bonin switched places with him in the dawn hours, and he went back to the hotel to shower and get an hour of sleep. Now he and Annabeth were heading back to the body dump.

"You're sure about the camper?"

She sucked on a bottle of orange juice. "Am I sure as in, it's fact? No. But my gut is positive."

A camper made sense. Easy to pick up and take off, with enough amenities to survive.

"I think Lyric is still alive."

Giving her false hope would hurt her more than the truth. "He killed her after you escaped. I'm certain of it."

Annabeth shook her head. "You're wrong."

"Okay. Then how do you explain your vision? How did her spirit come to you?" Cage still believed it was her memory breaking through, but he needed to prove a point.

"Gran taught Lyric Voodoo her entire life. She told me that I—Lyric—had as much skill as she did. And there are ways to call on the spirits to help you make contact with another living person."

He understood taking comfort from her religion, but she was setting herself up for major disappointment. "I know you think her being alive will make you feel better."

"No," she said. "I just know she is."

He kept his mouth shut and focused on the road. Annabeth would have to deal with the reality soon enough. The more important question was Lyric's role in the kidnappings. What had she done to stay alive after he took her? Or had she gone willingly instead of going back to Charlotte like everyone wanted to believe?

RANGER LEWIS SHOOK Cage's hand. "The land owner's name is Joel Rogers. He lives up north in Illinois. Leases four hundred acres to hunters through a local company and probably makes a ton of money."

Cage liked the brawny Texas Ranger immediately. He didn't seem to have any issue with Cage being out of jurisdiction or getting glory. He wanted justice.

"Rogers bought the property at auction in fall 2010 after the owner defaulted on the loan," Bonin said. "The previous owner was L.M. Gaudet. Bought the land in November 2005."

"Sonofabitch. He used her name. And she never came up as a missing person because everything went to shit during Katrina. Is the realtor still in town?" Cage prayed that was the case. Lyric being complicit would add to Annabeth's guilt, and she would obsess over Charlotte's spirit never being at peace. She would never be able to move on.

"The ground was purchased from the bank," Bonin said. "They want a warrant, all the bells and whistles. I'm working on it."

"I'll give the president a call," Ranger Lewis said. "He's

helped out on a couple of fraud cases."

Small and compact, her eyes hidden behind her sunglasses, FBI Agent Tims had listened to the briefing in silence. Her youth made Cage nervous. Inexperience came with the drive to prove you belonged on the job. She stood like a solider at attention, a kinetic energy radiating from her.

"Lyric Gaudet may have been an accomplice," Tims said. "It wouldn't be the first time it's happened."

"No." Annabeth's sharp voice cracked. "She was a victim, and she let me go."

Tims didn't look at Annabeth. "I'm aware. But the reality is she could have started out as a victim and ended up an accomplice. Or she was in on it all along. I'll need to debrief the witness before I get started."

Bonin gave Cage a knowing look. Ranger Lewis jammed his hands in his pockets and sighed.

"Annabeth's been debriefed. Detective Bonin and I can fill you in if that becomes necessary."

"If it becomes necessary?" Tims said. "This case is FBI jurisdiction. It's mine."

"How many major cases have you worked?" Ranger Lewis asked.

"That's irrelevant."

"So, the answer would be not too damned many," Lewis said. "All due respect, ma'am, but you need to prioritize. Instead of worrying about calling the shots, focus on solving the crime. That's what matters."

"I am focused on solving this. But rules are rules."

"You sound like a stereotypical feeb," Bonin said. "Not the way to make a solid reputation."

Tims glared at her. "Look, if we don't have a structure in place, this investigation will be a muddled mess. It's bad enough you two just rode into town and started digging on private property. How do you think that's going to come off in court?"

"Who gives a shit?" Annabeth's face burned pink. "You think these girls give a rat's hairy ass who's in charge? Stop waving your dicks around and start digging!"

Ranger Lewis stared. Tims's face pinched into a scowl. "I'm not sure who you think you are—"

"She has a traumatic brain injury," Bonin said. "Sometimes she can't control her anger. You'd know that if you read the full briefing we emailed."

Annabeth shook her head, eyes flashing. "I know damn well what I'm doing. These girls were used and discarded like trash. One of them helped me escape, and she planted those flowers so the rest of the victims could get home to their families. I'll tell you again, stop waving dicks and dig." Her last few words became a scream. She looked ready to pass out.

Cage stepped between Annabeth and the others, blocking her view. "Look at me."

"I swear to God, if you try to make me go to the car, I will fight you."

"I can toss you over my shoulder and carry you back without much effort."

"As temping as that is, Agent Sexy, try and you won't be making any more babies for a while. I have a right to be here."

"I get it," Cage said softly. "But you have to handle these people the right way—even if it means swallowing some pride—so let me deal with them."

"When are they going to start digging?"

"The forensic anthropologist from Texas State and her team have to do that, or we'll destroy evidence," Cage said. "They should be here soon."

Ranger Lewis cleared his throat. "I apologize, miss. You're

right. We all need to work together, and we will. Just let us get the logistical bullshit out of the way so we're ready when the doc gets here."

"And I still want to talk with you," Agent Tims said. "We need more information about your escape and abduction."

"There's no more information right now." Cage spoke before Annabeth exploded. "It's coming back to her in bits and pieces."

"Once Mickie's body is identified, we'll have proof he crossed state lines. Then it's officially my case. You won't be able to shield her."

"I won't work with you," Annabeth said. "You're a stuck-up bitch who's looking for glory. Cage and Detective Bonin are the only ones I trust."

Agent Tims looked ready to slap the girl. "There are legal ways I can make you talk."

"I'll sit in a cell," Annabeth said. "And Miss Alexandrine will fix you. Promise that."

Cage didn't get off on making people feel stupid, but he'd had a bellyfull of Tims. "You understand she's in my custody? Or did you miss that in the email as well?"

"I don't care if she's in your custody," Tims said. "Once I take over the case—"

"I'm not discussing that right now. We needed FBI resources. That's why you're here. Annabeth stays with us."

Tims jaw looked tight enough to shatter. "We already have Mickie's dental records and the DNA sample provided by her parents. The match shouldn't take long. I'll wait in the car until the dig team gets here."

"Christ," Bonin hissed as the agent stalked off. "What a shitshow."

"Junior agent with no damn clue. I can't stand cops who

don't put the victim first," Ranger Lewis said. "Listen, I've worked with the forensic anthropologist and medical examiner out of Houston. I'll talk to them and see if I can express how very carefully they need to examine all the remains before making any formal ID. We don't want to rush things."

Cage grinned. Sometimes he loved the good ole' boy network. "Thanks."

"I don't know how much time I'll buy you, but I'll do my best."

39

BODY RECOVERY SUCKED. Every single detail was vital, making the process agonizingly slow. Cage fought the urge to ask the dig team to work faster.

Dr. Carrie Metz from Texas State University was considered among the best forensic anthropologists in the country, and her work with the school's body farm was nationally recognized. She was meticulous to the last detail.

"These flowers are only over part of the remains." Metz walked away from the mess of flowers. "This ground is different than the rest of the pasture."

Cage hadn't noticed. He still didn't see any difference.

"It's about soil density," Metz said. "We marked off a perimeter much larger than the flower patch and probed through it. I think there are more bodies to the left of the flowers."

"How many?"

"I can't say until we start digging," Metz said.

"Lyric planted the flowers over Mickie and the final girls. Different burials mean different times of death."

Metz eyed him over the rim of her sunglasses. "You're inferring. I don't do that."

After a small back hoe removed the top layer of soil Metz had marked off, four graduate students set up tents over the dig and began documenting and photographing the site. A third sifted through the soil and destroyed sunflowers. Metz laid out multiple shovels and small trowels on the blue tarp she'd placed next to the sunflower pit. "Let's see what we've got."

"Freaking media is shady as hell. Some woman conned her way past the barricade up the road and nearly made it to the barn before I caught her. She wasn't happy about being escorted off the property." Bonin handed him a bottle of water. "I pulled dental records of the other girls you believed may have been victims. One family had already provided DNA samples to local law enforcement, so I've requested that as well."

"Let's hope we find enough teeth on the remains to actually get a dental match," Cage said. "I don't like the idea of contacting families based on a hunch one of these bodies might be their kid."

He turned to Annabeth, who sat in a canopied lawn chair Ranger Lewis had brought to her. "You okay?"

"Fine."

Her pale skin and perpetually wide eyes said differently, but Cage didn't waste his energy. She wasn't moving from that spot.

Metz worked the area where Mickie's necklace had been discovered, and it wasn't long before she'd reached bone. "This one's buried shallow. We may not have a full skeleton. Critters like human remains."

"Once he discovered Annabeth escaped, he had to clean up quickly." Cage lowered his voice and leaned toward Bonin. "If Lyric's buried here, she'll be in the same grave. He wouldn't have time to dig two."

"Or he dumped her somewhere else."

"Ranger Lewis checked the state's unidentified remains database," Cage said. "No matches."

"State line isn't all that far from here."

"I've already checked Louisiana's. Maybe he didn't kill her.

He kept her for five years. She might have been able to convince him Annabeth escaped on her own. If she survived for five years, she knew how to deal with the guy." He didn't believe it, but if Lyric had somehow survived, Annabeth's guilt would be partially alleviated.

"You know better than that," Bonin said. "And her body would have been scavenged quickly if he didn't have time to bury her."

"He buried her. She meant too much to him not to, even with her betrayal." The kidnapper's relationship with Lyric was the key to blowing things wide open. She meant something more than the rest—a prized possession.

"Female," Metz said. "Probably under twenty-five and likely an adolescent. Tibia's growth plates haven't fused. Ranges of fusion vary, but she definitely wasn't done growing. Teenager."

Cage had memorized Mickie's outfit from that fateful day. "Any clothing?"

"Not so far, but it likely disintegrated." Metz continued carefully removing the soil with her trowel while a graduate student bagged and tagged remains.

"She's got a Mickey Mouse watch on her left arm."

The words sucker punched him. "That's how she got her nickname."

Metz didn't reply. She wouldn't make the official ID until she'd completed the entire process.

Cage glanced at Annabeth, who'd come to stand beside him. Silent and pale, she watched the bones being removed. "How many bodies are in that grave?"

"So far, just one."

"I sneaked Lyric's missing persons case file out of your briefcase," Annabeth said. "She wasn't wearing any jewelry. Will we have to wait for dental records to match?"

"Yes," Bonin said. "And the FBI's forensic odontologist knows he's about to get hammered. He'll work as quickly as he can. Speaking of the FBI …" Bonin pointed to the barn where Tims and her crime-scene techs had converged. "Searching for trace should keep them occupied for a while, but she'll eventually get her way."

"We'll deal with that when it happens," Cage said.

Metz called for one of her graduate students. "I need separate evidence collection bags."

Annabeth grabbed Cage's arm. "What does that mean?"

"Two sets of remains in this grave," Metz said.

"Male or female?" Cage asked.

"Not there yet. Let me do my job."

Annabeth's short nails cut into his skin. "She's not dead."

"It's not your fault," Cage said. "Lyric knew the consequences of letting you go."

Annabeth backed away, shaking her head. "You're wrong. I don't care what the bone doctor says. Lyric is alive." She spun on her heel and stalked off.

"I'll make sure she doesn't get far," Bonin said. "She's too attached to you, and this is your show." She jogged to catch up to Annabeth.

"It's another female." Metz's voice sent ice down his spine. "Skull's in bad condition, but it looks like she had her wisdom teeth."

The second body was over eighteen.

40

FOUR VICTIMS SO far. And Metz's team was still digging.

Sickness rolled through Cage as he watched Metz's team working beneath the blaring Klieg lights. The FBI techs found broken fingernails wedged into the horse stall doors along with a makeshift bathroom area consisting of a five-gallon bucket and long-since degraded toilet paper. A pack of sanitary wipes had also been recovered from the muck. Hopefully the lab would manage to extract DNA.

He'd kept the victims in the barn and probably taken them to his camper for the assaults. A search for an RV in Lyric's name turned up empty. Looking for a camper registration from seven years ago was like digging for a specific piece of hay in a giant stack, especially since he could have registered it in any state. And Annabeth couldn't remember specifics about the camper—if it existed. They didn't have a damn thing to start with.

Local media had discovered the dig. Sheriff's deputies had already run off three trespassers, but the national affiliates would arrive soon. Once the killer realized his burial ground had been discovered, he'd burrow deeper underground.

"I think this is the last grave, but it might be the most significant." Metz looked exhausted, a smear of dirt across her forehead. "All the others are female. But the remains in this last grave are male."

"Are you sure?" Cage expected the bodies to be identified as the missing girls he'd already flagged. This guy had a clear type: young, bi-racial girls with athletic builds.

Metz shot him a dirty look. "Pretty damn sure. He was rolled up in a tarp, so his clothing didn't completely disintegrate. The bones are nearly a complete set." She handed Cage a clear evidence bag containing a dirty, fragile knitted patch. He instantly recognized the famous basketball silhouette.

"2006 NBA All-Star game, Houston."

"I can't give you an exact date," Metz said. "But obviously he didn't die before 2006. The All-Star game is in February, I think."

Lyric had purchased the land in late 2005. "He was killed before the rest of them?"

"I can't tell with any scientific certainty until we've done a full examination in the lab," Metz said. "But going by the condition of the bones and the patch, I'd say it's likely."

It made no sense. Predators like this man didn't dabble in preference. Was it possible the boy had been dumped by someone else, years before? One hell of a coincidence, and Cage didn't believe in them. Not in murder cases.

"What else can you tell me about the boy?" Cage asked as Sheriff Michaels leaned closer to inspect the patch.

"Going by his skull and long bones, he was likely between eleven and eighteen when he died. There's blunt force trauma in the skull—I'll need to get it under a microscope to verify if it's pre-mortem."

The Sheriff stared at the patch. "It's Johnny Deitz."

"Who's Johnny Dietz?" Cage asked.

"Jasper County's a small place," the sheriff said. "Safe. We don't see too many kids disappear. But Johnny did. His sister was a problem kid, so no one believed her."

"What happened?" Bonin asked.

"Sheila Dietz was sixteen and wild," Sheriff Michaels said. "High school dropout and dragging Johnny down with her. He was fourteen and thought she was the coolest thing in the world. They both disappear one afternoon in spring 2006. No damned sign of them until Sheila shows up a couple of months later with a crazy story."

The gray-haired sheriff appeared suddenly exhausted. "She said Johnny followed her when she was supposed to meet her dealer. They got high. A man attacked them. She wakes up alone and tied up. Said she was assaulted for days and then escaped. Took her a while to come home because she was ashamed. She didn't think anyone would believe her, and we didn't." He turned to look at the barn, shoulders slumped. "She said she was kept in a horse stall and taken out to be raped. I might have believed her, but she talked about a girl helping him. I just couldn't get my mind 'round it."

Adrenaline rushed through Cage, wiping out his fatigue. "Did she describe the girl?"

"She couldn't remember," Michaels said. "Another reason it sounded made-up. Everyone thought Johnny OD'd, and she'd panicked and buried him, then took off."

"Were Sheila and Johnny mixed-race?" Bonin asked.

"Yeah. Genetics, man. Johnny looked more white, with reddish hair and a bunch of freckles. But Sheila, she had that pretty caramel skin, like yours." Michaels's wrinkled face reddened again as he glanced shyly at Bonin.

"Did you check out her story?" Cage asked.

"As best we could. I think she'd been strung out while she was gone. She was pretty sure she remembered where they were attacked, but she had no recollection of where she escaped from.

They were attacked about a mile south of here, near the creek." The sheriff's guilt radiated off him.

"Every one of us would have ended up with the same conclusion," Cage said. "Especially if she took so long to come forward."

"One of those cases that haunts you," Michaels said. "I felt sorry for Sheila, really. Her mama never forgave her."

"Is she still alive?" Bonin asked.

Michaels nodded and half-smiled. "I kept track of her. She got herself right. Owns a Cajun restaurant in Shreveport. Named it after her little brother. Best jambalaya I ever had."

CAGE DROPPED HIS overnight bag on the floor and sank into the hotel bed, ignoring the rough sheets and the stale smell in the room. After spending all day and half the night in the Texas heat, he smelled worse.

His eyelids were heavy, but his mind raced as it tried to make sense of the new information. Exhaustion turned his brain into a jumbled mess. His cell vibrated in his pocket; the glowing screen showed one new message from Dani.

Call me.

He didn't have the energy to argue with her again. But he needed to hear her voice, even if she was still pissed.

She answered on the first ring. "I wasn't sure I'd hear from you tonight."

"I just got to the hotel." Awkwardness swept over him. He loved this woman more than anything, but he didn't know what to say to make things right.

"Were you at the dig site all day?"

"Yeah."

She sighed. "I hope you wore sunscreen and drank water."

"I did."

"Emma misses you," Dani said. "She was asking for you all night."

Cage's throat tightened. He should have called earlier and talked to his daughter. "I miss her too."

"Doesn't this case belong to the FBI now?"

"Not officially. Not yet." He bit back the frustration and tried to look at things from her perspective. "I know you're lonely and worn out from getting ready to move and taking care of everything. You're having second thoughts about moving and I should be there. But I can't walk away from this now."

"From her," Dani said. "You can't walk away from her."

He sat up. "Is that what this is about? You don't seriously think I would—"

"It's not about trust," she said. "I'm not worried about you cheating. But you're swept up in this girl's well-being. You say you want to solve the case to save additional girls, but that's not really it. You want to bring her closure. Fix things for her. Because you still blame yourself for what happened to her."

"Dani—"

"Just listen," she said. "This is what I wanted to say before, but I was tired and fed up and it all came out wrong. You're a fixer, and that's one of the things I love most about you. Helping Annabeth is a good thing, but you can't trade your whole life and career for this case. Your boss is already pissed you didn't bring her home right away. He's going to be especially pissed if you're causing issues with the FBI."

"So I'm just supposed to hand everything over to Tims and walk away? She's too green, Dee. And she's more concerned with making a name for herself in the Bureau. And Annabeth will take off. I guarantee it."

"She's an adult now. You can't make up for what happened to her by sheltering her now. That doesn't help her."

"It's not just about Annabeth," Cage said. "Mickie's parents deserve answers, and so do the families of the other victims we found tonight. Five kids, Dee. How can I walk away without seeing this through and giving them answers?"

"You can't." He heard the tears in her voice. "I just don't want you to get caught up in something you'll regret. And I miss you. I hate being apart, even if it's only been a few days. It feels like years. Like you're just … separate from me now."

"Dee Dee." Cage barely managed to get the words out around the knot in his throat. "I'm still here. I'll always be here. I love you."

"I love you too." She sniffled, and he could see her in his head, sitting in her favorite chair in the renovated sun porch, her feet tucked beneath her. "Call me tomorrow when you can?"

"Thanks for putting up with me."

She laughed. "You are a giant pain in the ass."

41

JOHNNY'S CAJUN HOUSE reminded Cage of the backcountry barbecue joint his father loved. Several miles outside of Shreveport, the building looked like three country shacks sewed together. A hand-painted sign boasted the best jambalaya and crawfish broil in the state.

Inside smelled like heaven. Cage's mouth watered as they passed a couple happily eating gumbo.

"No time to eat," he said before Annabeth could ask. "We already had lunch anyway."

"A shitty sandwich," she griped. "I need something sweet."

Cage and Bonin quietly showed their credentials and asked to speak with Sheila. "She's expecting us."

Annabeth eyed the dessert menu. "Can I have an order of bread pudding?"

The waitress nodded and ushered them to a back table. Annabeth had finished half her bread pudding before Sheila Dietz finally joined them.

She was thicker than she'd been in her missing photos, but still a beautiful woman. She wore her black hair short and wavy now, her skin the same creamy, café au lait as the other victims.

"I thought most Cajuns were white," Annabeth said before anyone else could speak. "You're at least part-black, like me."

Sheila's eyebrows shot up. "You serious?"

"She has a problem with blurting things out," Bonin said. "Brain injury."

Sheila folded her arms across her plump chest. "Cajun on my mom's side. Dad is black. You happy now?"

Annabeth shrugged and inhaled her last bite. "This bread pudding is freaking amazing."

"Thank you." Sheila looked at Cage with weary eyes. "You said this had to do with my little brother's disappearance."

Sheriff Michaels had agreed to let Cage break the news to Sheila. "We've discovered remains in Jasper County that may belong to your brother. We're waiting on an official ID, but the victim wore the same NBA All-Star jersey as your brother had on when he disappeared."

Pain flashed over her face. "Where?"

"A few miles northwest of town," Cage said. "It's open fields and woods—hunting ground."

"A mile from where you said your attack happened," Bonin added.

"Charlotte." Sheila put her head in her hands. "If I'd never met her, Johnny would still be alive."

Annabeth jerked. Before Cage could dig the picture out of the file, she'd pulled it up on her phone. She slid it across the table. "Is this her?"

Sheila nodded and blushed. "She was gorgeous. I had a thing for her."

"Her real name is Lyric." Annabeth's hand shook. "Charlotte was her grandmother's name. You knew her?"

"I knew her as Charlotte—Char. I met her sometime in January that year."

"How?" Cage asked.

"At a gas station. She asked me for a lighter, then said she had some good stuff to sell."

"In town?" Bonin asked.

"An old station off 2800. Still had the slow-ass pumps. It's closed now."

"Was she alone?"

Sheila shrugged. "I was too interested in the meth she had."

He would have been nearby, likely watching Sheila's routine. Lyric showing up at that gas station was no coincidence.

Sheila picked at a scratch in the table, shoulders tense.

"Why did you take so long to go to police after Johnny disappeared?" Cage asked.

Sheila refused to look at them. "I knew no one would believe me. I was right, wasn't I? And I didn't even tell them everything."

Cage leaned forward. "We believe you."

"I loved Johnny. I didn't want him to end up like me, so I tried to make him stop following me around. I'd never do what they said I did."

"But you knew what really happened to him, when you went to the police, didn't you?" Annabeth said. "Why didn't you tell them?"

"Annabeth." Bonin's voice was sharp. "Please keep quiet."

Sheila's hands clenched into fists. "I can't relive all that."

"You're not going to be in trouble," Cage said. "I promise."

"You can't promise her that," Annabeth said. "If she withheld evidence, don't you have to charge her?"

Cage shot her a look. "Now I'm telling you to be quiet. And no, that's not true."

Sheila swiveled in the booth and started to get up. "I'm sorry, I can't."

"He did it to me too, and I don't remember," Annabeth said. "Please. Tell me what he did to us."

Sheila stared at her. "You can't remember?"

"From the brain injury. Everything before that is pretty much black."

"You're blessed," Sheila said. "You should keep it that way."

"I don't want to," Annabeth snapped. "And if you cared about your brother getting justice, you'd tell us the truth. Or did your brother die for nothing?"

Bonin looked like she wanted to choke Annabeth, but Cage shook his head. Her word vomit was getting to the woman.

Sheila's jaw worked, but she settled back into the booth. "Johnny died because of me."

"You didn't mean for that to happen," Annabeth said. "But you can help him now."

Sheila slumped against the booth, her body suddenly liquid. "I was meeting Char for a score. Johnny followed me, and we ended up getting high on Char's stuff. She went to pee, and then the man showed up. We were too high to fight. I can't even remember exactly what happened, just his hands around my neck until I passed out."

She looked at Annabeth. "Are you sure you want to hear the rest?"

"Yes."

"When I woke up," Sheila said. "I was locked in a horse stall and bleeding from my private parts. Both of them. He'd put a collar around my neck, and when he wanted to use me, he'd put a chain on the collar and drag me into his camper." Sheila took a long, shuddering breath. "He'd customized it so the main living area was his play area. That's what he called it. He had a special table with leather straps, plus a box full of sex toys and things to hurt me with. Bastard liked to talk. I think he got off on that as much as anything else. He'd tell me what he was going to do before he did it. He said that made me tighter."

Annabeth was silent, but her entire body vibrated against

Cage. He wanted to take her hand, but Dani's words from last night haunted him. Maybe he was getting too close.

"He kept my mouth taped so I couldn't scream. When I misbehaved, he burned me with a cigarette lighter. Kept me drugged so I couldn't fight. I lost track of the days."

"Did Lyric help him?" Bonin asked.

"Char." Sheila's voice was bitter. "I don't know if she was in the camper for the assaults. He had the bedroom and bathroom blocked off. Plus, I was always blindfolded. But when I was locked up in the barn, she brought me food and water. Kept saying she was sorry. That she had to give him someone else so he'd finally stop hurting her so much. I kept asking her where Johnny was, but she wouldn't tell me. I knew he was dead."

"How did you get away?" Cage asked.

"Char came to give me drugs—something strong that knocked me out. She was high, and I knew this was my chance. I asked to pee first. She untied me, and I attacked her and then ran into the woods. He came after me. It was night, and my body was wrecked. I found a hiding spot and just stayed put. I was so scared I pissed myself. But morning came, and he was gone."

"Why didn't you go to the police?" Bonin said.

"Because the whole time he was searching for me, he kept calling me a slut and telling me everyone knew I sold myself for money. He was an upstanding citizen, and I had drugs in my system. No one would believe me. Then he started threatening my mom and little sister. The baby was only a couple of years old. He knew her name and where we lived. He swore if I every reported it he'd kill her." She wiped her eyes. "Right before he stopped looking for me, he yelled that our goodbye was only temporary. No one got away from him."

"But you did," Bonin said. "And you waited a long time to tell someone."

"I didn't know who he was," Sheila said. "He said no one in town had ever seen Char, and he could make her disappear quickly. I'd sound like a drugged-out lunatic. So, when the sun came up and I got the nerve to come out, I went north through the woods. I jumped into the creek and cleaned off as best I could. Wiped away as much dirt and evidence as possible. I stayed in the woods until that night when I knew old lady Jones would have her laundry hanging out. I stole clean clothes and hitched my way out of town."

"The person who picked you up didn't ask questions?"

"He was a long-haul trucker passing through. I gave him a blow job for a ride. He was satisfied." She put her head in her hands. "I was young and screwed up, and the drugs he gave me caused the worst withdrawal I've ever experienced. By the time I got to my right mind, I'd been gone two months. You know what happened after that."

"You never saw his face?" Bonin asked her. "Or heard a name?"

"No," Sheila said. "But Char said it was useless to fight. He always got what he wanted, she said."

"What about when she sold you drugs?" Cage asked. "Did she mention where she got it from?"

"Just that she had a source with an endless supply."

"When you met her that day, was it where you always bought drugs?"

"No. We usually met at the gas station. But she wanted a new spot, said it would be more private." Sheila flushed. "She knew I liked her."

Four hundred acres of land. A woman no one else knew who'd likely been loaded into the camper as soon as Sheila escaped. All he had to do was drive to a local camping ground and wait until the dust settled.

Sheriff Michaels had checked who owned the land, found no record of Charlotte. He bought the story the townspeople believed, and their killer was quickly back in business.

42

I THROW UP the bread pudding outside. Dry heave until my throat is on fire and my stomach is one big cramp. My hands won't stop shaking. I go down to my knees because my legs have turned to jelly.

I don't remember being strapped to a table and raped. The first few days after my accident, I hurt all over. Gran said I was sexually assaulted, but I would heal. I never asked for more details. But I remember healing. I have little round scars on my thighs.

He did all those things to me.

Cage's tennis shoes are suddenly in front of me. I can't look at him.

I never thought of myself as a sexual assault victim. I didn't remember it, so I didn't have to deal with the all the psychological agony. Sometimes I even pretended the doctors had made a mistake. My private parts had been hurt in the accident. Easy peasy when I couldn't remember shit.

I can't do that anymore.

Cage dangles a bottle of water in front of me. I take it and drink slowly. I still can't look at him. I bet his wife is beautiful too. And not all shades of screwed-up and dirty like me.

I take the white doll out of my bag. She has no answer for me. Neither does the torn Tarot card.

Had Lyric lured me too? I pictured her approaching us at the lake, beautiful and mysterious. Maybe she offered to sell us pot and tricked us into meeting him.

Did she watch while he raped me? Did she do anything to stop him?

Anger goes off like a bomb in my head. I crumple the card in my hand and stumble to my feet. I'm screaming in English and Creole. My hands beat against something solid and warm. It smells like sandalwood.

Cage.

My fists pound against him until he gently grabs my wrists and holds me in place. I drop my head to his chest and bawl.

43

CAGE TRIED TO wake up as he followed Bonin into the downtown major crime offices. He needed a shower and sleep, but they had to debrief his boss and figure out what to do next.

At least Annabeth had slept for the duration of the drive. He and Bonin didn't discuss the details Sheila had given them or the way Cage held onto Annabeth while she cried. What else was he supposed to do?

"Sheila was different." Cage lowered his voice as they walked into the lobby. "No disaster as a distraction. Not as organized."

"She escaped and could have identified him," Bonin said. "So he changes things up, starts being more strategic."

Dani had been right about letting Annabeth take care of herself, but the kid was lost right now. Cage was responsible for her. He couldn't just stand around while she broke down.

Annabeth halted, and Cage nearly slammed into her.

"Shit."

The Georges waited in the lobby, Sam talking animatedly to the desk sergeant.

Krista had the sense to respect her personal space, but Sam strode forward as soon as he saw his daughter. "We allowed her to go to Texas with you. We'd like to take her home now."

Exhaustion shredded Cage's patience. "This has been discussed. She doesn't want to go to Roselea, and after your stupid stunt with the media, it's not safe for her."

"Are you accusing me of getting the news in on this?"

Cage shrugged. "Who else would be ignorant enough to think they'd benefit from it?"

Sam stepped into Cage's space and jabbed his finger into his chest. "You have a lot of nerve."

Bonin stepped forward, but Cage shook his head.

"So do you, putting your hands on a cop," Cage said. "I'll give you five seconds to back up."

"Sam." His wife's voice was strained. "Please don't get arrested."

He backed off but lingered close enough to land a punch. Cage glared back, daring the older man. He was done being compassionate. This fool was too caught up in his own misery to see the stress he'd caused his daughter.

"I didn't speak to the media," Sam said. "The NOPD and the LBI need to get their act together before I contact my lawyer."

"Just stop." Annabeth's voice surprised them all. "I can't deal with this shit right now."

"You look exhausted," her mother said. "What happened in Jasper?"

Annabeth's jaw went taut. She shook her head.

"Can we take you to dinner?" Krista asked. "There's a little diner just a block away."

"That's not safe. We have to assume he's already in town." Cage doubted it, but Annabeth twitched in panic.

Krista's hopeful smile turned to disappointment. "Of course."

Annabeth stared at her mother, a mixture of compassion and confusion on her face. Finally, she sighed. "I *am* hungry. Order me a pizza, and we can hang out here if it's cool with mustache over there." She waved at the desk sergeant. "But don't expect a heart-to-heart."

"You sure?' Cage asked her. "This has been a hell of a day."

"I'll call you if they piss me off." She gave him a strained smile. "And I'm starving, for real. Pepperoni, Mrs. George, please."

AGENT ROGERS'S VOICE crackled over the speakerphone. "You think that second body will turn out to be Lyric Gaudet?"

"Most likely," Cage said. "We're waiting on the official ID, but Metz discovered a pin in the arm from an old break. She's trying to get the serial number off it—metal's pretty rusted. But we'll see."

Johnny Dietz had been officially identified. Mickie would be next, likely by morning. Cage drained the stale coffee and tried to get comfortable. He'd eventually have his own office at major crimes—if he didn't lose his job first. For now, he was stuck with a folding chair in Bonin's cluttered cubicle.

"This Agent Tims—she's looking for her big break," Rogers said. "I can't stop her from taking the case."

"All due respect, sir, I want to keep working it," Cage said. "She has no compassion for Annabeth, and we need her to stay on our side. The kid's been through enough." Annabeth's parents had been waiting when they arrived. He'd been leery of leaving her alone with them. She looked ready to crack. But she was also hungry and reluctantly agreed to hang out in the lobby with them if they ordered her a pizza and didn't expect her to talk. The desk sergeant promised he'd keep an eye on things, and Cage reassured her that he could check on her via the lobby's security cameras. He glanced at the video feed on Bonin's computer. Annabeth was currently sitting several feet from her parents, waiting for her pizza.

"Let the FBI deal with her," Rogers said. "This case is a dead end that'll end up costing us a lot of money and time with no results—not to mention the bad press."

"We're closer than you think," Cage said. "And Agent Tims is only thinking about herself."

"Go home, Foster. Finish packing and get moved in. Start fresh with the LBI."

Bonin shook her head, lips pressed together.

"Annabeth trusts us," Cage said. "I can't just hand her over—"

"Not your problem anymore. It's over."

Bonin held up her hands in defeat and stomped out of the room. The door slammed behind her.

Cage couldn't walk away now. Especially if Tims had the case. She'd shove Annabeth aside while she focused on getting the glory. "I'd like to push my start date back a month, sir. I need more time to get ready."

"Christ, Foster. Does this case mean that much to you?"

"That's not what I'm asking."

"Don't play me. I'm done with that dance. This new division isn't just about you. My ass is on the line, and we've established a launch with my director. Full media coverage. I can't reschedule just because you have white knight syndrome."

"It's about being a hero. It's about doing the right thing and putting the victim first. Isn't that why you hired me?"

"I hired you because I wanted someone with a stellar record and integrity to make my department a success."

"Same thing," Cage said.

Rogers sighed. "God, you're a stubborn bastard."

"You aren't the first person to say that." He waited, thoughts spinning. How far could he push Rogers?

"Think of it this way, sir. If I don't catch this guy, I look like a fool. I'm operating on my own. But if I can bring him in and close this case, that's a huge win for the new Criminal Investigative Division. And you, of course."

Rogers didn't answer right away. Flop sweat trickled down Cage's forehead, stinging his eyes. "The FBI expects me to hand everything over to Agent Tims."

Cage slammed his fist on the desk and hoped Rogers heard.

"I'll tell them I can't reach you. You're following a lead and ignoring me."

"Thank you—"

"We never had this conversation," Rogers said. "Don't expect this to buy you more than a day or two."

Cage's pulse sprinted as he ended the call. He slipped his hand into his right pocket for the gris gris bag Bonin had made him. He'd never hear the end of it if she knew he actually carried it around, but he needed some serious luck in the next twenty-four hours.

The door swung open, and Bonin leaned inside. "Is it over, then?"

"Not yet. But don't expect to get any sleep tonight."

44

OH MY GOD, why did I agree to this? When will the pizza get here?

Krista's sitting a few feet away and telling me how I used to be a track star with scholarship offers from division one schools. Apparently, that's a big deal for a small-town kid.

My grades were excellent too. I had it all, until I didn't.

I don't want to hurt her feelings, but hearing how great I used to be isn't exactly an ego boost.

"What about my horse? Does he miss me?"

Her eyes light up. "You remember Charlie?"

"Cage told me about him."

"Right." She messes with her wedding ring. "Charlie died a couple of years ago. He was an old horse."

This shouldn't upset me. But it's the final chunk of sliding rock that starts a landslide. Tears well in my eyes. I rub them, disgusted. I don't cry. I yell and throw things. But I'm so tired, and my head feels like it's swollen and dumb.

"I'm sorry, honey," Krista says. "I know how much you loved him."

"I don't." The words spew from my mouth. "Why can't you get that through your head? I don't remember. I don't remember Charlie, or you, or him." I'm horrible, but it's like I'm split in half—part mean, part shameful. The mean side usually triumphs.

Sam is staring at me. I bet he doesn't have it in him to love the daughter he's stuck with now. "You may not remember her, but you will not talk to your mother that way."

"Whatever *Dad*."

"Have you stopped to think about how much your mom and I are suffering? Seven years not knowing if you were dead or alive, and then we find out you don't even remember us. You have no idea how much we've gone through."

"And you can't imagine what I've gone through."

"Neither can you," he shot back. "So that's a lousy excuse."

I want to hit him. I'm out of the chair and only a foot away from him when I see my mother's frightened eyes. I dig in my bag for the torn Tarot card and pray for Ezili to keep me calm and give me strength.

Sam steps closer, disgust on his face. His breath smells like one of the bars on Bourbon.

I have to get away from him. And Krista. I can't take her tears right now. I've already scouted the lobby. The restrooms are on the other side, not far from the exit.

"I need to pee." I glance at the security camera. Cage said he'd be watching, so I wave and point in the direction of the bathroom.

As soon as I'm—hopefully—off camera, I start sprinting. I'm pretty sure my legs aren't as fast as they used to be, but they move well enough. I skirt around people on the sidewalk, but I'm not familiar with this part of town. Where do I go?

I hear Sam shouting behind me.

A yellow cab is sitting at the stoplight a block away. I run harder, dashing past the woman and little kid I'm pretty sure had hailed the cab.

I fall into the backseat and lock the door. "Go! My dad's a maniac!"

Sam's big hands slam against my window, and he's screaming.

The cabbie locks the other doors and peels off into traffic.

When I finally get the nerve to look back, I see Sam doubled-over, his hands on his knees.

And Cage running toward him.

I turn away before I can see the disappointment on his face.

45

CAGE AND BONIN hopped out of the car as the Georges squealed to a stop behind them. "Let me do the talking," Cage said. "She trusts me."

Bonin had berated the cab company into telling her Annabeth's cab had dropped her off near Canal Street. She'd likely hopped on the streetcar that would take her within walking distance to Alexandrine's house.

By the time they navigated through the evening traffic and the chaotic French Quarter, Annabeth had at least a thirty-minute head start. Twilight had given away to a clouded, dark sky.

Cage doubted she'd gone to Alexandrine's—she knew the Quarter well enough to easily disappear.

Damn her. She knew better.

"We're her parents," Sam said.

"Not in this new life." Cage would have slapped cuffs on Sam and left him at the police station if Bonin had let him. His beer breath and red eyes confirmed the long-whispered rumor that he'd become a drunk after his daughter disappeared. Cage might have felt sorry for him if Annabeth hadn't taken off. "If we don't find her soon, she'll be in danger. Thanks to you."

Krista grabbed her husband's arm before he could say anything. "Just let them do their jobs, please."

The small cottage was mostly dark, but a light shined from one of the back windows. "Don't just go bursting in. Alexandrine might be with a client."

"Client for what?" Krista George asked.

"Miss Alexandrine is a Voodoo priestess," Bonin said. "People from all over the city come to her for help."

"Is that the mumbo jumbo she was muttering?" Sam asked. "This woman taught her?"

"Charlotte Gaudet taught her," Bonin said. "She was also a priestess."

"Blasphemous," Sam said. "She's forgotten God. That woman knew Annabeth wasn't her granddaughter. How dare she teach her black magic?"

"That woman," Bonin said, "took care of your daughter through the worst times in her life. And Voodoo is steeped with Catholicism. God is very important."

"She kept her from us!"

"She didn't know her real identity," Cage said. "And she kept her survival a secret from her kidnapper. Too bad you couldn't do the same."

"I did not speak to the press," Sam said.

A sudden wind cut through the stillness but did nothing to lessen the humid night air. Coldness grew in the pit of his stomach. Static electricity swarmed around him, but he hadn't touched anything. The breeze faded away, but Cage could have sworn …

"Did you say something?"

Bonin shook her head and banged on the door again.

The static electricity turned to a spark of unease. "You know where she keeps an extra key?"

"I doubt she does," Bonin said. "Too risky for a woman living alone, especially around here."

Cage peeked between the curtains of the nearest window. The front room appeared normal, but he saw no sign of either woman. He caught the scent of a strong, musky perfume that wasn't Bonin's. It made his eyes water.

Go to the back.

The iron gate protecting the narrow alley between Alexandrine's cottage and her neighbor clanged in the wind.

"She'd never leave that unlocked."

Cage was already ahead of Bonin, running down the alley and into the tiny courtyard of sweet-smelling plants.

The back door opened easily.

"Sonofabitch."

Miss Alexandrine lay crumpled against the wall in her narrow hallway, shards of glass littered around her.

Cage rushed to the woman's side, sidestepping the broken glass and gagging on the same musky scent he'd noticed outside. The bottle of heady oil had toppled off the built-in shelf, coating the other bits and pieces that had fallen.

He tried to block out the scent and checked Alexandrine's pulse. "Her pulse is steady, and she's breathing. It looks like she passed out."

"Low blood sugar." Bonin raced back to the kitchen and quickly returned with a paring knife and a red onion. She sliced the onion in half and stuck it under Alexandrine's nose. "My brother used to faint as a kid. Mama always got him back up with a good, strong red onion."

"Lord." Miss Alexandrine's trembling hand shoved the onion away. "Get that thing out of my face, Myra." She tried to sit up straight and swayed.

Cage gently took her arm. "Easy."

"Eat." Bonin handed her a candy bar.

Alexandrine slowly chewed, her eyes still glazed. Cage

snagged a towel from the kitchen and started wiping up the stinking oil. The built-in shelf contained an altar, and the oil had soaked part of the red velvet lining the bottom. "You're going to need some adhesive remover to get the oil out of this wood."

The priestess reached for a small statue of an African woman cradling a bright red heart with a sword running through it. The statue's painted toenails peeked from underneath her blue dress. A book of matches and a painted card with the same sword through the heart design and a busted red candle were scattered around her.

"My offerings."

"You must have been praying when you passed out." Bonin carefully picked up the statue and sat it back on the alter.

"That's the same as Lyric's Tarot card," Cage said.

"Ezili Dantò," Alexandrine said. "One of my Mét Tét."

"Master of the Head," Bonin clarified. "Like a guardian angel."

Cage nodded, his throat tasting like he'd swallowed the perfume. "I can't believe how strong that stuff is even with a window open. You'll never fully get it out of the woodwork."

"No window open in August," Alexandrine said. "The air's running."

"Well, the stench of this stuff leaked outside then," Cage said.

The priestess's eyes brightened, and a soft smile played on her lips. "You smelled it outside because Ezili Dantò knew I needed help. She was guiding you."

"Right." Cage checked the back of her head. A good-sized lump had already bloomed, but her coloring was almost back to normal. "You should keep better track of your blood sugar. Next time you could really get hurt."

"That's not why I fainted." Alexandrine grabbed Bonin's

hand. "Li rete, Li rete."

Bonin fired off a question in Creole. Alexandrine nodded. "Li rete."

Cage only understood a single word of the conversation, but the older woman's adamant tone let him get the gist of it.

"You're wrong," he said. "You have to be."

46

I FIND JOE in his favorite spot, an alley near a liquor store on St. Louis Street. He reeks of piss and booze, and his clothes are dirtier than they were the other day. I squat next to him; no way in hell am I sitting down. The streets around here are like a giant petri dish.

"What're you doing?" Joe looks at me with glassy eyes.

I hold up ten bucks. "I need your help."

JOE AND I wait until it's good and dark. St. Louis No. 1 is closed and locked, but I don't have anywhere else to go. I'm safer in here than on the streets. And Cage will eventually figure out where to find me.

"Conti Street side's the best option." Joe points to the ratty housing development across the street from the cemetery. "Ain't no one hanging around here this time of night."

Unless they're up to no good, like us.

The wall's not too high, but I need help getting over it. Joe glances around and motions me over. I step into his cupped hands, and he gives me a good boost. My fingers bleed as I fumble and hoist myself over the wall and onto the top of one of the old oven vaults. Brick crumbles from the crypts as I shimmy to the ground, and I feel like a destructive piece of shit.

"Sorry," I whisper.

"You okay?" Joe calls from the other side of the wall.

"Yeah. Go on back to your spot."

"You sure you don't want me to stay here and make sure no one else is sneaking around?"

He'll just piss Cage off and if my kidnapper really is lurking, he'll kill Joe. "No. Go get something to eat."

Clouds shroud the half-moon, and despite the light pollution surrounding it, St. Louis No. 1 is blacker than the lodestone in Miss Alexandrine's altars. Using my cell as a light isn't an option. Turning it on means GPS tracking, and Cage is probably already on that.

I just need to get my bearings. I've been here dozens of times.

Relax.

The wall vaults are on the southwest corner, toward the front. I just need to follow this path to the main alley by the front. The way is easy from there.

Blood pounds through my ears as I tiptoe past the tombs. The city may surround St. Louis No. 1, but the old cemetery makes me feel miles away from the chaos. Gran used to say the dead live in the waters of time, influencing all existence, that our living reality merges with the dead as their spirits anticipate the call for guidance.

The wall oven vaults that make up St. Louis No. 1's perimeter wall don't allow an ounce of breeze, and the air is so thick it's like wading through three-hundred years' worth of spirits. The silence is even worse.

My nerves ease when I turn left onto the center alley and head toward the Sanité tomb. I need to sit down and plan, figure out what to do. And wait for Cage to find me.

My heart snags in my throat. Sweat drips down my neck.

Who is that?

I duck behind one of the taller vaults. The figure stands silently in front of the iron fence surrounding the Sanité tomb. It's so freaking dark I can only tell it's human-shaped.

What if it's a ghost?

What if it's Sanité coming to kick my ass for impersonating his family?

I touch the mourning ring hanging from my neck. Charlotte's here. She'll make Sanité understand.

I tiptoe closer, ready to dive behind another vault.

The clouds drift enough for moonlight to slip through.

My insides feel like they've come loose and are rattling around. My brain is ready to explode.

I force my dry lips to move. "Lyric?"

47

"LI RETE," MISS Alexandrine repeated for the third time. Cage had helped her to a chair in her front room. "She lives."

"Honey, I think you're just confused."

Alexandrine shot Cage a glare so reminiscent of his paddle-carrying grandmother he shrank back.

"I'm not some confused, old woman," Alexandrine said. "I was making my offerings when someone knocked at the back door. The hairs on the back of my neck stood up because the gate was locked. Spirit was agitated. Warning me to be careful."

She did have a direct line of sight from her altar to the back door, but white, filmy curtains covered the small window. "How did you see her from here?"

"I went to the door and saw her through the curtain. It was like being hit with a stun gun. My mind worked but my body was frozen. She left. The girl always was impatient."

"You came back to the altar to pray about it?" Bonin asked. "And fainted?"

Alexandrine nodded and then smiled warily at Cage. "You don't believe me, but I know what I saw."

"I don't want to believe you," Cage said. "Because it changes the entire case."

She stared at him until he felt like she'd crawled inside his mind. "Spirit says you misunderstand."

"What the hell does spirit know?" Cage's temper flared. "And who is this spirit? Do you mean God? Or your guardian angel spirit? Or some other Voodoo entity?"

"Spirit is the force within us all, the energy that connects us to the Loa," Alexandrine said. "It's our own essence that has a much deeper understanding of life than our conscious mind."

"Like a fortune teller? A psychic? Or some other supernatural crap?"

"Your mind is too narrow and too tired," Alexandrine said. "All religion is supernatural. God isn't of this earth, no matter your faith. Let go of your fears and accept your deeper instincts, and only then will you be able to see. And remember, Ezili Dantò sought your help for me, and you listened. She will repay your kindness."

"Enough of this Voodoo spirit bullshit. Where is our daughter?" Sam and Krista had been hovering quietly by the back door, but now Sam stood in the hallway in front of the altar. "Are you hiding her?"

Alexandrine stared at Cage. "You're supposed to be taking care of her."

"I'll find her."

"You and that Gaudet woman filled her head with this Voodoo nonsense," Sam said, "and now she's wandering around at night, thinking some stupid ring will protect her."

"I don't like her wandering at night any more than you do. If I knew where she was, I'd tell you."

"Back off," Cage said. "She's been good to Annabeth."

"Filled her head with crazy, you mean." Sam snatched a mini bottle of rum from the altar. "Alcohol? Cigarettes? Are these more offerings? You call this a religion?"

"You're out of line," Bonin said. "Why don't you step outside and let us finish here?"

"Because she knows where our daughter is, and she's going to tell us." He glared at the priestess with intense hatred.

Cage blocked the path to Alexandrine. "Put her things back and get out."

He saw the fight in Sam's eyes; the man desperately wanted to take his anger out on anyone but himself. Cage no longer gave a damn about the consequences. "Leave right now, or I will arrest you."

"On what grounds?"

"Drunk and disorderly sounds like a good one. How much did you drink on the drive over here?"

"What's your deal, anyway?" Sam sneered. "I never saw a cop take such a personal interest in a victim. You got a thing for my daughter? Married man, looking for some vulnerable brown sugar on the side?"

"The only thing I'm afraid of is pushing Annabeth so hard she breaks down." The hell if Sam George was going to start a bullshit rumor that would hurt Dani. "And it is personal because it's partially my fault she was kidnapped."

Sam's meaty hands fisted, and Cage braced for the hit.

Bonin grabbed his arm. "Don't be an idiot. Listen to him."

Too bad. Tossing Sam into a cell would be worth taking the punch. "Two days before they disappeared, I pulled her and Mickie over. They'd been smoking pot. I let them go in exchange for information about their dealer. If I'd hauled her in, maybe she would have been grounded and safe. And if I'd caught her dealer—who was probably her kidnapper—this would have stopped then. So yeah, it's personal."

He waited for Sam to swing at him and threaten him with legal action. But he sagged against the wall, all his bluster evaporating. "I caught her coming home that night. Smelled the weed on her. She promised me she'd never do it again, she knew how important track was for getting a scholarship." He turned around to look at his wife. "I didn't punish her. Didn't tell you, either. I thought I was the cool dad. If I had—"

"Stop blaming yourself," Krista said. "Both of you. I'm tired of trying to make everyone else feel better. This is about Annabeth." She shoved past them and knelt in front of Alexandrine.

"Thank you for your kindness toward her. Do you have any idea where she might have gone? It's late and so dark—does she have a safe place? Friends who would let her sleep on their couch?"

"She still has the key to Charlotte's house in the Quarter. I would look there first," Alexandrine said. "As far as special places she runs to when she's upset … I just can't think of any." Her dark eyes locked onto Cage.

He had no idea how Annabeth could get into a locked cemetery at night, but he didn't doubt she would find a way.

Cage could be at the cemetery in five minutes. But he needed to get rid of Sam first.

48

HER SKIN IS a bit darker than mine, her silky, jet black hair shimmers around her face. A jagged scar runs diagonally through her lips. She's majestic and terrifying.

"Are you a ghost?"

She smiles, and she's even more beautiful than the pictures. "No, Annabeth. I'm real. And so are you. All these years, I thought you were dead."

My knees knock together, and I'm afraid I might piss my pants. Then the alarm sounds in my head.

I'm not falling for it.

"You're the bait. Just like you were with Sheila. He's here, isn't he?"

She flinches. "I'm here alone."

"Then where is he?"

"I don't know, but he's probably coming after you. Maybe both of us." She edges forward.

I step back. "He wanted you the most."

She's looking past me, her expression haunted. "He dumped me a long time ago, long after I was broken." She's only a foot away from me now, close enough to attack. But I can't move. I just stare into her eyes like I've been put into a trance.

Has she put a spell on me? Charlotte taught her the ways—Lyric must remember some of them.

My brain is so screwed up I don't know if I'm nuts or just dumb, let alone what's real and what isn't.

I know damn well I should turn and run, but I reach out and touch her cheek instead. Panic wells from my gut—what am I doing?

She smiles and takes my hand in both of hers. They're calloused and delicate at the same time. And cold. "He said you were dead. I saw your body."

She's still holding my hand, and it feels nice. Maybe she's not here to hurt me. "When he discovered you were gone," her voice drops to a whisper, her hands trembling, "he whipped me until I begged to die. I still have the scars on my back. I passed out, and when I came to the next day, there you were, lying dead. Your face was beaten to hell, but the body looked like yours. He'd stripped you naked. I'd never seen you that way, but I just assumed ... and I was in so much pain. He buried you with Mickie, and we took off."

Her grip tightens, her hands getting warm. "I prayed he would kill me. But I didn't get that lucky. I paid for my decision for a very long time."

I finally pull my hand away. She's come back to exact her revenge. She's probably not sane after what she's lived through. And I'm living a peachy-keen life compared to hers.

"I don't resent you," she says softly. "I made the choice to let you go. God, you're alive." She touches my uneven face. "Different, but the same."

I should jerk away, but I edge closer. "He just let you go?"

"He wanted to own me, and he did. I was used up and broken and couldn't even gain a new girl's trust. I lost all my value." Her eyes narrowed, her chin setting, the scar through her lips pure white. "He thinks I'm worthless, but he's wrong. You and I are going to find him and end this once and for all."

49

I KEEP MY phone in my hand and some distance between us, but I'm not going anywhere.

"What's his name?"

"He goes by a lot of names. Different names in different states."

"What's his real name?"

She looks up at the moon, her face twisting in anger. "I lured Sheila Dietz for him. Poor little Johnny was collateral damage. But he didn't kill him quickly. He kept him for days, close enough he could hear Sheila scream when he raped her."

My stomach churns. "How many times did he rape me?"

"We lived in a camper—an RV, I guess. It was thirty feet long or so. One side was his 'play area,' as he called it. When I wasn't fishing for him, he kept me chained up in there." She looks at me with sad eyes. "He brought you into the camper several times."

I try not to think about the things Sheila told us. "He sent you for other girls. Why didn't you run?"

"He was always close by back then, with his gun. He was a good shot. And what was I supposed to go back to?"

"Charlotte! She was looking for you."

Lyric shakes her head. "New Orleans was underwater. He showed me the pictures from the first few days after levees broke, the people stuck on the bridges and in the Superdome. I kept asking about the French Quarter, but he wouldn't answer. And then he took away the television and the radio. I went for months before I knew anything else, and by then I was so destroyed it didn't seem to matter."

I still don't get it. How could she stop fighting? I would never stop fighting.

You don't remember. Maybe that's the only reason you can still fight.

"He only gave me freedom to leave when he knew I wouldn't," she says. "By that time, I'd been with him for almost four years. He'd destroyed my body and my soul. Those girls in the graves are my victims too. And he made me believe I'd be punished, same as him." She lowers her head. "I was dirty and worthless, with nowhere to go."

"Charlotte never stopped looking for you," I say. "Katrina ruined everything. The police shit a lot of things up. Your missing persons report got lost. But she never stopped looking. She tracked you down to Sean Andrews. Remember him?"

A smile flickers across her face. "Big Sean from the Lower Nine. He made it through Katrina?"

I nod. "I met him, and he thought for a second I was you. Then he saw my saggy-ass face and realized I was too ugly."

She brushes the tear off my cheek. "You're not ugly. You're a survivor, and you're beautiful. I saw it in you. You were so strong. I knew you were our best chance."

I swallow the lump in my throat. "I swear to God I didn't know who I was after the car hit me. I guess I kept telling people your name and Gran's phone number. That's why they called her."

"Those were the last things I said to you before I shoved you out of the barn's back door," she says. "We do resemble each other, because that's what he likes. He specifically searches for girls who meet his perfect criteria."

"You."

"Light-skinned black girls, silky hair. Young teens, past puberty, but far from grown. I was fifteen. He would have taken me years earlier, but he never had the chance. I think that's why he kept me so long." She turns back to the monument. "Gran's name isn't on here yet. You're working on that, right?"

My throat tightens, my hand reflexively grabbing the ring hanging around my neck. "Sure."

"You're alone now. Except for your parents, who you don't remember."

"I have Miss Alexandrine," I say defensively. "I'm not that pathetic."

"The Voodoo Queen of St. Ann Street. I stopped by to see her, but she didn't answer the door. Probably with a client. She still peddling that nonsense?"

"You don't believe?"

"In magic? Or some sort of God?" She scowls. "Not anymore. I used to steal her and Gran's gris gris bags and use them for pot. Miss Alexandrine threatened to curse me forever when she found out."

"But I saw you the other day." I reach into my back pocket and show her the ripped Tarot card. "I found this in your things from Gran's room, and when I touched it, you came to me in a vision. You said to look for the purple flowers."

Something's been nagging at me this whole time, and now I know what it is. My vision wasn't young Lyric from her picture. It was this one, older and angry. Lyric stares at the card. She looks pissed and sad. I stick my hand out for her to take it—it's hers. She cuts me off with a flash of her hand.

"I don't need that. There are no such things as visions or Loa or Bondye the Supreme or a Christian God. There's only life and death and nothing in between."

I want to cry, but I won't be able to change her mind. "Who is he?"

"I haven't seen him in a long time," she said. "We were at a truck stop when he told me he was done with me." She chokes out a bitter laugh. "Can you imagine? The only human you've had any real contact with for more than a decade sends you away?"

"No." Something else bugged me. "Mickie was white. Why did he take her?"

"She was a witness." She closes her eyes. "'You never waste a live pussy.' He lived by that motto."

I feel sick, but I need to know the truth. "Did I abandon her? Was she alive when I escaped?"

"No," she says. "He choked the others—I think it was something sexual for him. But he sliced her throat right in front of you. To break you."

I sink to the ground. She's so blunt and cold. But I understand why. She doesn't have much soul left.

Lyric drops to her knees in front of me. "He said you were a track star. He'd gone to one of your meets, just to watch you. He talked about letting you get a head start and then gunning you down when he was done with you. I had to give you a chance to save other girls."

"How many more did he kill after you left Jasper?"

Lyric takes my shoulders. "Too many. But we can end it. I can draw him out."

"You said you haven't seen him."

"That doesn't mean I don't know where to look," she says. "He's older now. But so are we. We're bigger, stronger. Colder. We can kill him."

Slice his throat just like he did Mickie's. Dump him in a shallow grave.

Cage said the only thing that gave his family any peace was having his sister's body to bury. "If we kill him, there are families who don't get closure."

"I can give them that closure," Lyric says. "I was there, remember?"

"That's not good enough," I say. "Those families deserve the right to see him go to trial. To see him be executed." I push myself to my feet and reach for my cell.

Lyric slaps it out of my hand. "I'm not dealing with any cops."

"You won't be in trouble," I say. "You were the biggest victim of all."

"I've had plenty of time to come forward. I know how the cops in this city work."

"Things have changed since Katrina, I promise. And Cage is different."

"Don't you understand? He'll come for you now. He obsessed over you for years. I promise you he doesn't give up. He didn't get what he wanted from me the first time, so he waited almost five years to make his move."

My head throbs. The stress is building up in me. I don't know how much more I can take. I suck in deep breaths, but they're hot and foul and make my stomach turn.

Lyric's fingertips dig into my shoulders. "We have to stick together. We're family now. And I can give you back your memories."

"Only the bad ones."

"But you'll have answers."

My throat burns. "You'll only tell me who he is if I help you, right?"

She nods.

I close my eyes and try to think. Lyric is all I have. Except for Miss Alexandrine. And Cage. They would both be so disappointed. So would my real parents, who haven't done anything but want their daughter back.

I open my eyes. "I'm sorry. I just can't."

Her jaw tightens, her mouth drawn into a tight line. Her chin trembles. She releases my shoulders, and I take her hand.

"Please, trust me. Cage won't blame you."

Lyric sighs and nods. She bends over to pick my phone up off the ground. "I'm really sorry. For everything."

Her hand swings up. She's not holding my phone. She's got a chunk of concrete that's fallen off a tomb.

"Lyric, no!"

50

CAGE'S CELL RANG as he drove toward St. Louis No. 1. He hit the touchscreen, and Dr. Metz's voice filled the car.

"We have an ID from the pin found with the adult female in the first grave," Metz said. "Shannon Powell, a twenty-five-year-old waitress from a town about twenty miles away from Jasper. Weird thing is, she went missing the morning after Annabeth escaped."

She lives.

Lyric's humanity had been destroyed long before she helped Annabeth escape. Returning to New Orleans after Annabeth's story made the national news meant she was probably looking for Annabeth—and likely still working with her kidnapper.

"She was grabbed walking to work," Metz said. "She left her parents place in the country at 5:30 a.m. It was a nice spring morning, and she had a fifteen-minute walk to work. She never showed up."

Why take this woman? She was too old for his tastes. "Any luck on cause of death?"

"It's hard to say if the trauma came before or right after death, but her skull was bashed all to hell. From the fragments we recovered, her nose was shattered, along with both eye sockets and one side of her jaw. She would have been unrecognizable."

Rage at Annabeth's escape, and this poor girl ended up a scapegoat? But why not take that out on Lyric for her betrayal? "You have a formal ID on Mickie yet?"

"We're stalling, but we're going to have to announce it by mid-morning tomorrow. Her skull was intact enough that matching dental records is relatively easy. Sorry we can't hold it off any longer, but I've got my job to do too."

Cage understood. "Thanks for getting us this far. Let me know if you ID any of the other victims."

The cemetery's border wall of crypts loomed ahead. Cage parked a block away, grabbed his weapon out of the glove compartment and holstered it, then stuck his badge under his T-shirt. Strolling around this neighborhood at night was dumb. Hopefully, Annabeth had gotten inside safely.

Sweating, he jogged around the cemetery's perimeter. The walls were at least a foot taller than Cage. Annabeth couldn't have jumped them without help. Maybe she'd already come and gone or hadn't even been here.

He rounded the corner at Conti Street. A figure slouched near the end of the cemetery, knees drawn up to its chest. "Annabeth?"

A foul aroma of body odor and filth hit him, and Cage halted a foot away. The man snored softly, a cookie wrapper in one hand and an empty beer bottle in the other. Layers of dirt covered his white shirt and cutoff jeans. Cage had been told most of the homeless stayed in the more traveled areas of the French Quarter, partially for safety and to ask tourists for money. The remnants of the dangerous projects across the street were the perfect place for drug deals and God knows what else.

He nudged the sleeping man with his foot. "Sir, wake up. It's not safe for you here."

The man stirred and opened his eyes. They were bloodshot

and cloudy. "I grew up 'round here, boy. Can take care of myself."

"Then maybe you can help me. Have you seen a young girl trying to get over the wall tonight? She's got long dark hair and is wearing a blue shirt."

"You Cage?"

Cage stilled. "You know Annabeth."

The old man got to his feet and stepped closer. The stench rolling off him turned Cage's stomach.

"I went and got something to eat. She told me not to come back but," he glanced over the wall, "this place ain't safe at night. And I don't mean spirits. Guess I fell asleep waiting."

"She was okay when she went over the wall?"

"As right as she could be," the man said. "She's off sometimes, but I got no right to judge. And she's a good girl. You want me to boost you over too? Twenty bucks."

Cage dug the bill out of his pocket and handed it to the man. "I can get myself over. Thanks for helping her."

"All right." The man reached for Cage's hand. "She said you were good people."

Cage shook it and felt guilty for wishing he'd brought hand sanitizer.

"She's scared and worked up about something," the man said. "You take care of her and get her on back to Alexandrine's. She can't be wandering 'round at night like this. And tell her I said I'll see her soon." He stuck the bill in the front of his pants and headed down the street.

It took Cage four trips to get enough bricks from the torn-down building. He climbed the wobbly stack of bricks and hoisted himself over. Pain shot through his shins when his feet hit the ground. He wiped the sweat from his eyes and tried to figure out where the hell he was. The night seemed twice as dark inside the concrete walls, and the jumbled rows of stone crypts robbed him of his sense of direction.

The place swallowed him. The air felt thick, like walking through vapor. Inside the concrete walls, the night was completely silent, as though they were still in the wilderness and the city hadn't grown up around St. Louis No. 1.

Cage navigated around the vaults as fast as he dared. Uneven flagstones covered the winding, narrow aisles and some of the smaller brick tombs had worn down to a single layer. Falling in the congested cemetery pretty much guaranteed a head wound.

The short, white pyramid tomb loomed to his right. He cut left down the wider path. The Sanité family tomb was just ahead.

"Annabeth!"

She lay on her back in front of the tomb, arms outstretched. Blood streamed from a gash in her forehead.

Cage dropped to his knees and scrubbed his hands against his jeans and then pressed his left hand over the gash. Her pulse beat steadily beneath his fingers.

The wound wasn't as deep as it looked, but he kept pressure on it. "Annabeth, wake up. It's Cage."

She moaned but didn't open her eyes.

He patted her cheek. "Please. I don't want to carry you out of here."

"Mmm." She licked her cracked lip and raised her right arm. "Yes, carry me, please, Agent Sexy."

He sighed in relief. "Look at me and tell me who did this."

Her eyes finally fluttered open. "Lyric did this to me."

MISS ALEXANDRINE CAREFULLY cleaned Annabeth's wound. "Girl, you know better than to be running 'round that cemetery at night." She pulled back and examined the dried wound on her forehead.

"Can you stitch it up? I don't want to go to the hospital."

"Of course I can." Alexandrine dug through her kit. "Butterfly bandages should work. Why would Lyric hurt you now? Are you sure it was her?"

"She told me about the pot gris gris bags. And I know she came here first."

Alexandrine nodded at Cage. "And this one thought I imagined her."

"He wouldn't believe me if the bone doctor hadn't found out that wasn't Lyric in the grave."

"Lyric is going after her," Cage said. "She wanted Annabeth to help her kill him."

He still wasn't sure Lyric hadn't been sent to trap her. She had to be angry knowing that Annabeth had taken her place instead of bringing help.

"She doesn't blame me." Annabeth resumed the argument they'd had on the drive back. "She understood."

Cage didn't buy it. Any normal person would be out for revenge—Lyric had suffered through unimaginable abuse and then endured years more because Annabeth never brought help.

"What else did she say?" Alexandrine asked.

"That my kidnapper couldn't handle that I got away, even though he claimed I was dead. Lyric said he couldn't get what he wanted from her the first time he tried, so he waited."

Alexandrine's hands stilled. "What did you just say?"

"Lyric said it, not me."

Alexandrine took her by the shoulders. "Tell me exactly what she said."

Her tone must have scared Annabeth; she shrank back and tried to wiggle free. Alexandrine didn't let go. "What did she say?"

"That he didn't get what he wanted from me the first time,

so he waited almost five years to make his move. Please let me go."

Alexandrine released her and touched the ring that rested on Annabeth's collarbone. "Bondye mwen. Charlotte, out e konnen. Mwen te antò."

Annabeth's fingers closed over the priestess's. "Kiyes li ye?"

"It's my fault," Alexandrine whispered.

"What's your fault?" Cage didn't understand a damn thing the women had said, but he knew it was important. The air in the small cottage shifted and compressed. Pressure built in his ears the same way it always did when he flew. He sensed someone in the hallway, just out of his field of vision, but it was empty. The reek of the spilled oil in the hallway magnified, even though the liquid had been cleaned up.

"When she first filed the report," Alexandrine said, "Charlotte swore she knew who took Lyric. I talked her out of putting down the name because he'd left town years ago. It was too outlandish, and I thought the police would be wasting their time. And Charlotte always blamed him for … I thought she wasn't thinking clearly."

Cage rubbed his eyes and forced his head to clear. The stench of the oil was getting to him, making him feel uneasy and half-sick. "What's his name?"

Alexandrine sagged in her chair, suddenly fragile and old. "Anthony Thomas."

51

ALEXANDRINE TOLD THE story through teary eyes. Seeing the woman cry unnerved Cage. He'd focused on taking notes and trying not to puke from the damned oil spill stench.

Charlotte Gaudet had insisted Anthony Thomas caused her daughter's overdose. The police didn't agree. Thomas disappeared, and Lyric came to live with Charlotte.

Lyric's mother caught Thomas watching a video he'd taken of a twelve-year-old Lyric in the shower. They fought, and Lyric had fled to her grandmother's. Lyric's mother was found dead from an overdose the next day.

Cage jogged to his car, taking in deep breaths of air, but the musky scent seemed to have nested in his nose. Blocks away, the party at Bourbon Street emitted a smoky glow. Across the road, the arched entryway at Louis Armstrong Park illuminated the north end of the street. Headlights turned off the main road onto the narrow, cracked road. Sam George jumped out of his car and stalked toward Cage, Krista and Bonin hurrying behind him.

"You tell me where my daughter is right now, or I'm calling your boss."

"She's inside with Miss Alexandrine." Cage blocked the man's path up the slanted stone steps. He hoped their mutual guilt party earlier would make it easier to get through to him.

"There's been some developments in the case. We have a lead on the kidnapper. Annabeth needs space right now." He looked at Bonin. "A real lead."

Krista joined her husband. Dark circles rimmed her eyes, and her cheeks were red from crying. She looked past Cage at the old cottage. "We'll give her space, I promise. But can I speak to her, just for a moment?"

Cage glanced over his shoulder. Annabeth stood on the other side of the screen door, only her silky black hair visible. "If she's okay with it."

"Stay here," Krista told her husband. "You'll just make it worse."

She climbed the two steps, her hands raised. "I'm not going to try to talk you into anything. I just want to tell you something."

Cage tried to watch Sam and Annabeth at the same time. He wasn't going to let her be upset again. Her memory might give them more vital details.

"Go ahead," Annabeth said.

"We love you more than anything," Krista said. "We want to be there for you, however you need us. I know things will never be the same, but I hope you'll allow us to start fresh when this is all over. On your terms," she added.

Cage strained to see the girl's expression, but the meager porch light cast her in shadow.

"Krista," her husband demanded, "what are you saying? She belongs in Roselea with us."

Krista still faced the house, but her words sliced through the air. "Sam, enough. She's not the same person. After what she's been through, she's earned the right to call the shots."

Sam said nothing, but his veneer appeared to crumble as it had done before. "I just want her home."

"She is home," Krista said softly. "And only a few hours away. We can see her on weekends. Right?"

Annabeth slowly opened the screen door. "I'm okay," she said at her mother's gasp. "Just smacked my head, that's all. Miss Alexandrine already stitched it up."

Krista's hands flexed at her side. Her desperation to touch her child made Cage long to see his own.

"As for the weekends," Annabeth said. "I'd like that."

Krista's entire body seemed to melt. "Thank you, sweetheart. We'll leave you with Miss Alexandrine. I know she'll take good care of you." She edged forward, fingers trembling. Cage tensed, but Annabeth remained steady, her eyes focused on her mother.

Krista brushed her fingers over her daughter's cheek. "We'll see you soon."

"OVER A HUNDRED Anthony Thomas's in Louisiana and Texas combined. About half of them are the wrong age or skin color, but I can't narrow things down any further." Bonin snapped her laptop shut.

Alexandrine said Thomas was around the same age as Lyric's mother, which put him around fifty. She described him as white, wiry, and shifty-eyed. He and Lyric's mother lived in the Lower Ninth Ward until her death. Anthony left town shortly after.

Katrina had swept their old house away, along with half the others on their street. Bonin and Cage had gone door to door in a four-block radius in the Lower Nine, asking if anyone remembered the couple or Lyric as a child and came up empty.

"A lot of Katrina survivors didn't come back," Bonin said. "But this is the Lower Nine. The people here are proud. Most of the families go back generations, and a lot of them have stuck around to rebuild. Someone here has to know something."

Cage popped two aspirin and wished he had more coffee.

Ranger Lewis had called an hour ago. The associate who handled the sale of the land to L.M. Gaudet died of a heart attack last year. No one else at the bank had any memory of the sale. Too many years had passed.

"Sonofabitch blends in," Bonin said. "Knows how to work the system."

"Anthony Thomas isn't his real name." Cage was certain. "Lyric said he had aliases."

Cage had left a message for Sean Andrews. He was the only other link to Lyric's past and their best hope for getting Thomas's real name.

Alexandrine had found a picture of Lyric and Charlotte around the time her mother died. Lyric looked more like a grown woman than a twelve-year-old. "He would have been in his early thirties when he first tried to molest her, right?"

"Roughly, if he's around the same age as her mother."

"He wouldn't have waited until his thirties to start molesting girls," Cage said. "Lyric's age didn't bother him as long as she looked older. He probably started in his late teens or early twenties. So, we're talking around 1989 and later."

"The national sex offender registry wasn't started until '94," Bonin said, "and it didn't really get organized until the mid-2000s—around the same time Lyric disappeared. People didn't register, and the states didn't have an adequate tracking system. We're looking for a needle in a scummy haystack if we don't have his real name."

"Go into the NCIC's main database—not the registry—and go back pre-2000 and look for white men with a preference for biracial teenaged girls," Cage said. "And don't limit it to assault. Look for guys arrested for stealing underwear or hiding out in girls' locker rooms, that sort of thing."

The FBI's National Crime Information Center had been cataloging cases for fifty years. As long as the record had been entered, it would be accessible.

"If he's got a juvenile record, I can't access it."

Cage shook his head. "You can if it was reported. The FBI usually leaves them in the NCIC. They battle with the states on that, but the feds usually win and keep it in the system."

It was a long shot, and going through decades of records would take time, but right now this was their best option.

A rap on the window made them both jump. Sean waved a grease-stained hand at them.

"Idiot." Bonin motioned for him to back away. They slowly exited the car.

"You ought to know better than to sneak up on cops," she said. "What are you doing here?"

Sean still had on his work uniform, his clothes streaked with grease. "Agent Foster called me earlier. I meant to get back to you, but I been helping a friend get his car running. Then my brother said you two were in the neighborhood."

Bonin grinned at Cage. "The Lower Nine. Just as unique as the French Quarter. No matter how rough it gets, they stick together, right?"

Sean nodded. "My mom's house got washed away in Katrina. We rebuilt it, even though this one's not as big. Our family's lived here since my great-grandpa came in off the plantation looking for paid work. We're not going anywhere. You guys looking for Lyric's mom's ex? The pig who took the video of her in the shower when she was a kid?"

"You knew Lyric back then?" Cage asked.

"Nah, but she told me about him. Real creep. Used to brag about getting away with selling because his cousin covered up for him."

"His cousin?" Bonin asked.

"Officer Lionel Pietry. I think he still patrols the Quarter."

52

I'M TRAPPED INSIDE the barn again. My fingernails rake down the wooden stall. My weak voice begs for help. There's no answer, and it's only a matter of time before he comes to drag me back to the camper.

"Please, God. Let him kill me. Don't make me endure it again."

Cigar smoke hits me, sweet and pungent. I shrink away until my back slams against wood. I rub my watering eyes, and a scream strangles me.

A tall man emerges from the tornado of smoke, but he's just a skeleton, with gray shadows along his cheekbones and around his eye sockets, red blazing where his eyes should be. A snake curls around his shoulders and winds around his walking stick. He blows a ring of smoke in my face and tips his tall hat.

I'm paralyzed.

He holds out his hand. I shake my head, pinning my hands behind my back. But my hand is suddenly trapped inside his, and we're running. Out of the barn, into the fields.

He stops. I yank free.

I still see the barn and the camper from here. A light's on. It's only a matter of time before he sees us.

"We have to go."

The skeleton man belly laughs, even though I'm pretty sure

he doesn't have any flesh underneath his suit. The noise echoes through the fields and into the valley where the man lives.

He tucks his cigar into the corner of his mouth. "He cannot hurt me."

"Who are you?"

The thick snake winds around his neck, and the skeleton pats it affectionately. "You know who I am. And you know why we're here." He points his gnarled walking stick at the ground.

Mounds of dirt, side by side.

The faces of other victims.

My teeth chatter in fear. "Are you the Grim Reaper? Am I dead?"

His laugh is deep and raspy. Shivers race down my spine. "You are not dead. And I am not the Reaper."

I can't stop staring at the graves. "Why did you bring me here?"

He leans down until his face is close to mine, smelling of rum and spice. The white cross on his black top hat sparkles in the moonlight. I should be terrified, but I feel only peace.

"It was not your time to die." He points a long, bony finger at the graves. "And they were innocent children, robbed of life by a cruel man. He must be stopped."

"I can't stop him."

He smiles, his cigar wedged between his teeth. "She will never draw him out without your help. You must show her the way."

"Who? I don't even know where I am." I turn in a circle, seeing the moonlit fields and the fat blob of trees.

But the smoke has turned into a cyclone, carrying him away.

"Please, don't leave me out here."

He tips his hat again. "Ale kounya a."

Go now.

I'm staring at a familiar ceiling, with white paint peeling away from the exposed beams. I sit up on the couch. My head feels like a watermelon, and my hair is plastered to my face and the back of my neck.

Miss Alexandrine is asleep in her chair, her chin on her chest and her Bible in her lap. Her reading glasses dangle from the bridge of her nose.

Dizzy and jelly-legged, I slowly stand. The house stinks like cigar smoke.

His seductive laugh still echoes through my head, his silky voice beckoning me.

I know what I have to do.

53

BONIN ACCELERATED THROUGH a yellow light. "Pietry was the arresting officer. I should have put two and two together."

"Why does that name sound familiar?" Cage asked.

"He's the asshole who gave you a hard time after Annabeth hit you."

"The sweaty redneck you shot down?"

"The very one."

Cage dreaded the answer, but he had to know. "How did you get him to drop the charges?"

"Promised him we'd go for a drink this weekend."

Talk about taking one for the team. "What do you know about him?"

"He's a twenty-year patrol officer who never moved up the ranks," Bonin said. "He claims he wanted to work the streets, but he applied for detective twice. The second time, I got the job."

Cage grinned. "How did that go over?"

"As well as you can imagine. I made detective fairly young—right after my thirtieth birthday. So that pissed him off even more. We both worked at the Eighth District in the Quarter, and he either put me down or asked me out. He's only got two gears."

"If he ran interference for his cousin's drug business, he might be helping him with other things. Like kidnapping teenaged girls."

A homeless man leaned against one of the Eighth District's white pillars, smoking a cigarette and talking to himself. A woman sat on the steps, playing a game of solitaire, her backpack tucked underneath her. While most major cities tried to keep their homeless population out of the public—and tourists'—eyes, New Orleans appeared to embrace it, at least in the French Quarter. Some of them eked by entertaining tourists, while others congregated in the dirty alleys and narrow corridors between the buildings.

Twenty feet from the front steps, several people enjoyed coffee and beignets in the next-door café's courtyard. The dichotomy between tourists blowing money on alcohol and trinkets in the shops while the homeless suffered in plain site was unsettling.

Bonin checked in with the night sergeant, who said the evening had been unusually quiet. Cage showed his old badge and signed in.

"Where are we going?" He followed her down the dim hallway toward the back of the station.

"Locker room." She stopped in front of the men's. "Make sure no one's in there."

Cage gave her the all clear. Bonin scanned the lockers until she found Pietry's. "Thankfully these lockers haven't been updated since the '80s." She pulled a nail file from her pocket and stuck it in the lock.

"You sure this is a good idea?" Cage asked.

She raised an eyebrow. "Are you really asking me that? Remind me what you told your supervisory agent—after you lied about being employed by him."

"All right."

"We just need to count clicks to the flat spot." Bonin used the nail file to twist the dial, listening to the clicks. "Ten." She twisted in the opposite direction. "Twenty-seven."

"Guess you weren't always a cop," Cage said.

"I couldn't remember my locker combination in high school to save my life." Back the other way. "Two."

She entered the combination and opened the door. A picture of a smiling woman and a gap-toothed little girl was taped to the inside, along with a newspaper article about Pietry reaching the twenty-year mark.

Cage moved to go through the locker's contents, but Bonin waved him off. "This is on me. Oh, gross."

Pietry had left a half-eaten sandwich along with smelly shoes and a dirty uniform.

"The sweat stains are never coming out of this shirt. The thing could walk on its own." She pulled a baggie out of the shirt pocket. "Weed. What an idiot."

Bonin yanked the uniform pants out, and a couple of folded papers fell off the shelf.

Cage picked them up and opened the first one. "Looks like a picture, printed from a crappy—Jesus."

Bonin already had her cell out. "I think Pietry and I should have our drink tonight."

CAGE LEANED AGAINST the wall, sweating and hoping Bonin pulled this off. A formal request for an interview with Pietry would tip him off. He heard voices and strained to make out words.

"I need to show you something." Bonin opened the door. "Have a seat, Lionel."

Pietry crossed his arms and glared at Cage. "The hell is this?

Myra, I thought we were going for a drink."

"You're off shift," Bonin said. "And I have some questions for you."

"Too bad." His club-hands shoved the table away, and he started to stand.

"Sit," Bonin said.

"You kiddin' me, right? You're a fine piece, and I'll drink with ya. Take you to bed. But I ain't bowing down to you just 'cause you got that shield."

Bonin tossed the baggie of marijuana on the table. "This was in your locker."

His pockmarks turned red. "You got no right to go through my shit."

"The door was open," Bonin said. "I wanted to make sure nothing was stolen."

"You just hanging out in the men's lockers?" Pietry spat. "Looking for a good time?"

"I noticed it," Cage said.

"I'm not that stupid, pretty boy."

Bonin laughed. "You sure about that? Want to guess what else I found?"

"That muffuletta I forgot to take home. You think the olive salad makes it soggy?"

"A couple of grimy pictures of a girl who doesn't look legal doing some nasty things with you." The image of a naked Lionel Pietry had been burned into Cage's brain.

"You can get the fuck out." Pietry pointed a stubby finger. "You don't work here. Ain't even a cop right now. Everyone knows your fancy new dick-sucking job don't start for two more weeks."

"You're not wrong," Cage said. "But that means I don't have to follow the rules, either."

Pietry snorted. "What the hell do you two want?"

"How much were you paid for the story about Annabeth George?" Bonin asked. "I should have known when you agreed to drop the charges you had something planned."

"Sweetheart, I dropped those charges 'cause I thought I'd get you drunk enough to finally get in your pants. I didn't say shit to the press."

"You're not the only one capable of getting information," Bonin said. "I checked in at your favorite bar. You made it easy since you were shitfaced and bragging about the money."

Pietry's lip curled. Fat made up the majority of his bulk, but his big fists could do some damage. Pietry's hostile eyes followed Bonin as she strolled over to the wall.

"Go ahead," she said. "Come at me. I'd love to throw your ass in jail."

He wouldn't attack. Pietry was too much of a coward—a man with a big mouth who made sure the women he abused couldn't fight back.

"What about you hiding her identity?" he said. "I sent the information to the Adams County Sheriff, and this piece of shit shows up. I figure he's going to take her home, but I wanted to know why the hell she was claiming to be Lyric. Then you arrest her again and book her as Lyric. Bet your Commander won't be impressed with that."

"You're not going to tell him. Because then everyone knows you're the leak." Bonin waved the baggie. "And then there's this."

"How did you know Lyric?" Cage stepped forward, adrenaline pumping. The dumbass hadn't even realized his own slip.

"You said "claiming to be Lyric." No last name. You knew Lyric Gaudet, and I'm asking how."

"My cousin dated her mom back in the day," Pietry said.

"Billy hated losing her after her druggie mom OD'd and she went to live with Grandma."

"You didn't know Lyric was missing?" Bonin asked.

"Not until I realized you two were up to something. Crazy ass girl, believing she was someone who drowned in Katrina. That grandma must have been nuts too."

"I can't imagine why you didn't make detective," Cage said.

Pietry's neck bulged. "I never wanted that."

Bonin snapped her fingers. "Focus. Let's talk about your cousin who dated Lyric's mom. Is he still dealing?"

"Billy? He's all about the Lord these days. Ain't touched anything in seven years."

Unbelievable. It couldn't be this easy. "Seven years this month, maybe? Did he have some kind of come-to-Jesus event?"

"None of your business, asshole."

"It's my business." Bonin held up the printed off pictures from his locker. "Child pornography carries a hefty sentence."

"Them girls are seventeen, and that's above the age of consent in Louisiana."

"Maybe," Bonin said. "But I think between these and the weed, you're looking at getting shit-canned and maybe lose your pension. And that's if you slither out of the charges."

Pietry dragged his hands through his mass of gray hair. "Goddamn, Myra. I can retire in four years."

"Then answer our questions, and we're done. What did Billy go through seven years ago?"

"Billy's a good dude. He's changed."

"I doubt it," Bonin said. "I'm tired and hungry. You don't start talking I'm taking these to the LT."

"All right," Pietry said. "The girl he'd been with for a few years was all strung out. He had it bad for her, but she wasn't getting no better. He was going to cut her loose, but she starts bringing home girls for him. Teenagers. Says he can do whatever he wants and she's cool with it as long as he lets her stay and keeps the drugs coming."

"And good guy that he is, he agreed," Bonin said.

Pietry shrugged. "Was all good for a while. She had her drugs, and he had some hot ass. Willing, too, from the way he talked about them. Then one night, she brings two girls. Billy said those two broads were up for anything, and they had fun for a few days. Then the girlfriend—whatever you want to call her—went nuts. She locked both of them in the barn, in a horse stall full of shit."

"His girlfriend did this?"

Pietry nodded. "That ain't the worst. She lost her shit and made one of the girls kill the other."

"That's the story your cousin told you?" Disgust rolled through Cage. Had Billy made up the narrative for the cousin, or did he really see his victims as willing?

"Sure is."

"See, I think it's the other way around," Cage said. "I think his girlfriend had been held against her will for a long time, and when he was done with her, he made her bring in new girls. Usually it's just one, and he keeps them for a few years. Does a lot of really shitty things. Then he kills them, and she finds another. Only seven years ago, he ended up with two. He slit one's throat and planned to keep the other one. But she escaped, and his ass nearly got caught."

Cage spread his hands wide. "Come-to-Jesus, maybe. Or he's a lot smarter and more careful. Either way, I think your cousin's a kidnapper, and a rapist, and a killer."

Bonin held up the picture of the girls. "These pictures make me think you might have been in on it with him. Did he give you these girls?"

"The hell you talking about? Those girls come from Tulane Avenue, paid for in cash."

"Prostitutes?" Bonin said. "Is that what you're telling me?"

"Damn right."

"And you like light-skinned ladies, right? Creoles, like me?"

He licked his lips. "Sure do. I'm still willing if you are. I'll make an exception on your being over thirty and all."

She slammed one of the pictures down in front of him and pointed to the girl tied to the bed, spread-eagled, staring straight at the camera. "See her?"

"She liked bein' tied up."

"It's a good shot of her face," Cage said. Pietry wasn't just a scumbag; he was an idiot for leaving the pictures in his locker. "Helped us find her in missing kids database. She's a fourteen-year-old runaway suspected of being sold into sex trafficking."

Pietry's smug attitude had disappeared. "I didn't know. The place on Tulane said she was seventeen. They had her birth certificate."

"How did you survive as a cop for thirty years?" Bonin said. "You know how easy it is to fake a birth certificate? If you even checked, which I highly doubt."

Sweat beaded across Pietry's wide forehead. "I swear to God, she said she was seventeen and fine with it, Myra. Just a prostitute, that's all."

"Like the girls your cousin tortured? I suppose the girl asked him to slit her throat?"

"He didn't do that." Spit flew out of Pietry's mouth. "I got the tape to prove it."

Cage stilled, his stomach lurching. "What?"

"The crazy bitch didn't know Billy had a security camera in the barn. He got it all on tape."

54

I DON'T CALL Cage. He'll say I've lost my mind and rush over here to stop me. But the Baron, the leader of the Ghede Loa who watch over the dead, has shown me the truth: Lyric can't stop him on her own. She needs me to draw him out.

Cage and Bonin might find him one day, but how many more girls will be tortured and killed before they do?

Lyric and I can stop him now. I just have to find her.

I gather everything I need and sneak out the back door into the tiny courtyard. The clouds are gone, and the moon lights up the entire courtyard, but it's still muggy and the mosquitoes are dive-bombing.

Better make this quick. Lyric may not believe, but I have enough faith for both of us.

I sit down on the stones and set out my things. I hope I have enough to make the ritual work. Ezili Dantò won't like my borrowing from Miss Alexandrine's altar, but I'm desperate.

I place the little statue of Ezili in the center of a flagstone and put the torn Tarot card next to it. I offer her a fresh red candle, a stick of sweet-smelling incense, and a hot pepper that's close to rotting. She probably won't appreciate that, but it's the best I've got.

Finally, I offer her the white Voodoo doll with my own hair tied around it.

I slap a mosquito off my arm and begin to pray to Ezili Dantò, explaining that I call on her because of Lyric's card and needing her guidance. I make my offering and ask her to lead me to Lyric so we can protect other innocent girls.

Impatience makes me want to open my eyes, but I keep them closed, waiting for the vision. She must come and show me where to find Lyric.

Alexandrine's gate opens and shuts. I want to believe the spirit has delivered Lyric to me, but I'm not completely stupid.

I jump to my feet and tiptoe to the door, crouching behind the big hydrangea.

My heart's pounding.

Her footsteps thud against the flagstone, and then she's standing over my pathetic altar. Her black hair shines in the moonlight, and she's shaking her head. She thinks I'm silly. Wait until I tell her I've called her to me.

I edge out from behind the big plant, but an alarm buzzes in my head.

Lyric's wearing different clothes.

And she's thicker. A good twenty pounds thicker.

Like an idiot, I gasp.

She turns her head.

Angry eyes meet mine, a wicked smile on her face. "Hello, Annabeth."

55

CAGE HIT PLAY, his stomach already sour. The camera had been mounted high in a corner so that it captured most of the barn's floor and the stalls.

"Lionel swears this is the only video his cousin sent him." Bonin yawned. "I'll get a warrant for his computer as soon as the judge is in. William Thomas Pietry, by the way. Anthony was his father's name. Billy's been off the grid since Katrina, of course."

"Any chance we can trace where Billy sent the video from?"

Bonin shook her head. "He sent it years ago, from an online storage drive. We'd need to subpoena them, and that's not happening."

Despite the low-resolution, he clearly saw Mickie, naked and bruised and dirty, hands zip-tied in front of her, backed up against the horse stall's closed door.

"That's definitely Lyric." She stood in front of Mickie, wielding a Bowie knife. She looked thinner than she had when she disappeared, her naturally curly hair longer and stringy. Lyric gestured with the knife as she spoke, her mouth moving too rapidly to lip-read.

He didn't need sound to understand that Mickie was begging for her life. "Are we seriously supposed to believe that Pietry thought this girl was naked, dirty, and bound because she agreed to it?"

"Billy told him she looked like that because she and Lyric fought, and the girl ran for her life. Lyric caught her and made her strip."

"He's an idiot if he believed that," Cage said.

If Lyric knew about the camera, she didn't seem concerned. Suddenly her head whipped to the right, and Cage made out the dim profile of Annabeth crouched in the corner.

"Can you tell what Lyric's saying to her?" Bonin asked.

"The resolution's not good enough." Lyric shook her head as she spoke, stomping her feet. "Maybe she's insisting she's got no choice."

"Or she's telling her to shut the hell up," Bonin said. "At this point she's been held captive—assuming she didn't go willingly—for what, six years? Between the drugs and the trauma, she might enjoy hurting someone else at this point."

Lyric turned her attention back to a weeping Mickie. She squared her shoulders and raised the knife.

Annabeth charged from the corner and pulled hard on Lyric's arm. Lyric backhanded her, brandishing the knife in her threat before kicking Annabeth in the throat.

Annabeth dropped to her hands and knees, mouth open in pain.

Lyric jabbed the knife into a screaming Mickie's throat at the same time Annabeth reared up and grabbed her arm. The women struggled as the blade sank deeper. Mickie's bound hands raised to pull out the knife, but Lyric slammed her elbow into Annabeth's eye and drove the knife in to the hilt.

Breathing hard, Lyric stepped back. Annabeth tried in vain to pull out the knife, getting Mickie's blood all over her.

Cage swallowed vomit. "Now we know why she dreams that she killed Mickey. It's all mixed up in her memory of trying to stop it."

Mickie went still, and Annabeth rested her forehead on her friend's, her body shaking with sobs.

Lyric grabbed her by the hair, sinking a needle into her neck. Thirty seconds later, Annabeth had dropped to her knees, succumbing to the drug while a motionless Lyric watched.

"What's Pietry's excuse for not reporting this?"

"He didn't want to get involved," Bonin said. "Frankly, I believe him. He's scared shitless and telling me everything else he knows, which is damn little. Billy's mom lost everything in Katrina, and he didn't stick around to help her. Pietry had to step in, and he's got serious resentment. If he's guilty of anything beyond the underage girl and the dime bag, it's keeping this to use as revenge when he was good and ready."

"Still a scumbag. Where's his cousin now?"

"Living in Arkansas with a new girlfriend," Bonin said. "I can't find any Bill or William Pietry. He's probably off the grid or using an alias. He did give me Billy's cell number. I'll contact the carrier in the morning and see if they can locate it."

"If the GPS is on," Cage said. "And it is morning."

Three a.m. The last time he'd been up this late, Emma had been teething.

"Go back to the hotel and catch a few hours," Bonin said.

Lyric had stood silently for two minutes until Annabeth lost consciousness. Then she whipped around and walked toward the camera. She stared up at it with undisguised hate.

"Sonofabitch."

The camera zoomed closer until Lyric's sneering face took up the entire frame.

He read her lips easily this time. "Happy now?"

56

CAGE SAT UP, disoriented and searching for the digital clock on the nightstand. He'd slept less than an hour, and his alarm was set to go off in thirty minutes.

Bonin had put out a BOLO for Lyric Gaudet, using an image from the video along with the description Annabeth gave after their encounter at the cemetery.

Even if Lyric had been forced to kill Mickie, the video could very well send her to prison. She may not know of the video's existence, but she certainly knew she was being filmed. And she knew Annabeth was getting her memory back. He had to assume Lyric saw Annabeth as a threat.

If Billy really had kicked her to the curb, Cage doubted she knew where he was. She'd probably tried to lure Annabeth.

Then why hadn't she killed her in the cemetery? And had she been forced to bring in girls? Had she acted on her own after years of horrific abuse? Or had she been a willing accomplice the whole time?

That didn't add up with Sean Andrews's story about Lyric's reaction at the party. Cage believed she must have recognized Billy and realized he'd come for her like she'd always feared. Going with him willingly didn't make sense. But taking a ride from him in pouring rain as a hurricane swept in certainly did.

He swung his legs over the side of the bed. A cold shower

might wake him up enough to survive until the first four shots of espresso.

If he managed to keep his eyes open long enough to reach the shower.

He heard a familiar soft giggle in the hallway, then a child's voice. A hoarse stammering followed—a monosyllable repeated over and over. An older female spoke in a language Cage couldn't understand. The unmistakable stink of Alexandrine's spilled oil washed over him.

He jerked awake in time to keep from falling face-forward off the bed. His mouth had gone dry, his memory of the oil so strong his nose burned from it. The scent must have been embedded in the shirt he'd fallen asleep in. He'd never get the smell out.

His cell's loud ringtone startled him, and he nearly pitched off the bed again. Cage snapped it up. "Bonin, I'm too tired to think straight right now."

"Get dressed," she said. "Annabeth is missing."

57

"WHAT THE HELL happened?" Cage scrubbed the sleep out of his eyes and gulped lukewarm coffee. In the early morning, the French Quarter streets and sidewalks were nearly empty. A dense fog hung low over the old buildings, eclipsing some of the iron balconies and colorful flags. The thick vapor matched the haze in Cage's head. Part of his exhausted brain wondered if he was really awake or stuck in yet another powerfully vivid dream.

Bonin drove through a pothole, and Cage nearly smacked his head on the top of her car. Definitely not a dream.

"Alexandrine woke up an hour ago, after falling asleep in her chair," Bonin said. "She assumed Annabeth had gone to bed. She went into the kitchen to start coffee and saw remnants of a spell in the back courtyard."

"Remnants of a spell?"

"It looked like Annabeth was using a piece of a Tarot card in a spell to try to contact Lyric."

"You've got to be kidding me."

Bonin glared at him. "The spell itself doesn't matter. The point is, that statue of Ezili had been knocked over, and the Tarot card was still there. Annabeth wouldn't have just left things like that."

"She wouldn't have left that card."

"Exactly," Bonin said. "Alexandrine checked the guestroom. Annabeth hadn't gone to bed, and she left her phone."

Miss Alexandrine had insisted the house was secure. If anyone tried to force his way into the house, the shrill alarm would sound, simultaneously contacting the police. "Annabeth promised she would stay inside."

"This isn't exactly the first promise she's broke."

Last night, Annabeth wanted nothing to do with helping Lyric. Had her TBI caused an impulse decision, or had something else changed her mind?

A PATROL SERGEANT briefed Bonin as soon as they reached the squad room. "Every unit has her last booking photo and the physical description of the other woman. You don't know her name?"

"Nope." Bonin wondered if going to the media about Lyric's reemergence would draw her out, but Cage had argued against it. She knew how to disappear, and the attention would drive her underground. Only four people knew Lyric was alive, and they needed to keep it that way as long as possible.

"Did Pietry make any calls last night?" Bonin asked.

"Not on the official log book," the sergeant said. "But he's one of us. Someone might have covered for him. I'm heading out to search. I'll call you if we get anything."

"Thanks. Does your commander know?" Bonin had called her boss, Commander Starr, after picking Cage up at the hotel. Starr wanted absolute secrecy for as long as possible—preferably until Annabeth was quickly found—and stressed making sure her parents were told before the story was leaked to the press. He'd also told Cage to call Rogers at the LBI.

Cage planned to put that off as long as he could.

"He's due at the station in an hour," the sergeant said. "If you want this kept quiet, I suggest talking to him right away."

Cage waited until the sergeant was out of earshot. "What about the aged-up photo of Lyric?" A forensic artist from the criminal investigations unit had been given Lyric's old picture and a description from Annabeth in order to create an up-to-date composite photo.

"They didn't get the information until late last night, and I didn't ask for a rush because I didn't want to tip anyone off. I just told them we needed the digitally enhanced photo because we knew she'd been kept alive for several years. You think Lyric's responsible?"

"The only thing I know is Annabeth didn't go willingly. And either Lyric's involved or she can help us find Billy. Either way, she's our best option right now."

Bonin rolled her shoulders and fought off a yawn. "I'm going to visit Pietry in the holding cell. You stay here. I've got a better chance at getting him to talk without you antagonizing him."

He sat down at an empty desk. Lack of sleep and the memory of his strange dream just before Bonin called made Cage sluggish and half-disoriented. The dream-voices played on a loop, and each time he seemed to hear them a little better. He closed his eyes and tried to focus on just the older woman's voice. He'd never admit as much to Bonin, but Cage couldn't shake the feeling that she'd been talking to him instead of the girl. At the time, he thought he smelled the oil from the altar because his shirt still reeked of it. But thinking back, replaying the dream, it seemed like the oil somehow came from the woman—Ezili. The same Loa Annabeth had been praying to before she disappeared.

God, he needed coffee. And an energy drink. Sleep deprivation and stress made his mind play tricks on him.

"Agent Foster?" A second patrol officer who didn't look old enough to be out of the academy had appeared out of nowhere.

Cage blinked. This must be what sleepwalking felt like. "Yeah?"

"The front desk sergeant said to tell you Lyric Gaudet is in the lobby. She's demanding to speak with you."

The knot of tension between Cage's shoulders loosened as he hurried toward the lobby, his anger rising with every step. When would Annabeth learn to think things through? Had she considered her parents? Or Alexandrine? Cage and Bonin had both stuck their necks out for her. Did that even compute?

No coddling this time. Let her lose her temper. Stupid decisions have consequences.

Cage slammed into the front lobby. The French Quarter station had once been a bank, and the lobby's focal point was a long, L-shaped counter with dozens of pamphlets for tourist attractions. Its front panels had been painted by local artists, depicting scenes of New Orleans and NOPD history. A glass case near the front door featured police T-shirts and other items. The tired front desk sergeant and NOPD flags were the only things that kept the lobby from looking more like a visitor's bureau than a police station.

Annabeth stood in front of the soda machine, no doubt in desperate need of sugar and food. She must have stopped at Charlotte's to shower. Her still-damp black hair hung in a long braid down her back, and she'd changed into a black cut-off shirt and faded denim shorts.

Cage strode past the sergeant and pushed through the old bank-style short doors into the lobby's public area. "What the hell were you thinking? You could have at least let someone know you were okay before taking the time to go home and shower."

She slowly turned, her mouth curling into an amused smile.

"Holy shit." Had Cage fallen asleep at the desk and been sucked into another realistic dream? Or was the real Lyric Gaudet standing ten feet away?

58

"AGENT FOSTER?" HER low voice had a sultry, feminine tone. Her striking beauty remained, although her face seemed hardened and fixed into a wary expression. A thin, fading scar streaked diagonally across her full lips.

"Yes." He glanced at the desk sergeant, who seemed to be focused on paperwork. But the raised counter prevented Cage from knowing for sure. "Would you mind talking in private?"

Lyric's calculated gaze wandered over him. Unlike Annabeth, she emanated confidence likely gained from her years of hell. Reading people's intentions had become second nature to her.

"I'll follow you."

Cage led her through the front entrance and cubicles, past the squad room and to the first interview room. What was she doing here? Did she have Annabeth stashed away somewhere?

Lyric hesitated in the doorway. "I can leave anytime I want."

"Of course." Cage held up his phone. "Detective Bonin is working with me. You okay with me letting her know you're here?"

"I'm only talking to you. Annabeth said I could trust you."

"That's fine." Cage pointed to the ceiling corner behind him. "I'll let Bonin know to watch on the camera."

Anxiety flashed through her eyes, evaporating into a grim determination. "Whatever. As long as it's just you and me in this room. And leave the door open a couple of inches."

He did as she asked and sent the text. Hopefully no one eavesdropped at the door and Bonin kept the camera to herself.

Lyric sat down in the same chair Annabeth had occupied days ago. "I know Annabeth's gone again."

"How'd you find out?"

Lyric's face briefly softened. "I stopped by to see Miss Alexandrine again this morning. She answered the door this time. She looks exactly the same. She told me about Annabeth."

"Last night, before you knocked her out, you made it clear to Annabeth that trusting me wasn't an option. You wanted nothing to do with legal justice." Cage might have to walk a tight rope with this woman, but he wasn't going to pretend she hadn't assaulted Annabeth or that he believed she was truly here out of the goodness of her heart.

"I still don't," Lyric said. "Laws never did anything for my mother or me. But Miss Alexandrine took care of my gran, and the old lady's even more persuasive than I remembered. She says you're a good man trying to do the right thing."

"I am," Cage said. "Right now, I don't care what you've done to survive, and I'm willing to overlook your attack on her last night. Catching Billy and bringing Annabeth home are all that matters." For now, at least. He and Bonin couldn't pretend they hadn't watched the video of Lyric slitting Mickie's throat.

"She told me you guys figured out who he was." Lyric didn't seem surprised or impressed. "Do you know where to look for him?"

"I'm hoping you're here with that information."

"How do you know I'm not trying to protect him? You know about Sheila. You know what I've done, that I stayed with him." Lyric leaned forward, the thin, white scar through her lips matching the dark gleam in her eyes. "Why trust me?"

"I know enough about kidnap victims and trauma to understand why you didn't escape. I'm hoping your time away from him has helped break some of those ties. But I don't completely trust you."

"I'm all you've got right now."

"Pretty much."

"I appreciate the honesty." Lyric sat back and rested her clasped hands over the table. More faded scars marked her wrists and hands, including what appeared to be a branded 'B' on the inside of her left wrist. "Yes, he branded me with his initial. The other scars are from trying to get free when he first took me."

Sick bastard. Cage had to find Annabeth before the same thing happened to her. Billy didn't intend to kill her, at least not for a while. She was unfinished business for him.

"You know Alexandrine really believes all that about the spirits and her magic," Lyric said. "In her mind, she's witnessed a thousand things that validate that faith. Gran was the same way. My mom, she might've been, but she liked drugs more."

"And what about you?"

"I stopped believing in anything a long time ago," Lyric said, "and ninety-nine percent of me still doesn't believe."

"And the other one percent?"

Lyric pulled part of a faded card from her pocket. "This was my mom's half of the Ezili Dantò card. When I was a kid, she'd take off for nights at a time and leave me with Gran. She said she had to work, but even then, I knew she was doing what she had to do to get her drugs and put a little food on the table. You know who this spirit represents?"

Cage nodded. "I've had a crash course in Voodoo the past few days."

Lyric snickered. "Have they made you a believer?"

"Not just yet."

"Keep it that way," she said. "Anyway, my mom tore the card in half. She said the card was blessed with a spell that would allow me to see her when I needed her most."

Lyric stared at the card, her eyes blazing with hate. "I never saw a damn thing, of course. My mom and Gran said it was because I didn't have enough faith. That's the key element in Voodoo—faith at all times so your mind tricks you into seeing results. You have to believe in order to see."

"I'd argue that's pretty much the same across all religions."

"Fair point," Lyric said. "Mom had this card in her pocket when they found her. You've heard what happened?"

"Your mom caught Billy watching you in the shower and let him have it."

"I took off and made my way to Gran's. She kept calling Mom, but we knew they were fighting. Gran called the police the next morning. Mom was already dead by then." Lyric traced the ripped edges of the card. "The thing is, I'd been using my half of the card all night trying to see what happened to her. When I found out she had the card in her pocket, I got so angry."

"Why?"

"Because if she really believed in all the spells and crap she and Gran tried to push on me, she'd have used that card. At least that's what I thought as I kid. I stopped trying to believe in any magic and put my half of the card away. I kept her half as a reminder of how foolish I'd been."

"Annabeth told you what happened the night she picked up the other half of the card?" Cage asked.

"She insists her vision looked like I do now, scarred lips and all. Her mind just filled in those blanks when she saw me."

"That's what I told her, but she wanted nothing to do with that explanation. Even when the pathologist told us the second body buried with Mickie's was an adult female, Annabeth refused to consider it might be you. She believed in her vision."

"The decoy," Lyric said. "I didn't know it wasn't her."

"I know," Cage said. "If you don't believe in any of this, then why bring up the card? Why are you here?" He felt for Lyric, but he still didn't trust her.

"You think Annabeth's a liability to me," Lyric said. "That if she gets her memory back, she'll be able to incriminate me. But if I've come to get rid of her, why didn't I just kill her last night?"

Telling her about the video would take the power of Annabeth's memory away. Was Lyric trying to negotiate?

Screw it. Might as well go all in and pray he didn't regret. "Annabeth's memory isn't your only problem. Billy sent the video of you killing Mickie to his cousin."

He'd thrown her with that one. Her tough veneer dissolved, her face paled. "I didn't have a choice."

"I believe you," Cage said. "But there's no audio, so ultimately, it comes down to your word against the video. A jury could go either way on that. If you had a damned good defense attorney, you might walk. But there's no guarantee."

Lyric recovered some of her composure. "If I'm so concerned about Annabeth getting me in trouble, then why am I here to help you?"

"Is that why you're here?" Cage asked. "Or are you here to negotiate? Your freedom against Annabeth's location?"

"I'd argue those are essentially the same things." She smirked, turning his earlier comment around.

"They might be, if your information is solid enough."

"I read the paper," she said. "You're not really a cop right now, are you? That means you can't offer me any deal."

"Correct. You'd have to take that up with Detective Bonin. Want me to call her in?"

Lyric banded her arms across her chest, her scarred lips curled. "I'm not worried about a fucking deal. I want to help Annabeth because she doesn't deserve this shit. If that means I go to prison, then fine. At least I'll know where my next meal's coming from."

Cage waited.

"You couldn't find Bill Pietry on the grid, right? No William, Billy, whatever. He's too smart for that."

"My guess is he's living with his new girlfriend and keeping everything in her name." Time to gauge Lyric's loyalty. "She the same one he left you for?"

"Leaving me isn't the right term," she said. "I never wanted to be with him. He forced me to rely on him for everything. But yeah, it's the same bitch. He'll stick with her to the end."

"Even when she gets too old, like you?"

Lyric rolled her eyes. "First off, it's not nice to say a girl is old. And secondly, stop trying to rile me up. I'm not jealous. I fucking hate him, and I hate her more, but I'm not jealous."

"Why hate her if it's not about her replacing you?"

Lyric pointed to her scarred lips. "Because she did this to me."

"He broke her just like he did you," Cage said. "Until she did whatever it took to survive."

Lyric's bitter laugh set his nerves on edge. "He didn't need to break her. That bitch was willing from the start."

59

HER CRAZY EYES scare the shit out of me. She licks her lips like she can't wait to get started with whatever they have planned for me.

He obsessed over the ones who got away.

She stuck the gun against my ribs and licked my ear. "Let's go, sweetheart."

My guts knot in fear. I'd rather die than go with her. No chance of forgetting any of the abuse this time.

"I'll kill the old lady. Nice and slow too. You can watch."

Tears pop in my eyes. I can't let Miss Alexandrine die for me.

She walks me through the narrow alley and out the gate. I expect a camper or the blue pickup, but she opens the passenger door of a sweet Mercedes. Guess Billy's terrorizing in style now.

"Get in, bitch."

I obey, staring out the window at the house, silently begging the Loa to help.

The woman gets in the driver's seat, and I wait for the needle. She jams it into my neck, and I'm dizzy, my eyes crossing. My tongue is numb, and my fingers are tingling.

I shake my head, trying to clear my vision. My forehead lands on the window. I blink, my eyelids heavy as a rock.

"Lyric," I whisper. "Help me."

The woman snorts like a pig. "She's probably dead or whoring her way to her next fix. You're all alone, baby."

60

"WHAT'S HER NAME?" Cage asked.

"Bitch. At least that's what I call her."

"Please." Cage gestured to the camera. "While we're talking, Detective Bonin can search the state and local databases. But we need a name."

Lyric drummed her fingertips on the table.

"Every second you delay decreases our chances of finding Annabeth alive."

She gritted her teeth as if saying the name caused physical pain. "Cathy Chambers, from Louisiana. At least that's what she always said. Bitch probably lied."

"Thank you. Did she resemble you, like all the others?"

"Except for being fat and ugly, yeah. She's mixed, and she's got black hair. Kinky shit that she straightens."

"How old is she?"

"Older than me, which is the real kicker. Early forties, I think."

"Tell me about her."

"I already did," Lyric said. "She's pure evil. He never told me how they met—just that fate brought them together. Ridiculous coming from his controlling ass. He brought her in and said we'd all work together. I decided right then to find the guts to leave. It didn't take her long to make her mark. Literally." Lyric closed her eyes. "He used to say my lips were his favorite feature. Then he lets her cut me so she can be the alpha female."

"He used that term?" Cage asked.

"He acted like we'd been partners and suddenly some new chic had come to challenge me."

"He never used any other girls to lure victims?"

"Only me," she said. "After Annabeth escaped, he got organized. Started 'holding out and saving up.' His term, not mine. He only took a girl every two or three years and made do with me after he'd used her up. Once he finally picked a new girl, it was my job to bring her to him."

"In these downtimes," Cage said, "he made do with you …"

"Sometimes he put me in the stirrups like he did before I brought him the first girl. And he was just as brutal. Others, he just told me what he wanted, and I did it." She looked down at the brand on her wrist. "Most days, I felt like I'd left my body, like I looked down and watched him rape me over and over. When the time came to get a new girl, I did everything he told me to. He could hurt someone else for a while."

"But when Cathy came along?" Cage asked.

"Everything changed. First time he brought Cathy to his toy shed, they had a girl with them. Strapped her down, and Cathy started in on her. I went into the house and locked my door, but I could still hear her screams. I should've done something then, but I didn't think anyone would believe me. And he held that tape of me killing that girl over my head."

"He didn't have the camper anymore?" Cage asked. "Annabeth remembers a camper."

"He trashed that when she escaped," Lyric said. "Listen, I'm not sure you're getting this. Cathy is worse than him. That first girl they brought? She was Cathy's stepdaughter. Her husband had died in some freak accident just a few months before, and

Cathy had inherited a shit-ton of money. But she was saddled with a fourteen-year-old girl."

"Where was this?"

"Nacogdoches, East Texas. Not far from the state line."

"I know where it's at. The police didn't suspect Cathy?" Even an unexperienced cop would question a husband's death from a freak accident followed by a stepdaughter's disappearance.

"I only know what I overheard," Lyric said. "She and Billy seemed to think they'd covered their tracks. Must have, because no one came looking for them before I left. And with Annabeth gone, I'm guessing they're not in jail."

"You told Annabeth he made you leave," Cage said. "Is that true?"

"It's a version of it. I didn't feel like going into the whole thing, so I told her what she needed to know."

"Then you did escape?"

"No," she said. "I wanted to, but after so long … I couldn't get the nerve. A few months later, Cathy made it easy for him. He went to work, and she packed up my shit and dumped me off at the truck stop. I couldn't decide whether to thank her or hit her."

"Because you cared about Billy?"

Lyric chewed her bottom lip, fighting for composure. "Attached is more like it, and I'm ashamed to say that. The shower wasn't the first time he'd spied on me. I started developing that summer, earlier than some girls. And he used to watch me get undressed. I'd see him peeking through my bedroom door. I would have told my mother, but he always waited until she was passed out. One time, I confronted him. I had more balls at eleven than I did when he took me. I told him that if he didn't stop, I'd have my gran curse him good. That's when he said we belonged together. I was made for him, and one day, it would happen. I just needed to get a little older."

An eleven-year-old child, and probably not the first one he'd victimized. "Where did Billy work?" If he had a trade, something Cage could track …

"Odd jobs, always for cash. Lots of carpentry stuff. And he loved scavenging for old shit he could fix up and sell. Never online, though. Always at some crappy local flea market."

Smart sonofabitch. "The day he kidnapped you, did he force you to get into the truck after you left Rouse's, or did he use the storm to entice you?"

"No hurricane would have made me get into a vehicle with him." Lyric spit the words. "He pulled a gun on me and threatened to take me home and kill Gran. That was enough."

"Did he have the camper set up by then?"

"Ready and waiting," she said. "I'm not sure if I was the first, but I was the goal. The practice run, until he needed fresh meat. I know you're wondering why I didn't take off. I had multiple chances after a few years." She lowered her eyes, staring at the table. "You can't possibly understand the mind games. He raped me, burned me, beat me. Told me I belonged to him and no one would want me now, anyway. But then he'd bring me water or ice cream. Or let me take a shower. He bought books for me to read—textbooks, so I could halfway keep up with high school. He even studied with me. And then he'd strap me to the table and start over."

"He manipulated you," Cage said. "These people are skilled at tearing you down to nothing and then making you completely reliant on them. You're certainly not the first one to stay."

Lyric's face tightened, the scar across her mouth white. Seeing her fighting off tears struck Cage harder than anything she'd told him.

"You may not believe it," she said, "but I never considered hurting Annabeth when I found out she was alive. He took me to one of her track meets, right before he kidnapped her. She just took off like she was flying. I knew then she was my only hope."

Cage shouldn't have been surprised, but the wind had been knocked out of him. That meet had been a state qualifying meet, and Annabeth had been expected to break records. Most of Roselea came to watch, including Cage.

"When I heard she was alive, I broke down and cried. Talked to God for the first time in years. And then I realized what I needed to do. I lost my cool with her last night, and I'm sorry. I'd just convinced myself that she would agree, and I had this fantasy of finding them and killing them both, to bring us closure. I realized this morning, before I went to Alexandrine's, that killing him would destroy Annabeth. She's still special, and better. I guess that's why I'm here."

Cage's phone dinged with a text from Bonin. A picture of a dark-haired, round-faced woman popped up. His already tight chest took another sucker punch. He recognized this woman from somewhere.

He turned the phone and showed Lyric the picture.

"That's her. She doesn't look that good in real life. Hard drugs do that to a person."

He confirmed the identity to Bonin, his pulse racing.

Bonin's quick reply: *OUTSIDE NOW.*

"Would you excuse me one second?"

"Whatever."

Bonin prowled outside the door. "Cathy Chambers, forty-five, owns a house a few miles south of Shreveport. That picture's from a recent driver's license."

"I've seen this woman somewhere," Cage said. "I just can't

place it."

"I can," Bonin said. "She showed up at the Jasper dig site, claiming to be from the local news. I ran her off, remember?"

Cage snapped his fingers. "Sheila Dietz's restaurant. Remember I ran back inside to give Sheila my card and cell number? This woman had sat down at the bar. She must have come in while we were outside with Annabeth."

Bonin shook her head. "I saw the woman you're talking about. She had her head down, but that girl had a full Afro. The woman at the dig site had a weave."

"Then she took it out," Cage said. "Sheila was talking to her, and this woman looked pissed when I interrupted them."

His knees turned to liquid, and he sagged against the wall. "He obsessed over the ones who got away, and we led him right to Sheila."

61

MY HEAD IS pounding. My hand and feet are zip-tied, the plastic digs into my wrist. It's freezing in here.

I'm naked.

I start full-body shaking. Even my teeth knock together. I'm so freaking scared my brain is slower than usual, and my nerves feel like someone threw a match on me.

I force my eyes open, but it's pitch black. I'm close to going into a full-blown panic attack. I suck in deep breaths, and I realize I'm lying on moldy smelling blankets. The floor beneath is cold and hard. Metal, I guess.

My brain's caught up. Has he already … the rest of my body feels okay. He hasn't attacked me yet.

"This is your fault."

I freeze at the sound of her voice. It's not the nasty beast who brought me here.

"Who's there?"

"Sheila."

It takes me a second to get it. Lyric's warning from last night torments me. He obsessed over the ones who got away.

Did she know about Sheila?

"How long have you been here?"

"He took me last night when I left the restaurant. He knew I was closing by myself."

"Did we somehow lead him to you?"

"You think? I told your cop buddy that the night I escaped and hid in the woods, he kept telling me he'd find me one day. That he would never give up."

I can't stop myself from asking the question. "Then why didn't you have a weapon or something? Why did you leave by yourself?"

I feel her shift toward me. Suddenly her hot breath is on my face, and I think I can make out the outline of her hair.

"Are you seriously blaming me?" She sounds ready to fight.

"I'm sorry. I said it without thinking." I still want to know the answer, but I manage to keep my mouth shut.

"I did have a gun," she snaps. "He jumped me in the dark. I didn't have a chance to get the gun out of my purse. Believe me, we wouldn't be here if I had."

I rub my neck. Whatever Crazy Eyes injected still burns my skin. "What about the woman with him? Who's she?"

"What woman?"

"The bitch who kidnapped me this morning," I say. "She's biracial, but she's older and mean, and she's doing this because she wants to."

"I haven't seen anyone since he dumped me in here," Sheila says. "He must have found someone else to train and lure girls."

She doesn't know. Should I tell her? Can he hear us? If he can, maybe he'll be stressed enough to make a mistake. "Lyric is alive. I talked to her last night."

Sheila's practically whispering in my ear now. "What did you say?"

I tell her what happened last night—except for the part about Lyric hitting me and taking off. If he's listening, I want him to think she's still on my side.

"I was actually trying to contact her through the spirits when the woman showed up," I say. "It was dark, and for a second I thought the spell had worked."

I waited for her to ridicule the spell or ask me what the hell I was talking about, but she was silent for a while.

"Are you sure it was Lyric in the cemetery?"

"Totally sure."

"Do you think she really knows where he is?" Sheila's voice is shaking. "Even if she does, she took off, right? She isn't going to know you're gone, and no one knows where she's at."

I think back to last night. Fog was creeping in when crazy eyes took me to her fancy car. The drug made me feel like I'd floated into another dimension or something. Am I sure?

Something bangs hard on the metal wall behind us, and then it rattles and groans.

The door is opening. I twist around and shrink away, but there isn't very far to go. Sheila scoots next to me and takes my hand.

Her lips are against my ear. "Fight."

The door swings open and sunlight blinds me. My eyes water, and I can only see a blob of light.

"Welcome home, ladies."

62

BONIN ENDED THE call. “Sheila’s roommate called the police when she didn’t come home last night. Shreveport police found her car parked in its usual spot behind the restaurant. The driver-side door was open, but no sign of Sheila.”

“You better find a way to charge Lionel Pietry with this,” Cage said. Pietry must have told his cousin more than he admitted to. The guy knew how to snoop and stay in the background. “He told him about us going to Jasper.”

The small interview room was just around the corner from the storage area Bonin had commandeered for a temporary workspace. Cage slipped down the hall and peeked into the interrogation room. He’d left the door partially open so that Lyric wouldn’t feel trapped and would hopefully learn to trust him.

She waved at him. “Can we finish this?”

“Couple of more minutes.”

“Little Rock’s about a five-hour drive,” Bonin said when Cage rejoined her around the corner. “An easy road trip for Billy and his new lady.”

“Billy didn’t go to Jasper,” Cage said. “He’s too smart. He sent her, she comes to the dig site, and probably finds a way to spy even after she’s run off. We led her to Sheila.”

“I can’t decide if he’s got balls of steel or a massive ego.”

"Lyric said he obsessed over the ones who got away." Acid rolled in Cage's stomach. His investigation had given Billy Pietry the information he needed to find both women. "I need to get back to Lyric. I've already asked her to wait twice. She's probably ready to curse me."

The walk back to the interview room took less than ninety seconds.

"Shit."

Lyric was gone, and a note written on the back of a napkin left on the table.

Agent Foster,

I've told you everything I know, and I need to get back to Alex. She's pretty upset. Call us as soon as you know anything.

~L

Lyric's disappearing act left Cage uneasy. Alexandrine gave him the impression the two had never really gotten along, so why did she feel any sort of loyalty to the priestess? Then again, Lyric didn't have any other place to go.

The disembodied female voice from his dream revved up again, her words echoing in his head, louder this time, until he finally managed to make out some of the words.

"Lyric left." Cage showed Bonin the note. "We need to keep her and Alexandrine updated."

Bonin raised an eyebrow but didn't question Lyric's decision to bail. "The address on Chambers's driver's license is south of Shreveport, rural and well out of city limits. Caddo Parish Sheriff's office confirmed she's still the owner. Water and electricity are in her name too. Satellite photos show a storage unit in the back, roughly ten feet away from the house. They're getting a TAC team ready. Their K-9 has Sheila's scent from the car."

Shreveport was a half-day drive, and the women didn't have that much time. He hated being stuck on the sidelines, especially when Annabeth was so unpredictable. If she panicked and attacked a cop, she could end up shot. "You told them about her issues, right? Do they understand Annabeth may come at them?"

"They're aware. Are you going to call her parents?"

The Georges planned to go home this morning. Annabeth had promised she would call her mother in a few days. Walking away from her had taken its toll on Krista, and Cage didn't want to upset her anymore. "Not yet. They can't do anything for her, and they're probably on the road."

"Don't be an idiot and keep this from Agent Rogers," Bonin said. "He's a dick, but he stuck his neck out for you. We may need the LBI's resources, especially since the forensic anthropologist officially identified Mickie. Agent Tims arrives tomorrow for a full debriefing. Rogers won't be able to put her off anymore."

The shit just kept piling on. "Listen, I need you to translate something I overheard this morning. Please don't ask me to explain. Just tell me what it means. Sorry if I butcher the language."

He clumsily repeated the three Creole words.

"I'm not sure you have the whole sentence." Bonin chewed the end of her pen. "Where did you hear this? Who said it?"

Cage shook his head. "Just translate, please."

"Well, like I said, you're missing some words. But what you just told me means, 'she is revenge.'"

The words struck like shrapnel. "I need to make some calls."

63

HE'S TALL. TALLER than Cage, even. His potbelly lops over his jeans, but his legs are still skinny, his arms all wiry muscle. He doesn't have enough hair to slick back, so he's combed it over. If I wasn't paralyzed with fear, I'd make fun of him. I expected someone dirty and mean looking. This guy's dressed like my high school guidance counselor.

Was that a real memory? If I live, I guess I'll find out.

He steps closer, and Sheila and I are jammed against the wall. He crouches down so he's at eye level, but I can't look at him.

He inhales, and then chuckles. "You both stink of fear. My favorite scent."

My knees knock together. Sheila squeezes my hand.

"You ladies look uncomfortable, but I suggest you get used to it, because this is the best you're going to feel." He strokes Sheila's leg. "I bet you thought I'd forgot all about you."

She tries to kick him with her bound legs, but he anticipates it and slams her feet to the metal floor. "Now, you know that's naughty. I'm sure you remember how all of this begins. Why don't you refresh Annabeth's memory?"

Sheila glares at him, her mouth clamps shut. He lunges forward, backhanding her across the face. She spits blood.

"It starts with you telling us everything you're going to do, in detail."

He smiles. "Good girl. I'll take it from here because I've grown quite a bit since you and I last played. Obviously, my lady and I have brought you here to be our sex slaves." He sounds like we should be excited about this.

"You're not going to like it, and you're going to fight, but you'll learn pretty quick that just turns me on and causes you more pain. My lady too. You'll be kept naked and housed in here unless we have you in the straps. This slave pod is sound proof and escape proof. Our sex room is too. Plus, it's stocked with all sorts of equipment to satisfy us and bring you pain."

I remember Sheila's story about her rape and torture in the barn, and vomit bubbles in my stomach. I'm breathing too fast, my heart racing. Red clouds my vision.

Motherfucker.

"Understand your role here, and you'll survive, at least until we're done with you. Normally I'd say that's less than a year, but I plan to make an exception in your cases. As long as you behave, you'll be given enough food and water to survive. You'll be hosed off at the end of every session. If you're good, I'll even use soap." He laughs, and I'm shaking. Why the hell is he doing this? What gives him the right to act like he's God?

"I'm sure people are already looking for you. But don't waste your energy on hope. You'll need it for other things. No one knows about this place. It's quiet and secluded, and we've taken all the necessary security precautions. And if you try to run, the gators will probably get you before I do."

He's looking at me now, and I bite my tongue, trying to fight the explosion. I know it will only make things worse.

"So, what do you need to remember? You're slaves. You will obey our every command, and we will use you whenever we feel like it." He starts running his hand up and down my leg and then up my bare thigh. He forces my legs apart and crawls between them until he's on top of me. His breath smells like garlic.

"You don't say no, and you don't speak unless we ask you a question. Do you understand, Annabeth?" He's nose to nose with me. "Are you ready to play?"

I open my mouth and dig my teeth into his bottom lip.

64

CAGE'S KNEE BOUNCED against the desk. The Caddo Parish tactical team had surrounded Cathy Chambers's two-acre property more than five minutes ago. He and Bonin waited for the captain's phone call.

Stress knotted at the base of Cage's neck as his mind obsessed over the past few days. Even without Lionel Pietry's giant mouth, Annabeth's story frontlined the national news by the time they'd discovered the Jasper graves. Cage should have expected Billy to check in—and he shouldn't have been surprised by his having another sidekick. If he'd kept his head focused on the investigation instead of worrying about Annabeth's delicate psyche, she and Sheila would probably be safe right now.

Dani had tried to warn him. He should have swallowed his ego and listened.

Bonin's ringtone blasted through the small room. She put the call on speaker. "Detective Bonin, with Agent Cage Foster."

"Captain Mary Forbes, Caddo Parrish. Our K-9's been all over this property, including the shed in the back. He didn't scent on anything, and the shed's full of junk. Sheila's never been here."

"We confirmed Cathy Chambers owned this property," Bonin said.

"I hear you," Captain Forbes said, "but we've gone through the residence, the grounds, and the shed. If Sheila set foot here, the dog would have scented."

"What the hell?" Cage asked. "This is the only Louisiana address for Cathy Chambers. We matched her driver's license to the witness's description."

"Is it possible your witness is mistaken?" Forbes asked.

"It's possible she played us," Bonin snapped, glaring at him. "I'm sending a unit to Alexandrine's."

Cage dropped his head to his hands. "She won't be there."

65

"LYRIC NEVER TALKED to Alexandrine this morning." Bonin stood over Cage as he checked his phone for the umpteenth time.

"What? You think she's going to call and tell you where she is?" Bonin didn't give him time to answer. "She knew Annabeth was taken because she's in on it. You got played. Understand?"

He shook his head. "She's not working with Billy. You didn't see the hate in her eyes."

"Get a grip," Bonin said. "She manipulated you just like she did Annabeth. And she kept us sufficiently distracted while she met up with Billy and Cathy—if Cathy's even a part of this. I wouldn't be surprised if Lyric randomly chose her as a decoy. We are screwed."

Cage shoved his chair back, the metal slamming against the wall. "I'm not some bonehead country cop who doesn't know when he's being conned."

"Really? What's your grand plan then?"

"Lyric said Cathy Chambers was a widower when she met Billy and that their first victim together was Cathy's stepdaughter."

"So what?"

"Chambers is likely her married name. Lyric also said Cathy's husband had only been dead a few months, and Billy brought the stepdaughter into his toy box. This happened in Nacogdoches. Since Billy only takes a girl every few years, I'm betting he and Lyric had some kind of permanent setup there, and that's where he met Cathy."

"All right," Bonin said. "But Cathy could have been from anywhere."

"Billy told Lyric that fate brought him and Cathy together. When I asked her about the local police not questioning Cathy after her husband died and then her stepdaughter went missing just months later, she didn't say anything about moving. In fact, when the stepdaughter was being abused, Lyric went into the house, but she could still hear the girl screaming from the toy shed. You follow me?"

"You think Cathy Chambers is local to Nacogdoches or at least lived there when her husband died."

"Or somewhere relatively close. Cathy came into the picture four years ago. Her husband died in a freak accident shortly before that, last name Chambers." Cage held up his phone. "Ranger Lewis is on it. I'm just waiting for him to call me."

THERE'S BLOOD EVERYWHERE. Running down his chin and pooling in my mouth. Before I can spit it out, Billy punches me in the face. My head snaps back and bangs against the metal wall.

"Fucking bitch." He kicks me over and over as Sheila screams, wiggling so she's between his boot and my ribs.

He's suddenly calm, breathing hard, blood dripping from his mouth. He stares down at us, his eyes flat, pure evil.

"You're going to suffer dearly for that." He walks to the door and screams for Cathy.

My ribs throb, and my throat's so dry I can't talk.

"What the hell?" Cathy's inside the metal pod now. She's ditched the black clothes she wore last night for a pair of cut offs and a skimpy-ass tank top that makes her boobs look like they're ready to spill out.

"This little bitch bit me." Billy points to me, and Cathy sneers.

"I knew she'd be trouble. Why don't we take her to the play room and show her who's boss? You can go first."

Billy stares me down, rubbing his crotch. "I'd like that. Bet she hasn't had any since the last time I played with her."

He walks toward us, and Sheila tries to block him, but he yanks her by the hair and throws her to the side like a ragdoll.

"You know what?" He unzips his pants. "I think you can start right here, so Sheila can get a show."

I lock my jaws.

He laughs. So does Cathy, her big boobs jiggling.

She doesn't see the shadow behind her. An ear-splitting boom rocks the metal pod, and Cathy stops laughing. Her eyes pop wide. A sliver of blood seeps out her nose before she pitches forward and hits the floor.

Blood pours from the hole in the back of her skull.

Billy drops to his knees and screams like a little girl. He's trying to plug the bullet hole and stop the bleeding even though it's obvious Cathy's dead.

"Hi Billy." Lyric's scar disappears with her wide smile. "Miss me?"

66

BONIN SLAMMED HER fist on the horn. "Get out of the way."

They'd been stuck at the light at Rampart Street for ten minutes. A second line parade had jammed up half the quarter, and traffic backed up all the way down Royal.

"Lewis is sure?"

Cage yanked the collar of his Kevlar vest. "One-hundred percent. Cathy O'Dell bought a place on the edge of Ponchatoula late last year. It's practically in the swamp and totally secluded."

Self-made Nacogdoches millionaire John O'Dell had died from a fall down the stairs four years ago, leaving behind a wife, Cathy, and a daughter, Sydney—who disappeared two months later, leaving a note saying she was running away.

"Remind me to send Ranger Lewis a thank you gift," Cage said.

"Ponchatoula is about an hour drive—if we ever get out of the Quarter." Bonin ran the yellow light and turned onto Rampart. "If Lyric's telling the truth about Cathy getting rid of her, then why is she working with them again? Why would Cathy allow it?"

"So Lyric could deliver Annabeth and make Billy happy."

"Given Lyric's track record, I'm not convinced that story is true. They may have been a trio the entire time."

"We'll find out soon enough," Cage said. "Lyric thinks she's in the clear."

"Hopefully she takes her time getting her revenge on Annabeth," Bonin said. "At this rate, we'll be lucky if we make it in two hours."

Cage thought about the warning from the woman in his strange dream and silently prayed for her to protect Annabeth and Sheila.

THE GUN'S POWER vibrated through Lyric until her entire body seemed charged. She held the power now. "God, the look on your ugly face. It's worth the wait."

Annabeth and poor Sheila cowered against the back of the storage pod, Annabeth holding her side. She rested her head on Sheila's shoulder. Blood streaked down her chin to her chest. Since Billy's bottom lip looked like hamburger meat, it was a safe bet Annabeth had done the damage.

"Sit up straight," Lyric said. "Makes breathing with broken ribs a little easier."

Annabeth didn't move, didn't react. Was she in shock or just plain pissed off at Lyric?

"Give me that gun." Billy raged over Cathy's body, his fists ready to do familiar damage.

"Fuck off," Lyric said. "You move toward me, I blow your brains out. Move toward them, I blow your brains out. Nothing would make me happier, so feel free to test me."

"You betrayed me."

She burst into laughter. "You can't be serious. I'm supposed to be loyal to you?"

"I gave you food and shelter for years. Treated you all right."

"You stole me from my family and raped me over and over!" she screamed. "And you forced me to hurt other people. What the hell is wrong with you?"

"Same thing that's wrong with you," he said. "I want what I want, and I get it."

Lyric imagined what it would be like to put a bullet in his head and watch the life drain out of his eyes. Better yet, injure him first. Shoot him in the leg, hit the big vein, watch him bleed out.

"I'm not like that," she said. "I did what I had to in order to survive. And that's only because I wanted to see my gran one last time and tell her I was sorry."

"Why didn't you?" Annabeth's voice cracked. "If you've been free four years, why didn't you come home?"

"I did," Lyric said. "And I saw that Gran was happy taking care of you. You needed her, and I was too broken to fix. New Orleans is a big city."

She had really believed Annabeth was the beaten woman Billy had forced her to bury that last morning in Jasper. She hadn't put things together until she'd been home a few days, watching from the shadows—a trick Billy drilled into her head years before.

"I saw you this morning," Annabeth said. "I was in the car, and she drugged me. I thought I saw you in the alley."

"I knew one of them would come for you," Lyric said. "I'd planned to hide and wait, take care of them before you or Alexandrine had a clue. But she beat me to it. She was shoving you in the car when I showed up. I couldn't risk shooting her then. And I was too far away, I was afraid I'd hit you."

Lyric glared at Billy. "Get on your knees."

"I won't kneel for you."

She could shoot off his dick. Put a round in his shoulder. But the bullet might go through and hit one of the women.

"Do it, or die."

"You're going to have to kill me." He smiled the same creepy grin he'd given her since she was ten years old. She'd known right then Billy would destroy her life.

"Here's your mistake," Lyric said. "You think I have something to live for. There's nothing left for me but killing you. Once help's on the way for these two, I end it. Peace, finally."

"I've loved you, girl."

She nearly gagged. "Like you loved all the other girls you tortured and killed?"

"I left you alive, didn't I?"

"Because I was useful. And too ashamed to run."

"That's not why," Billy said. "It's always been you. Even after all the fight went out and you turned into a meek mouse, I wouldn't have turned you out. Why you think I kept calling after Cathy kicked you out?"

"Because you're an idiot," Lyric said.

"I sent money so you could get back on your feet. Helped you get that car."

"You could have done better than an ancient rusting Beetle with no shocks and shit tires."

Billy sneered. "Always ungrateful. Your mama used to say the same thing."

"You killed her, didn't you?"

"Did what I had to do."

Rage shot through her like an electric current. "Kneel, bastard. Your time's up."

"Lyric, please."

"I said kneel!" The metal walls amplified her piercing scream.

She saw the shift in his eyes, the absolute defeat. Billy did love her, in his sick, twisted way. That's why she'd always known her betrayal would destroy him.

"You have plenty to live for," Annabeth said. "Me, for starters."

"You'll be fine," Lyric said.

"Take him outside and shoot him," Sheila said. "One body in here is enough."

Lyric wasn't going to take any chances. Billy had a lot more room to maneuver outside, and he knew the swamps.

"Then you can toss the body to the gators," Sheila said. "The gun too. We find our clothes, and we all leave here. No one speaks about it, and we get on with our lives."

"You could live with covering up a murder?" Lyric asked.

"Killing him isn't murder. It's justice. And a gift to society."

"What about all the others?" Annabeth asked. "The girls he killed after you left, and the ones after Jasper? Their families deserve closure."

Lyric didn't want to hear the closure argument. "Cover your ears."

Billy started to sniffle like the little coward he was. "Not so tough now, are you? Consider yourself lucky I'm not strapping you to that table and shoving things inside you until you tear and bleed."

She pressed the gun to his forehead. His tears flowed, snot oozing out of his nose.

"Goodnight, sweetheart."

67

THE SKY HAD turned pitch black by the time Cage and Bonin found the address. A beat-up Volkswagen Beetle was parked halfway off the dirt road. Bonin ran the plates.

"It's registered to Cathy O'Dell."

Cage shined his flashlight through the window. "That's Lyric's bag sticking out from underneath the seat. She drove here. Right-side tire's flat."

Cage double-checked the Google Earth map he'd printed. The dirt lane ran deep into the woodlands south of Ponchatoula, not far from the big wetlands. "This lane dead ends at their house."

Bonin swatted away a mosquito. "We're seven miles or so from the swamp. Keep an eye out for gators and black bears. They wander."

She secured her Kevlar, and they headed down the narrow lane. The woods surrounded them, blocking out the partial moon. Every breath in the dense humidity felt like inhaling water. Mosquitos and gnats swarmed. The still air and silent woods set him on edge.

"See that?"

A football field away, miniscule light peeked from the trees. The vein in Cage's neck pulsed with a familiar adrenaline rush. They crept forward, guns ready. The trees gradually thinned, allowing the moon's light to break through. The lane turned into a circular drive in front of a single-story house with old clapboard siding.

Underneath the slanted porch roof, Lyric relaxed in a lawn chair, a pistol on her lap. Bug zappers at either end of the shabby porch crackled with activity.

"Back me up," Cage said.

Bonin caught his arm. "You've got a wife and kid. Let me go first."

"She won't talk to you. I won't get close enough for her to get a good headshot." Cage wiped his forehead and patted his bulky vest. The Kevlar made them both sweat like pigs.

Bonin grumbled but took position behind a giant tree stump. Cage holstered his gun and moved into the round drive, hands in the air.

"Agent Foster," Lyric said. "I'm impressed. I wasn't expecting you until morning at the earliest."

"You didn't expect me at all."

She stopped rocking, her hand on the gun. "Not true. I gave you enough information to put it all together. Fast work, though. Beauty and brains. I bet you've had girls falling at your feet your whole life. Some guys too."

He closed the distance between them, stopping about ten feet away. "Where are Annabeth and Sheila?"

"I didn't expect to see Sheila," Lyric said. "Talk about a blast from the past."

"We can get you help," Cage said. "With all the psychological trauma, you'll probably be put in a care facility instead of prison."

She laughed. "A care facility? You mean mental hospital. No thanks." Lyric ran her fingers along the pistol's handle. "And no jury's going to let me off easy once they see the video of me killing Mickie."

"They will if you get a good defense attorney," Cage said. "And if you didn't hurt Annabeth or Sheila."

"Why would I hurt them?"

"Because of what Billy's done to you. It's called Stockholm syndrome or trauma bonding. He's made you believe that he's your only option. That's not true. You have a way out. I promise I'll fight for you as long as Annabeth and Sheila are okay."

The bug zapper popped and sizzled as Lyric appeared to consider his offer.

A mosquito dined on his cheek, but he didn't dare move.

"You've got this whole deal twisted," Lyric said. "I didn't do all of this to hurt Annabeth. I did it to bring Billy fucking Pietry and that crazy bitch to justice."

"If you wanted justice, then why did you send me on a wild goose chase?"

"Because legal justice is a joke. You know Billy's cousin is a cop, right? He was dealing drugs and messing with young girls way before me. His cousin always covered for him. Everyone knows you can't trust the NOPD."

"Things are better," Cage said. "Katrina changed a lot of things. And Lionel Pietry's in jail for having sex with an underage girl. He can't do a thing for Billy."

"Doesn't matter," Lyric said. "I'm not interested in legal justice."

Could he believe her after so many lies? He doubted she was capable of being completely honest about anything.

"Where's Billy?"

She shrugged.

"What about Cathy?"

"Lying in a pool of her own blood in the storage pod behind the house. I put a bullet in her head before she could hurt

Annabeth."

A sliver of hope rocketed through him. "Are Annabeth and Sheila all right?"

She picked up the gun. "I thought about calling you, but the cell service out here sucks. Couldn't keep a signal long enough. Freaking boonies. Billy always fantasized about having a place in the swamps. Guess this is the closest he could get."

"Did you kill Billy too?"

Lyric raised the gun and pointed it at him. Bruises peppered her arm. "I bet you think I can't make a headshot. But I've had four years to practice."

Blood roared in Cage's ears. "That would be a really stupid thing to do."

"Yes, it would." Bonin spoke from behind him. "Put the gun down."

"Who the fuck are you?"

"Detective Bonin."

Lyric nodded, but she didn't lower the gun. "Annabeth thinks the sun rises and sets on you, Agent Foster."

Present tense … was Annabeth still alive?

Lyric pulled the hammer back. Bonin strode forward, her own weapon ready to fire.

"But even if she didn't, I'm not a cop killer." Lyric swung the pistol around, pressing the tip against her forehead.

The cabin door banged open, but the shadows from the porch roof prevented Cage from seeing anyone but Lyric in her rocker, ready to kill herself.

"Stop!"

Annabeth.

68

I SERIOUSLY CAN'T believe Lyric. It took a lot of begging and pleading, but she'd finally promised to stick around. Now she's ready to splatter her brains everywhere.

I'm so pissed off I yank the gun right out of her hands. "You promised."

Lyric's mouth opens in shock. I realize I'm holding the gun that killed Cathy, and it's loaded and ready to fire.

"Annabeth." Cage is at the front steps. "Give me the gun, slowly. We don't want it to go off."

My heart is flying. I thought I wouldn't see him until we talked Lyric into giving us a ride out of this shithole. "How'd you find us?"

"I told you he would," Lyric said. "He's just early. See, Agent Foster?"

Cage moves to the bottom step, his arm reaching toward me. He wiggles his fingers. "Give me the gun. Slow."

The thing suddenly feels like a bomb. I hand it over, and he puts the trigger-thingy back in place and drops the ammunition to the ground.

"Christ." Bonin's beside him, pointing her own gun. "Now will one of you explain exactly what's happened here?"

I answer before Lyric can open her mouth. "It was self-defense. Cathy was going to attack me."

"What about Billy?" Cage asks. "And Sheila? Where is she?"

"Unbelievable." Lyric's still salty with me. Too damned bad. I might be brain damaged, but I'm not an idiot.

"She's out back. She's fine." Even though he's standing a couple of feet away, it's so dark I can't see Cage's expression. That's probably a good thing because I don't want him to be disappointed in me.

"I did what I had to do," I say. "Lyric's in enough trouble as it is."

"What exactly did you do?" Bonin asks.

"She charged me," Lyric snaps. "Sheila helps her get untied, and then Annabeth's coming at me like a bulldozer."

"She was going to shoot him point blank in the head," I say. "How's she going to explain that to a judge?"

"You did the right thing," Cage says. "Where is he?"

"Good damned question." Lyric turns to glare at me. "You better hope he's gator bait."

Cage steps onto the porch, just inches from me. Sweat coats his face and stubble, his fair cheeks are pink, and his hair's standing on end. "He's not here?"

"I really wish you weren't married."

He closes his eyes, and Lyric snickers. Bonin shakes her head.

"I totally didn't mean to say that out loud."

"Billy?" Cage is irritated now.

"He bolted when she came after me," Lyric says. I managed to get a couple of shots off and hit him in the calf. He kept going—you can probably get a dog and follow the blood trail." She points to the woods on the side of the house. "I would have gone after him, but Rain Girl over here was hanging onto my arm and screaming like a banshee. Freaked me out."

"Is that why you were sitting out here with the gun?" Cage

asks.

Lyric nods. "I got them dressed, and we found Billy's shotgun. It was getting dark, so we headed to my car."

"The tire was flat." Cage has already figured it out.

"And by then it was good and dark. Billy and the bitch have been living out here for a while, and I know he always has contingency plans. He's probably holed up, waiting. We decided to stay here and keep praying for a cell signal. My data plan sucks, and he got rid of theirs."

Cage and Bonin are staring at us like they don't believe. It does sound like a soap opera.

"Shouldn't you call for a search team?" Lyric asks. "He couldn't have gone too far."

Bonin checks her phone, so does Cage. No signal.

"Get Sheila," Cage says. "We're leaving."

69

BONIN COORDINATED A search of the woods and surrounding areas with the Tangipahoa Parrish Sheriff's office while the three women gave their statements. A crime-scene crew collected Cathy O'Dell's body and large amounts of trace evidence in both the storage pod and the house.

Cage refused to let the women out of his sight. He didn't trust them, and he didn't believe their story. Lyric had world-class deception skills, but Annabeth and Sheila didn't. As soon as Lyric started telling the story, Annabeth stopped looking at him, watching the bugs get zapped. Sheila talked too fast, nodding her head like she was mentally checking off plot points.

Each woman gave her statement separately, to different deputies. Cage sat in with Annabeth, and she refused to make eye contact with him. When the deputy finished, she bolted for the bathroom.

With their statements finished, Sheriff's deputies directed the women to a large breakroom with a couple of couches. Annabeth whined about going home, but Cage put his foot down. They weren't going anywhere until Bonin returned. Annabeth flipped him off and flopped face first onto one of the sofas. Sheila did the same, and both fell asleep in minutes, leaving only Cage and Lyric in uncomfortable chairs.

Black hair in a loose knot, sweat stains on her tank top, and circles beneath her eyes, Lyric appeared years older than she had this morning. Her steely resolve remained. "Are you going to charge me?"

"I'm off the clock." Cage shrugged, folding his hands in his lap. "That's up to Bonin."

"Freaking girl." Lyric glanced at Annabeth snoring softly on the sofa. "She should have let me pull that trigger."

"You need each other," Cage said. "Although you need her more."

Lyric half-smiled, her head lolling back against the chair. "I don't need anyone. Besides, I'll be happy to have a cell and three square meals. Being on my own the past four years has sucked."

Cage had been running various scenarios in his head, and only one made sense. "You and Billy stayed in touch, he sent you money. Hooked you up with a car in his girlfriend's name."

Her eyelids drooped. "He didn't have the balls to stand up to Cathy when she dumped me off, thank God. I hid for like three weeks, thinking he would show up to haul me back and trying to figure out what the hell to do next. I didn't want to go back, but where else would I go?"

"Did he find you?"

"Nope, but he called. I had one of those pay-as-you-go phones back then, and only he had my number. He told me to stay gone, that he had Cathy now." She banded her arms over her waist and shuddered. "I wish you could understand how screwed up I was. I'd spent eight years living in hell with him. He didn't just let me roam free. Ever. He lurked in the background when he sent me to bring in girls. The rest of the time, he locked me in my bedroom. I got a little more freedom when Cathy came along, but not much."

"You went to Annabeth's track meet," Cage said. "I was there. Other cops were there, in uniform. All you had to do was speak up."

"I wanted to." Her face hardened. "But I told you why I didn't. And you said you understood."

"As much as I can," Cage said. "It's just impossible to put myself in your shoes, especially when you've lied so much to me."

"Not really," Lyric said. "I lied to you about Cathy's last name. Everything else is the truth. And I gave you enough information to put it all together."

"Don't bullshit me," Cage said. "Annabeth and Sheila aren't accomplished liars like you. What really happened to Billy Pietry?"

She stared back at him, unfazed. "If I cooperate and tell you the names of the girls he took up after Jasper, do you think the courts will go easier on me?"

"You know their names?"

"Someone had to give them a proper goodbye." She glared at the wall just long enough to grab her composure.

"That's why you put the coneflower seeds down."

"And as a marker in case I ever got away," Lyric said. "They were just beginning to grow when we left Jasper. He never had a clue. But I didn't have anything to leave for the girls after. I can tell you where each one is buried."

"Because he made you bury them?"

"Yep."

"What about Mickie? Annabeth saw her in the grave."

"He made her watch." Lyric seemed to look past Cage, her eyes unfocused, caught up in her horrific memories.

"And what about the girls from the past four years?" Cage asked. "If he's not found, those families have nothing."

Her gaze snapped back to him, sharp and challenging. "Surely you don't think he would have confessed? Billy thinks he's smarter than everyone else—and he's usually right. He plans and practices. And he's always got at least three backup stories. He never goes for a girl until he knows her entire routine—and he got even more careful after Jasper."

"But you outsmarted him." Cage played to her ego, knowing damn well she wouldn't bite.

"After eight years of captivity and another four dealing with his pathetic phone calls." She rolled her eyes. "He kept calling. Cathy would have killed him if she knew. I thought about telling her, but why should she get to have all the fun? Anyway, when he called just to talk—like we'd been some couple that broke up after years together—I saw my chance.

"I hitched a ride home, got a job waiting tables, and planned. Lived off the streets for a while, but eventually got a shitty apartment and this phone. I kept the number. He kept calling. I paid attention and waited."

Cage still couldn't wrap his head around Lyric living in New Orleans all these years. Seeing Charlotte with Annabeth gave Lyric peace, and she didn't want her grandmother to know the things she'd been forced to do. He didn't know if that made her a saint or a martyr, but it bugged him.

"When I saw Annabeth's story on the news, I knew he would come after her. I couldn't let him destroy her life again."

Lyric's mix of hatred and kindness left Cage dizzy. Her obvious affection for Annabeth battled with her inner demons and need for revenge.

"I'm not a heartless monster." Lyric held up an old, beat-up cell phone. "Obviously not a shiny new smartphone, but this Razr records audio. Before Annabeth jumped me, I made Billy give me the names of the girls he and Cathy killed and where they were buried. He got smarter over the years, like I said. Four girls. Want me to email you the audio?"

Cage couldn't believe what he was hearing. "Let me hear it first."

"I'm turning it down low so these two don't wake up and freak." She handed Cage the phone, and he pushed play.

"Please don't do this."

Lyric smiled at the sound of Billy's terrified voice coming through the tinny speaker. "Pussy."

"Give me their names and where you put them, and maybe I'll reconsider." Her response burned with hatred.

Half-crying, Billy gave her four names: two girls were from Arkansas, one from West Texas, and a fourth from southern Oklahoma. Billy claimed all four were buried in an abandoned family graveyard about two miles away from his old place in Little Rock.

The recording stopped before Annabeth's alleged lunge for Lyric and the ensuing chaos.

"There you go," Lyric said. "If they don't find him, you have what you need."

He slipped her phone into his pocket. "I'm going to take this phone for evidence, since you handed it to me freely."

"Whatever. I don't have anyone to call now."

"If they don't find him, he's going to go back to taking girls."

Lyric stretched her legs out and craned her neck to stare at the popcorn ceiling. "He was bleeding pretty bad, and there are a lot of gators out there."

"You realize your car will be processed for evidence." With enough fear and adrenaline, the women could have carried Billy's body to the car and driven it to the swamp.

"Go ahead."

"It's interesting that you felt you needed to guard the cabin, yet all three of you took showers."

"These two were dirty. He hadn't gone for them yet, but you do things when you're tied up for a long time. And I was sweating like a pig."

"Will we find blood in the shower drains?"

"Cathy's sprayed all over, so yeah, you might."

Cage sighed and mimicked her posture, his eyes fighting to stay open. "Just tell me the truth."

"I have," Lyric mumbled. "You've heard all I have to say."

CAGE STARTED AWAKE. Bonin's hand gripped his shoulder, and she put her finger to her lips. All three women slept; Lyric had curled up on the floor in front of Annabeth's couch.

"I need to talk to you." Bonin led him out of the break room, quietly shutting the door.

"You didn't find him."

She made a face. "We found enough."

70

LYRIC CREPT AWAY from the door. She didn't need to hear any more.

The gator was just plain luck.

"Did they find him?" Annabeth was awake, all big-eyed and scared. All the years Lyric had kept on eye on Annabeth and Charlotte, she'd always known Annabeth was the one who deserved a real chance at life. The hell if Lyric was going to let that be taken away now.

"Sounds like it."

"He's dead, right?" Annabeth whispered. "You did kill him, didn't you?"

"Hush and go back to sleep. Stick to what I told you, and everything will be fine."

Lyric told Cage the truth—except for the part about Billy slipping off into the woods. Annabeth had charged her, Billy ran into the overgrown yard. Lyric shot him, and he went down but then scrambled to his feet and limped toward the woods. Annabeth had used up all her energy to stop her from blowing Billy's head open, and Sheila sat like a deer ready to get plowed by a truck.

Lyric managed to slam the door shut and half-ass lock the storage pod. She caught up with Billy at the edge of the woods. His bleeding calf left a nice trail as she put the gun to his head and forced him deep into the woods.

She didn't know exactly what she was going to do at that point. She had to make sure Annabeth and Sheila were safe before she put the gun to her own head.

Except Annabeth needed her.

And maybe Lyric didn't want to die.

"Shit, stop." Billy saw the alligator first. It lurked near a stream, eyes glowing in the twilight. "They're fast. Take the long way around him."

Lyric had known exactly what to do.

71

CAGE CRADLED HIS sleeping daughter against his shoulder and slipped his arm around Dani's waist. She leaned against him, wiping her eyes.

Annabeth and Lyric, along with Alexandrine, bowed their heads as Charlotte's ashes were interred in the Sanité tomb.

"Is she going to serve time?" Dani whispered.

Lyric had spent three months in the county jail while the prosecuting attorneys in different states haggled over whether or not to press charges. The Tangipahoa Parrish district attorney finally declined, accepting self-defense for Cathy's death and for the gunshot that turned Billy into alligator supper.

Cage still didn't believe the story. He also didn't care. The information Billy had given Lyric about his other victims had been correct, and the other four families received a bitter closure, along with the families of the victims buried in Jasper. Sheila buried her brother next to her mother and cut off everyone else.

Agent Tims had been livid about losing the opportunity to arrest Billy Pietry. Tims fought to have Cage brought in front of the LBI and FBI internal review boards, arguing that the Louisiana Bureau of Investigation existed to assist the FBI in criminal matters, and the LBI's new Criminal Investigative Assist Unit also fell under that heading.

Agent Rogers fought vehemently against it, using the media to paint the FBI as headline-grabbing vultures who didn't care about Billy Pietry's victims or their families.

The Jasper County district attorney waffled on prosecuting Lyric for Mickie's murder. Given Lyric's imprisonment and history of psychological abuse, capital murder charges weren't an option. Texas laws lumped both voluntary and involuntary into a single charge with mitigating circumstances, and the prosecutor didn't have a chance at convincing a jury that Lyric had willingly killed Mickie—even with the video.

Mickie's parents lobbied hard, but Sam George stepped in, hiring a top defense attorney and skilled psychiatrist. Lyric allowed Mickie's parents to hear much of her sessions with the psychiatrist—most of them detailing the extensive sexual and psychological abuse she endured.

Cage didn't know if Mickie's parents accepted her version of being forced to give up or just gave in to Sam George's unrelenting pressure, but they eventually agreed that taking the case to trial would be a waste of time. The Jasper County D.A. declined to prosecute but insisted Lyric agree to court-monitored psychiatric counseling.

Annabeth and Alexandrine believed Ezili and the other spirits led the way to Lyric's freedom.

With Alexandrine's forceful encouragement, Annabeth had started cognitive therapy again. A few bits and pieces had come back to her, and more importantly, she allowed visits from her parents.

"Lyric's not upset about Annabeth owning the house?"

"Who knows?" Cage said. "I'm not sure it's possible to really know what she's thinking."

"I hope the two of them living there together doesn't end up in a disaster."

So did he. But the women were stubborn and no longer Cage's responsibility. He'd told Annabeth if she wanted to do something as foolish as live with Lyric, then not to expect him to bail her out of trouble. He still hadn't figured out how the argument had resulted in Dani yelling at him for being insensitive and him being stuck helping Lyric move in.

Alexandrine made her way around the treacherous crypts, reaching for Cage's arm to steady her. "I'm just going to give them a moment alone with her." She beamed at Emma. "I'm so happy to have a little one around. You two bring her to see me or I'll sic Ezili on you."

Dani giggled.

"I told you all, it was a sleep-deprived dream. Period."

"Keep on denying," Alexandrine said. "Ezili'll still be there if you need her."

"I hope so," Dani said. "I'm used to living in a house full of ghosts. I feel kind of lonely without them."

"Come on," Cage said. "We've never seen anything."

"Just hearing someone digging through the hidden section of the house at all hours of the night and finding no one. Footsteps going up and down the servants' quarters, knocking …"

Alexandrine patted Cage's cheek. "He'll come around. New Orleans gets to everyone eventually."

Bonin told him the same thing at least once a week. He'd started to regret having his office next to her squad room.

Lyric and Annabeth joined them. Both wore bright purple as homage to Charlotte's favorite color. Lyric's newly shortened hair curled in ringlets around her face, while Annabeth's long waves hung down her back. Most people would mistake them for sisters.

"I'm hungry," Annabeth said. "And I want gumbo."

"Gross," Lyric said. "Let's have steak."

"You payin'?" Alexandrine asked.

"Do I look like I can afford to buy steaks?"

Alexandrine grunted. "That's what I thought. Ya'll come back to my house. I made a big pot of étouffée and baked mac and cheese for the little one."

"And me," Lyric said. "I hate crawfish."

She and Annabeth argued over gumbo all the way out of St. Louis No. 1, while Dani walked with Alexandrine. Cage switched Emma to his other arm. He thanked the attendant from the Archdiocese for allowing the private ceremony.

A soft November breeze swept down Basin Street, blowing bits of trash and debris across the sidewalk in front of the cemetery wall. As the old iron gate clanged shut, a sliver of cold ran down Cage's spine.

The fresh fall breeze carried the heady scent of musky oil Alexandrine loved to offer the Loa.

Please consider leaving a review for *The Lies We Bury.*

The second book in the Cage Foster series will release late 2018. Sign up for my mailing list for teasers, contest and news!

BOOKS BY STACY

The Delta Crossroads Trilogy

Tin God

Skeleton's Key

Ashes and Bone

Delta Detectives Novella Series (Cage Foster)

Living Victim

Dead Wrong

Night Terror

Last Words

Shots Fired

Dead Wait

The Lucy Kendall Series

She's no killer. She's just taking out the trash.

Hear No Lies

All Good Deeds

See Them Run

Gone To Die

All Fall Down

Killing Jane

Killing Jane

Standalone

Into the Devil's Underground

Welcome to Las Vegas

Twisted Minds

ABOUT THE AUTHOR

Stacy Green is the author of the Lucy Kendall thriller series and the Delta Crossroads mystery trilogy. ALL GOOD DEEDS (Lucy Kendall #1) won a bronze medal for mystery and thriller at the 2015 IPPY Awards. TIN GOD (Delta Crossroads #1) was runner-up for best mystery/thriller at the 2013 Kindle Book Awards. Stacy has a love of thrillers and crime fiction, and she is always looking for the next dark and twisted novel to enjoy. She started her career in journalism before becoming a stay at home mother and rediscovering her love of writing. She lives in Iowa with her husband and daughter and their three spoiled fur babies.

Stacy is represented by Italia Gandolfo of Gandolfo, Helin and Fountain Literary Management for literary and dramatic rights.

Stacy loves to hear from readers!

Website: stacygreenauthor.com

Facebook Facebook.com/StacyGreenAuthor

Twitter: @StacyGreen26

ACKNOWLEDGMENTS

I have to thank my readers for their patience and support of a new Cage Foster book. I hope The Lies We Bury lived up to your expectations!

Many thanks to my husband for supporting me through a couple of rough personal years and for being an amazing research assistant during our visit to New Orleans. Thank you to Alexandra Weiss for putting up with my numerous questions on Voodoo and sending me in the right direction. Thank you to my copyeditor and friend, Kristine Kelly, for your encouragement and support. Jonas Saul, you're an awesome development editor and a great cheerleader!

Special thanks to Sophia R. Mavroudas from Texas State University's Department of Anthropology for taking the time to work though my very specific body recovery questions, and to Dr. Stephen Andrews, Associate Professor of Neurology at the University of Iowa for helping me create a character with brain trauma.

A quick note on some of the terminology: followers of the religion use the spellings Vodou and magick, but I chose to use common spelling for my readers.

Finally, to the city of New Orleans: thank you for the push in the right direction.

Made in the USA
Las Vegas, NV
28 June 2023

74012105R00184